T0162741

Cabin by
BLACK LAKE

THE HORROR BEGINS

by
P.A. BRITON

iUniverse, Inc.
New York   Bloomington

iUniverse books may be ordered through booksellers or by contacting:

iUniverse
1663 Liberty Drive
Bloomington, IN 47403
www.iuniverse.com
1-800-Authors (1-800-288-4677)

Because of the dynamic nature of the Internet, any Web addresses or links
contained in this book may have changed since publication and may no longer be
valid. The views expressed in this work are solely those of the author and do not
necessarily reflect the views of the publisher, and the publisher hereby disclaims
any responsibility for them.

ISBN: 978-1-4401-3515-6 (sc)
ISBN: 978-1-4401-3517-0 (dj)
ISBN: 978-1-4401-3516-3 (ebook)

Printed in the United States of America

iUniverse rev. date: 10/27/09

CHAPTER 1

It was a warm spring day, after a cool snowy winter in Maine. The ground was finally clear of snow and the grass had turned a bright green and the air smelled fresh and clean. Jimmy Bentley was a young twenty two year old student at the University of Orono. He was in his room on the scent floor of the dome and he had been up at five thirty studying, for his test on Monday. The room had two bed one of Jimmy and one of his room mate Berry Bydean. The sum shown thought a little, seen there was only one window over looking the parking lot. It was now almost nine o'clock in the morning. Jimmy had nothing planned, but maybe he'd study and watch a little T.V. Jimmy know a lot of girls on campus, but didn't date very often. Because of college, he didn't have the time to date much and really don't have a close have a girl friend. Jimmy was a good looking young man and was well liked by the girl on college. Jimmy set in the chair and looked out the window on the second floor in room 214.

The University is one of the largest I the State of Maine, and covers almost square mile. The University also has a good baseball and football team. Jimmy was asked by the coach to play football, as he was a very good haft-back for Old Town a couple years ago. But Jimmy said "No!" he couldn't take the time off his studies, as he was attended college, to become a lawyer It had been a quit Saturday morning, as a lot of student had go home for weeks end. Jimmy was in his dome room, and it was almost eleven o'clock in the morning. And most of the student were gone for the week end, except for a few student that home for the week end. When Jimmy was younger he had seen a T.V. show about a lawyer, it made an great impression on Jimmy.. From then on he know he wanted to become a lawyer too. Jimmy had a dream and was studding hard at school to make it happen. Jimmy's father helped him as much as he could, but Jimmy's father did ran a small grocery store. A lot of small business had gone out of business do to big store moving in town. Jimmy hopped his father could keep the store going until Jimmy graduated for college. Then maybe Jimmy could help his father keep the store from closing. Jimmy had been thinking about his father and his family his mother how was quit, caring and sweet to him, when he heard foot steps in the hallway. Then the door opened and in walk Jill and Berry came throw the door. Jill was a pretty blond twenty year old with a cute twenty four that stood five foot nine inches he weight a good hundred ninety pounds with a round belly. Barry had brown hair with brown eyes. He was a happy go luck key guy. They walk a few feet to were Jimmy was sitting at his deck. Berry had Letters in his hand. He address Jimmy "You've got mail!" he handed Jimmy a letter, as he handed it to him he looked at the address it was for some lawyer how name, Berry chuckled to himself as he handed Jimmy the letter for the lawyer. Jimmy took the letter for Berry, "Thanks, Berry." Jimmy said. Jimmy didn't know anyone from Calais, Maine. It looked like a legal decrement from the court in Calais. Jimmy turned slightly so Berry couldn't read the letter. He'd open it after they left. Jimmy put the letter on top of his deck were had been setting. He'd open it later after they left "So what are you up to ,you going some wear good?" Jimmy asked Berry and Jimmy looked at Jill she was a very pretty girl, her blue eyes looked so bright. Jimmy was changing the subject away from the letter. It wasn't Berry business to know anyway. Berry looked back at Jimmy he could tell because Jimmy was staring at Jill. He went on to say, "We thought, we might go to a movie a bite later, if you wont to come, we'd like it?" He really didn't wont Jimmy come, but he know Jill would like Jimmy to come, so he asked him anyways.

"No, thanks, I thought I'd just like to say here and do some studying and maybe watch a little T.V. later." Jimmy replied. Berry put his hands on Jill's shoulder to turn her to the door and waved good bye to Jimmy. Jill waved to and bow him a kiss good bye. And they both turned and left the room, Berry said as he was leaving, "I'll see you in a few hours Jimmy. After they had left Jimmy room, he turned his attending to the letter on his deck. He picked the letter up and looked at it ones more. It was from the Court in Washington County and a lawyer, Jimmy didn't know. The letter read like these.

> *Dear; Jimmy Bentley.*
> *I'm sorry to inform you of the death of Orland*
> *Forster Gray. Mr. Gray died on problems of his heart*
> *on August twenty third. You, Jimmy Bentley, have*
> *been named in Orland Gray Will. You, Jimmy Bentley*
> *are ask to attend the reading of Orland Gray Will on*
> *the date of the reading of the Will. Mr. Jimmy Bentley*
> *must attend the reading of Orland F. Gray Will or*
> *you, Jimmy will lose you're part of the inheritance.*

Jimmy had not been told of his uncle Orland death back in August of late year. He felt bad that he didn't know, he might have attend his uncle funeral if he had a chance. Jimmy got up and walked to the window, and looked down at the parking lot below the build. His old red Mustang was parked down their, in the middle of the lot. Jimmy would call his mother and ask her if she know of Uncle Orland death. She must have know and didn't tell him about his Uncle dying back in August of last year. Knowing his mother she just didn't want Jimmy to weary about him going Down East. It was hard for Jimmy to believe that uncle Orland had named him in his Will, Jimmy hadn't seen his Uncle in five years. Jimmy couldn't get from thinking about his Uncle Orland. Jimmy decided to take a walk around the campest a clear his mind. Jimmy closed the book he was studding and turned to the door. Just very one had left the dome but Jimmy, so he closed the door behind him and walked down the hall. He thought he'd take a nice walk around the champs, it was a nice warm day, a good time for a walk. There was no wind and the sidewalks were clear of ice. He'd walk down by the sport arena with the big M on the top part of the building, passed the scorer and base-ball field, around the in door Hockey rink, and walk around the champs grounds back to his dome. Jimmy walked slowly by the Scorer field looking across the road, there was no one playing on the field. He walked on past the field to the big sports Arena. Jimmy had his cell phone in his pocket, he took it out.

Jimmy crossed the road to the Sports Arena. He thought he'd call his mother and ask her if she know about Uncle Orland's death. He dial the numbers to his mother's phone. The phone Rang and rang. As the phone rang, Jimmy was thinking maybe he could talk to his mother in person, about Uncle Orland's death. "Hello!', it was his mother on the phone. "Hi! Mon, it's Jimmy." He put the phone in his right hand and stopped walking for a moment. "How's things going in town," he didn't give her a change to talk. "I'll be come next week end, I thought I'd stay hear for the week end and do a little studying." He halted for a moment then went on to say. "Aunt May died two years ago is Uncle Orland still alive?"

"NO!" his mother replied, he just died last year, Why do you ask?" she said. Jimmy mother was a good looking woman for her age sixty. Yes she'd lost her slim girlies finger so years ago and her hair had turned gray, but she still was a good looking woman. She stood just over five feet tall, away had a smile on her face. She waited for Jimmy to answer her. "Mom, I received a letter for so lawyer in the mail from Calais." "Jimmy said to his mother. It seem as though I've be named in Uncle Orland "s Will. Orland Gray comes from a very big family to much about being named in her bother Will, Jimmy." You wont to talk to you're father, he can tell you more about it. She didn't give him a changes to answer, she call her husband to come to the phone. "Howard it's you're son Jimmy." She told him. Howard took the phone from his wife. "Hi! Jimmy, what going on, that you can't visit you're family?" he was joking to his son. Jimmy mother touched her husband shoulder and wisped in his ear he know about Orland dying late year, ask him about the letter?" she told her husband. Jimmy father turned and looked into his wife's eyes, he could see take she was concerned about Jimmy. "So what is going on Jimmy ever thing alright in school?" Jimmy said, "Ever thing just fine, dad," stopped talking and looked around him then added, "Mom, said she know about Uncle Orland death last year and didn't say anything to me "I know, like she says Orland comes from a very big family and him doesn't have that much. So I guess every body gets a little bite of the pie. Jimmy father told him. Why Orland was doing these he didn't know, but Orland wasn't a generous man. When he was alive he thought mostly of himself and cared from only a few people on these earth "Dad, I've have to go, I'll talk to you some, tell Mon and sister good bye for me bye for me."

He's father said "OK!" and hang the phone up. Mr. Bentley lived in the same house for twenty four years, Jimmy always lived their with his two sisters, Angela the oldest and Peggy the youngest of the three of them. Howard Bentley, Jimmy born. Like a lot of men Mr. Bentley had done a lot of the work on the house himself. Howard built the cabinets out of hard wood many years ago. The five bedroom house had one guest room on the second floor. It had been used quit often by June (Jimmy mother) family when their came to visit and go shopping in the area, their wound stay over night most of the time at Jimmy family home. June spook to her husband, "Peter, I didn't like Jimmy dealing with people like Orland, their could be trouble for him." She had a worried look on her face "Jimmy a bright young man, he'll be alright. He's got a good head on his shoulder, he'll think thing though and come up with the right answer. "He's going to be a big time Lawyer one of these days, June." Peter replied. "Well, I know but I'm his mother." June stated. Peter put his arm around her shoulder. "It will be all right! Jimmy put his cell phone back in his pocket and went on walking down the hill to baseball field. They was people playing on the baseball field and there was people also on the track field. Jimmy thought he'd walk over and see what was going. Jimmy know a good many student on champs and was well like by most people. Jimmy walked past the baseball field their wasn't much going on their. The track field had a lot of studied their, he'd seen who he knows on the field. Jimmy thought from time being he'd stop thinking about Uncle Orland Will. If Orland left him so thing, he'd fine out in time. Jimmy looked the track field and decided to go on the field. He seen many people he knows. He seen Glen running around the field with other student running with him. Like any young man he looked around and seen several young beautiful girls in their shorts. A few he know, one of there was a tall good looking sandy blond girl with long slim beautiful legs. Linda, know Jimmy from one of his class. She was a nice girl and liked him as a friend.

"Hi, Linda, how running going?" Jimmy ask her as she walked over to here he was standing.

"Ok, Jimmy, what are you doing these Saturday?" Linda replied back to Jimmy. "Oh, I talked to my parents about a Uncle of mine that die a wild back and then thought I'd take a walk and look at the beautiful girl on the track field Jimmy looked into Linda's brown eyes and smiled at her. She smiled back at him" You think with my long legs I'd be fast, I'm not. I just need to build up my straight and maybe the speed well come in time. I'm sorry to hear about you're Uncle dying." Linda said. "Oh, I didn't know till today, I was named in the he's Will," he with on to say, " Most likely it wont be much. My father didn't like him, thought he was cheap, I guess." Another girl walk up by side Linda, it was Rachel, a beautiful black girl with a grant finger and a pretty face with slim lips for a black girl. She was so good looking she could be a model almost any were in the country. Jimmy was greatly attacked to her, but he had no told her that he thought she so beautiful. Maybe so day he would tell her he had feeling of her, "Hi, Rachel, you're looking grant." Jimmy said as he looked her all over she smiled back, seen Jimmy was looking her over, she moved closer to him, she liked the idea that he was looking her over, she like at. Jimmy would be a nice man for he Jimmy was tilling me about his Uncle dying and her was named in his Will Maybe you'll get a million dollars from his Uncle and he can take us all out to dinner girl." Linda said. Jimmy know he could have said anything about his Uncle dying to Linda, but he did. And know she telling some one else. He'd be frank to her. "Linda, please don't talk about it any more. It's most likely, know big deal anyways." "Hey, boy what yours is mine, honey child." Rachel said joking as she winked at him and thought his cheek softly with her hand. "Please, no more, it's my business he died last year, it's know big deal" Jimmy said pleading for her to stop talking about his Uncle. "Jimmy she just playing with you, we'll all have to get together and have a drink or two some time. We have to get back to our practice. Jimmy watch the girl practice a wild then went back to his walk around the champs. Jimmy walked around the parking lot, past the baseball and Hockey Area then turned left and walked a haft mile around the champs. He still couldn't get

Uncle Orland Will off his mind. Jimmy checked the mail ever day. A week past, several weeks pasted then one day he checked the mail and their was a letter he'd be weighting for the letter from the lawyer in Calais, it said.

Dear; Jimmy Bentley
The reading of Orland F. Gray Will is to be held
in the Machias Court house on August 18, of this

year, at ten o'clock A..M morning time. You James P.
Bentley To attend the reading of Orland F. Gray Will.

The door open and Berry and his friends came in the room. Barry seen Jimmy with a letter in his hand said, "Good new I hope, Jimmy this is Amy," she was a very pretty white girl five foot four with short bond hair, "And there is Jill you all ready met her an LeRoy Barns." a tall black nice looking young man. Jimmy turned and greeted Berry friends. He put his hand out to the tall black young black man.

"Nice to meet you, LeRoy." Jimmy said to him, they shock his hands and then Jimmy saw the pretty blond girl stand beside LeRoy, "Hi, Jill we meet a couple days ago, I never forget a pretty face." Jimmy said as he smiled at her. There was another girl in the room, Jimmy hadn't meet before. she was a beautiful young girl with sandy blond hair that stood five foot four, just a little shorter then Jimmy. Her looked into her sparking brown eyes, And said in a caring voice to her, "Nice to meet you Amy, I've seen you around champs and know I get to finely meet you." Jimmy shock her hand hello. He went on to say, "So what are you taking of course, Amy?" Amy smiled back at Jimmy, "How, I'm taking Fine Art and Designing." Amy said in a soft voice. "What are you studying Jimmy?" "I'm studying Law, Criminal and Civil Law." Jimmy replied to her. Berry had been quit then he spook up and said, "We've been all studying hard isn't it time we all had a small party together?" They all looked at Berry, maybe it was time for a party.

CHAPTER 2

The party; Berry wasn't the best looking guy around, and he was a hundred pounds over weight and had a big around belly with a around fat face and a ball spot on top of his head. But when it came to having girls as friend around him he did better then most other guys. Maybe It was because the girls felt save around him. We all talk about having a party and Berry went to work on the idea from the start. He made a few calls and found a place to have the party not far form the dome. And it was still on champs just down the road on Main driver. Barry set the party up to be a week from today. And Jill said "Would help raise money of the party". The idea was to keep the party small just a few lose friends. Jill asked the people she called to help with cost of the party. Most of them give as much as they could. Jill and Berry raised quit a bit of money. With the money they bout case and case of Beer, they also had case of Whiskey, Vodka and so Gin. Jimmy know a friend had a Rock and Roll band, so they had music to dance too. Jimmy had raised only a couple hundred dollars, but Buddy said it would be alright as long as the drinks were free. Jimmy said "It would be fine with him." Thanked, Buddy for saying yes that they play at the party. So it was set a week from today they'd be a party at the Main road frat house. The house was away from the domes so the noise wouldn't bother anyone, and it was big enough to hold every body that came to the party. It would be a great time and Jimmy could forget about his Uncle Orland's Will for just a wild. Time would pass, and Saturday came the day of the party was here. The frat house was a big grand white with three story house with a large front lawn and plenty of parking space for the guest. Berry planned to have the party on the first floor of the building. Berry didn't have the money for a bartender, but there were planet of people that could mix drinks up at the party, of free most of the people that had came to the party had paid a small fee for coming to the party, so the drinks were free to ever body.

Jimmy wasn't much on large crowds, but he like to dance, and most girl like evening, Berry had been there for a hour and half getting thing ready for the guest. They didn't have a guest lest, but Berry know who he had asked to come to the party and so did Jill. It was seven o'clock and Jimmy walked throw the front door of the frat house. He hang his coat up as he came in the hall and walked in the large room, that had been made into a dance floor. He seen case of Beer that had been placed on the floor by truck driver, to be put way by who ever. Jimmy seen Berry at the far end of the room, and waved to Jimmy said to Berry "Has the band got hear yet?" Barry chook his head replied back "No, and" said to Jimmy, "I don't expect them tell eight o'clock maybe nine, were not paying them much money, Jimmy." Barry replied back to. Jimmy and Jill not hear either. but I know they will he hear, have you see her yet?!"

"No, I haven't seen her." Berry replied with a question in his voice. "I thought she'd be hear by know. She's been a great deal for help to me, in putting this party together. I thought she be hear, I'm shore she'll be hear soon. "Would you like me to put the beer away , Berry?" Jimmy asked him.

Berry shook his head Yes and pointed to the kitchen. and Jimmy went on to put the case of Beer away in the kitchen. At seven thirty people started arriving at to door for the party. There were snacks of people that came before the band started playing at nine O'clock. There was cheese and crackers on a large tray with chips and nacho on another tray. Amy arrived at the door of the frat house just a little before nine o'clock, and Buddy and his band have came in just head of her and was setting up their instruments, on the right side of the room. Jimmy seen Amy and her friends come in and went over to say hello to her. Amy had on a short blue jean dress with a pretty white blouse on. Amy had a nice slim finger with shapely legs. Jimmy looked at her and said "Amy, you look so beautiful tonight. Well have a dance with me?" Then the band started playing fast beat song. Jimmy took her hand, and they walk to wear the dance floor was. They were only a couple feet away for each other as they stared dancing to the music. Jimmy was a good dancer he had a lot of nice moves. Amy had a good flow to her dancing and their danced well together. Other couple joint in and started dancing as well, and before long the dance floor was fuel of people dancing. They danced on and then the music changed to a slow dance. Jimmy held her close to him and they danced to a soft slow dance. He could feel her nice warm body next to him. Amy passed closer to him, he looked down at her beautiful face, and she smiled back at him. Jimmy said softly to her, "it's nice to get away for the books for a few hours and hold a pretty girl in his arms. The music stopped, "Thank Jimmy." And turned and started to walk away., we'll have to dance again tonight, Amy?" Jimmy said, as she walked away to meet her girl friends. Jimmy went back to wear he left his drink, and so guy and girl was setting in the chair were he had been, he picked up his drink of the end table. A tall nice looking black girl walked by Jimmy and she turned, it was Rachel, a girl Jimmy know from school, and said the him "You're not a bad dancer, sweetie, we'll have to dance together later, honey." She was with a tall back guy The tall black guy, was LeRoy , he looked down at the little white boy, he had nothing to fear from him, he smiled and they walked away.

Jimmy took a drink he had just mixed it a bite strong. He looked around for a place so he could set down. All the seats were thanking. Jimmy took another drink, and looked around, he seen a very nice looking girl who had just came in the room. She was talking to her girl friend guest. Jimmy walked over to her and asks her if she like to dance? She shook her head, Yes. The music started to play once again, It was soft, slow dance. Jimmy held her in his arms and they danced to the music and the music played on. Jimmy looked down at her, she was a very beautiful blond girl, with a nice finger. He smiled at her. "My name is Jimmy Bentley, what is your name?" She answer back to him that her name was "Sarah. "About that time Jill came throw the front door and she was with a lady that looked a little like a gypsy, the lady was around forty years old with long black hair and a she worn a dark colored blouse with a long ruffled sleeve blouse and a dark granny dress. Jill looked nice with a short blue mini shirt and a white blouse that fit tied around her breast. She seen Jimmy and waved back at him a s they walked to the back of the room. Jimmy was with a blond girl and waved to her as Jill and friend walked by. Jill said some thing I couldn't hear to the lady with her and turned and started walking away from her on her way to the kitchen.

Jimmy turned back to the girl was with and looked into her eyes and said to her, "So, what is your name pretty girl?" Jimmy was tying to make a friend out of her, "So, tell me about yourself?" and then he when on to say, "Your a student, and you what?" Sarah pulled away just a little and she lower her eyes and looked to the dance floor. She said nothing.

Jimmy realized Sarah wasn't a student and changed the subject, "Can I get you something to drink." He asked her, Jimmy went on to say "My father runs a store in Bangor and my mother a house wife. Do you have any bother or sister, Sarah?" She looked at Jimmy and smiled, her face soften a bit. Her face had a little smile on it and said to Jimmy, "I've got three bother and I'm the youngest one in the family." "Well I guess I'll have to watch myself and a nice to you." Jimmy said almost laughing. Jill walked back to her friend , who looked a little like a gypsy, Jill was caring A card table with her and set up the table in front of her friend. Jill turned and went back in the kitchen a few minutes she came back with two folding chairs. She put one chair on one side and the anther chair on the other side. The lady set down in the chair her back to the wall. The music stopped, the band was going on brake. It was ten o'clock in the evening

Jimmy found a place for Sarah and him to set down in the chairs on the dance floor. "Sarah, Please save me a set and I'll go get use some thing to drink. What are you having to drink Sarah?" Jimmy asked her.

"You can get me a White Russian, please." Sarah told Jimmy' in a pleasant voice, Jimmy shook his head yes and went to get the drinks. Jill looked around the room it was a good size room about forty by A hundred feet long. The music had stopped of a wild it was a good time for Jill to go around and ask people about her friend, Hilgi and tell them that in sent nine o'clock and there was way more then the twenty that was asked to come. Jill didn't count but maybe there was forty maybe fifty people there know. Jill started going around asking people to have their fortune told and how grant it would be to know what was in store for them. Most of the people agreed to have their fortune told, it would be fun thing to do. The people started lining up in front of Hilgi, the lady fortune teller. Jill tell them it wound cost them only five dollars. And any other time it was twenty dollars fortune. Jill told their money as they lined up for the reading.

Jimmy went to the kitchen and asked Gorden, if he would make a White Russian for him. Gorden said "Yes." And made the drink for him. Jimmy handed Gorden a five dollar bill and said, "Thank You." To Gorden. And Jimmy went back to were Sarah was setting and handed her the drink. Jimmy had made himself a whiskey and coke and he set down beside Sarah.

Sarah, took the drink for Jimmy, her eyes told him, thank you. And she said to him, "What do you think going on down there, Jimmy." she pointed to the back of the room, were Jill and her friend was. and standing there in a line of people sending in front of Hilgi as she set at the table and Jill stood beside her.

Jimmy turned and looked down, to see his friend Jill and another lady setting at a table. So what is Jill up to now? Jimmy thought. "Well lest take a walked down and see what going on, Sarah." Jimmy and Sarah stood up and started walking to the back of the room.

Jill seen Jimmy and the blond girl with him and she said to Jimmy, "Hi, Jimmy." Jill waved her hand to Hilgi. She went on to say, "My friend, Hilgi is the best fortune teller in New England, Jimmy, I've know her for years. She lives just down the street for me, I asked her if she come and do her thing, tell fortune, and she said, Yes. It's only cost you ten dollars for the both of you, Jimmy." Jill looked at Sarah and smiled at her and said, "I'm Jill, Jimmy and I are in one of the classes together." She put her hand out to shake Sarah hand and they shook hands. "You wont your fortune told to don't you sweety?" Jill asked the girl with Jimmy.

Sarah shook her head Yes, and her face lit- up, Sarah was having a good time with Jimmy, who she just meet and thought it would be fun. She never had her fortune told before. Sarah looked at Jimmy with her pretty blue eyes. Jimmy put his hand in his pocket and pulled out his wallet and took out a ten dollar bill and handed it to Jill.

"Thanks, Jimmy, you won't be sorry, she really good." Jill said Hilgi was with another girl, and Jimmy thought he heard, the lady fortune stranger. Then Hilgi said to the girl in front of them, "I hope you meet him ,soon dear. The young girl stood up and walked away.

Jimmy thought he heard the fortune teller, say to the girl in front of them as she got up to leave. About a tall dark stranger. and then Hilgi, said to the girl in front of them "I hope you find him soon, Dear." Hilgi told the girl.

Jimmy was thinking, Oh Boy! The old, you'll meet a tall dark stranger routine story. Sarah set down in the chair in front of the fortune teller.

Hilgi, didn't tell many people her name. She was a thirty nine year old a divorced woman with two teen age children. Hilgi had been unmarried of the last ten year. And she didn't wont to get married ever again. Once was once to many of her. Hilgi's husband was in the Air Force and when they was married, they moved from place to place when ever the Government wonted her husband to be. Hilgi, was living with her family in Germany when she met Mark, she fell in love with him and two month later they got married and a week later moved to the United States and she never when back to Germany again. She remembered how lonely she was not Hilgi had always be a gifted child when she was younger, as she got older her mind became a force that she could tell the future. When she came to the United States her marriage wasn't going very good, they fort all the time they were together. Hilgi, know her marriage wouldn't last much longer. So, she started telling fortune of money, when they lived in Florida. The word got around and she started making a lot of money. when Hilgi mover to Maine, she went to a Lawyer and filled for a devoice and started telling fortune to help with the bills. Hilgi could look into the few dollars. She seen good and she seen bad things to come to them. After the devoice she moved in a nice three bedroom apartment, just up the road from Jill, and soon her and Jill became good friends. Jill was a nice single great mother to her children. Ten years had gone by and she was not as good at telling fortune, so she thought, when she was younger she was very good Hilgi could look into their eyes and tell them what tomorrow would be like. But now she wasn't as good, her heart was in her fortune telling. She was here at Jill college and would do the best she could to tell them what tomorrow would bring.

Hilgi took Sarah hand and turned it over palm up, so she could read her palm. Then a feeling that Hilgi hadn't felt in a long time came over her. It was true feel that something was terribly wrong. Sarah close to harm and something had to be done soon. Hilgi let Sarah's hand down and with both of Hilgi hands put them to the side of Sarah's head. Hilgi looked into Sarah's eyes.

Sarah had lost her mother six month ago to cancer and she couldn't make it to the funeral. She just didn't have the money to go back to Greenville, Mississippi and know one to watch the children. She know Jill would if she could, but Sarah didn't have time to get the money, so she didn't go. Plus she just broke up with her boy friend of five years. They was thinking of getting married and then he when out with someone else, and that was it. She told him good bye and good ridden. She had a child by her live in boy friend and when he moved out she was left with a two year old girl, how she loved with all her heart. Sarah found a job at a near by restaurant as a waitress and had to pay a baby setter. She needed something good to happen in her life. Sarah looked at the lady fortune teller for her to tell her something good. She'd just met Jimmy, he seemed to be a very nice man, one she could fall in love with and wouldn't hurt her. Sara looked at the lady fortune teller hoping that she was going to say Jimmy was the right man for her. Sara didn't see a smile on her face it seem to look twisted and up set as she held her hand. Hilgi was looking into Sarah's eyes to see Sara's future and Hilgi was felling something that was the dark and cool surrounding her all around her. The sprites of evil and death, Hilgi had to help the girl and maybe save her life. Hilgi could feel the cool hands of evil toughing her upper body. It gave Hilgi a cool chills that ran up her spin. It became so bad her body shook with the feeling. Hilgi need to go further and find out what the danger was, so, she could warn Sarah. Then Hilgi's mind started to receiving flash of Sarah's future. They was danger and death close and the young man she was with was also surrounded by death and evil too. Hilgi could see Sarah at here job as a waitress and she was safe there, but the dark side was telling her go with him some wear and be surrounded by evil? What did it mean, Hilgi thought? To go with them to meet evil! She tried hard to think why. Yes it was her job that would save her. Why Hilgi didn't know, but it clear to Hilgi the job would play a very important part in helping the young girl. Know Hilgi had to pull away from the power, and pull herself together, and warn Sarah, of things that may happen if she made the wrong choice. Hilgi put her hands down and pulled away just a little for Sarah. Now was the time to tell her of what could be. Hilgi wasn't smiling, her face gram and with concerning look about what might happen to Sarah's future. Hilgi's hand tying around Sarah's hand as Hilgi thought of what might happen, something terrible it was pure evil.

Sara's eyes wading as Hilgi's hands tying around her hands , it hurt her a little as Hilgi squeezed her hand Then Hilgi losing her grip and Sara eyes went back to normal. Hilgi lower her eyes and then she looked at Sarah. Hilgi had not had the felling of danger in a long time. Maybe Hilgi's powers had came back to her after all these years of mind reading? It was true the girl in front of her was in real danger of losing her life! Hilgi had to do something fast to save the young girl in front of her. So she said to the girl (Sara) with a in a concern kind voice. " In times Sarah, there is going to be good time and happy times in you're life. And I see a baby in time, but right now Sara, I see you could be in great danger and it's no to far away from you. You must make the right choice in your life first. Hilgi looked into Sara's big blue eyes as she spook to the young girl in front of her. Hilgi shook the girl hand be careful, very careful, if you do so you'll have a full life a head of you and if not?" Hilgi stopped talking, she thought she got her spot across to the young. Hilgi hope so enough to save her life Hilgi hoped! "Be very careful dear because I see damage around you." Hilgi was spending a little more time warring the girl in front of her then she had been, but Hilgi know it was important to tell Sara of the danger she felt that was so near to the poor girl You must make the right choose in what you do. I don't know why but you're job well play a big part in what may happen to you in the future. But first there is going to be hard and dangers things happen all around you. I can tell the young man behind you is a nice person. But it's up to you to make the right choose in you're life." Hilgi said almost pleaded with Sarah to lesson to what she was saying. The reading was over Hilgi pulled away from the young girl and dropped her hands to her side. Sarah lessoned to what Hilgi told her about her future and what might happen to her. Sarah wasn't excepting Hilgi to say anything like that to her. was Hilgi tying to scare her or was she tying to warn her of thinks to come? There was a line of people behind Sarah waiting to have their fortune to be told also.

Sarah got up to leave, realized Hilgi had scared her. She started to shake and felt a little sick to her stomach, as she got up and turned to leave. Hilgi looked into Sara's eyes and said "Child be careful be very careful danger is all around you young lady. Hilgi waved to Jimmy to set down, but Jimmy seen Sarah was up set waved her off.

Jimmy walked Sarah by the arm and said in a soft voice, "Let dance, Sweaty don't pay any thought to he. She just telling you a story that what she does to get your money, and then she tells story that all she is story teller, Sarah!" He held her hand and then walked off. Barry Band was playing a soft love song. It seemed to be just at the right Time. Jimmy held Sarah close to him, her warn breast pressed tie against the music. "Are you OK, Sarah?" Jimmy said as he pulled his lips from her lips. She looked at him and she was starting to fell better know that she was dancing once again. She shook her head Yes, as she looked into his eyes. Jimmy smiled back at her, their danced on to the music. The music stopped and changed to a nice fast beat song. Jimmy let her go and they moved apart to dance to the fast dance. Sarah had good moves, and she was a good dancer. Sarah's slam body had a nice, chare, chare It was almost eleven thirty and Sarah looked at Jimmy and said "I've to go pretty soon Jimmy, I've got to get up in the morning and go to work. I had a real good time with you Jimmy, I hate to go but I have to. "she told him. They danced one more slow dance together. Jimmy held her close to him as the Band played a soft song. And then their walked to the door. And Jimmy said to Sarah, " Please let me take you home?" he said. She shook her head O.K, and they started to leave together. .They passed a beautiful black girl that was named . Rachel and she waved at Jimmy as they went by and said, "What about that dance you promise me a dance Jimmy?" Jimmy replied," I will when I get back Rachel." She didn't think it was the right time to tell Jimmy about her little girl at home. Sarah looked at Jimmy he was a really nice guy. She could fall for a guy like him, she give him a big smile. But probable he wouldn't like the idea, that she had a small child at home. Dam it! She thought to herself. Sarah moved into his arms and looked up at he's and some face. Reached up and kiss him. She seen the pretty black girl wave at Jimmy and Sarah said, "Who was that girl, Jimmy?"

Jimmy replied, "Just a friend, Rachel." The got in Jimmy's car and drove, just down the road about five miles the Sarah's apartment house. Sarah told him the street and when they came to the apartment wear she lived, she pointed to the building and told Jimmy to pull in the driveway. Jimmy got out of his car and bristle walked around the car. So he could open the door for her. They walked hand and hand to the front door. Sarah stopped and turned to face Jimmy and said, "Thanks Jimmy, I had a great time." Jimmy put his arms around her and they kiss, good night. Jimmy said, " I have your number I'll call you tomorrow." Jimmy said. "I'll see you soon, I hope." She open the door and when in the building. Jimmy went back to the party, it was almost eleven thirty when he got back to the party. Jimmy walked in the frat house where the party was held and looked around for Rachel. He didn't see her at first and he walked to the back of the room, were he seen Rachel with a tall black young man. Jimmy walked up to were Rachel was and said, "Hi! Rachel, how about that dance, you promise me a dance?" Rachel heard Jimmy and turned to see him and gave him a big smile. She put her hand out and Jimmy took it.

LeRoy looked at Jimmy and was thinking. That little white boy came back tying to put the move on his girl. He keep it up and I'll bust his balls, if he keeps doesn't stop trying to hit on his woman. Rachel my bitch, LeRoy thought. They walked off to the dance floor. The band was playing love song. Rachel moved in very close to Jimmy. Her breast pushed again his warm chest. Rachel looked in to his face and kissed him softly on the lips.

Jimmy could feel her round fuel beast again his body. He liked it and he like her. Jimmy thought Rachel was putting the move on him, and he liked it. He'd never made love to a black girl and he thought he'd like it. They danced on as the music played on. Rachel was a good dancer, and so was Jimmy, but she moved just a bite to fast for the dance and they didn't seem to dance as good together, as they could have danced Rachel moved way to fast for the music and Jimmy to slow.

Rachel was a beautiful black girl, he kissed her and the music stopped. He did like her, they lips moved apart and she moved back just a little and, Jimmy looked in her eyes and smiled and said to Rachel, "We could go out some time. I know, I study a lot most of the time, but I'd take time off to go out with you, we'd have fun together."

"Sorry, I'd love to go out with you Jimmy. I'll give you my number. Call me any time. LeRoy doesn't mean anything to me, were just friends." Rachel said in a low sexy voice. And went on to say, "I've got to get back to LeRoy, he thinks he owns my, he don't!." Rachel turned and walked back to LeRoy. to leave. Rachel thought to herself she'd love to be with that nice looking white boy, Jimmy, he'd make her a

great man, any like her friend LeRoy. Jimmy one day was going to be a
big time lawyer and make big money and live in a real nice house and
LeRoy could do that, so he played baseball, he'd never make big money
like sweet little Jimmy boy. She bite they could make real good love
together. Maybe one day she'd see it happened. Rechel turned back to
Jimmy and throw him a kiss and waved good bye she'd see him soon.
There was no more beer left and little else to drink. But Jimmy loved
dancing it made him feel good. Maybe it was a Indian, native thing. to
do. But it was O.K. with Jimmy he like dancing and the girls liked a
guy that could to dance too. He thought he'd stay a few more minutes
and then go back to the dome. Maybe he could fine a girl to dance
with. He looked around and seen Amy setting in a chair over in the
corner by herself. Jimmy walked over and said pleasant voice, "Amy
would take she got up and took his hand. And they walk to the dance
floor, hand "It nice to see you, Jimmy." Amy said as they walked to the
dance floor. Amy was a pretty little brunette girl with a slim finger,
and beautiful brown eyes. Amy had a beautiful face with a nice smile
you couldn't forget. As it became later at night more and more people
showed up for the party. Bryan and Jill had only invited thirty people
and there was seventy and more was coming all the time, as the night
when on. It was almost a eleven o'clock at night and they was starting
to get low on beer and whiskey. People that came were asked to bring
they own drinks. And so people did just that. At times the small dance
floor became crowed when the band played the good dance. Jimmy
like Amy, he thought for her as his friend. He didn't know that well,
they was in a couple of class together in college. He thought she was
pretty, but he didn't get that far with her. Amy seem cold to man at
times. The band was playing a slow dance. He put his arms around her
and they danced to the music. Jimmy thought he wound mind getting
to know Amy better. The dance floor became very crowed with other
dances also dancing on the floor. Jimmy tried to keep for bumping
into other couples as they dance on. Amy looked at Jimmy and said,
" I heard that your Uncle died And left you a lot of money, Jimmy?"
Amy asked him.

Jimmy was surprised to hear her say that, had the hold campus
had heard about his Uncle Will? Jimmy thought to himself. What had
Jill was telling the hold campus about his uncle? Jimmy was thinking
to himself, for someone who's going to be a lawyer, some times he

talked to much, he'd better learn to do better in the future. Amy was a good dancer, these was the first time he'd ever dance with her and she had great dance move. The song ended and the Berry band started playing a great fast dance. Amy started to walk away, and Jimmy said out loud, "Amy on more dance with me?" he had a pleading sound to his voice. Amy stopped and turned around and walked back to Jimmy. The started playing a great fast dance. She was only a couple feet away for him. Jimmy took her hand and spun her around and her turned around to the music. Amy had good moves, she had great move to \ the music. They dance great together, around the dance floor. Amy had a big smile on her face. She was having a good time with Jimmy. If she was going to have a man friend Jimmy would be the one, most likely. Amy right now didn't care much for the guys, girl thing maybe she never be ready for sex with a guy? Amy really didn't no right now The music stopped playing. They walked off the dance floor Together. " Thanks Jimmy." She said and then added, "I'll see you Monday in class." Jimmy shook his head and they walked off the dance floor. Jimmy said to her, "Do you need a ride home, Amy?"

"No, I've got a ride with Jill." She said quietly. Amy thought Jimmy was a real nice good looking guy and she had fun dancing with him but she already had a boy friend in the Army and she was going to wait for him to come home so one day they could get married. If Amy had met Jimmy first he might have became her boy friend but he didn't and she already had a man.

Jimmy thought Amy was very nice looking but she seem a little cold, maybe she had a boy friend or she just didn't care for him

CHAPTER 3

It was a warm day and Jimmy only had a week of left to go, before finals. And Jimmy was doing good effect to have a little fun. He had played a little golf in High school and with summer coming he won't to just get out in the sun and play a game of something, anything just to get out. It had been a long cold winter in Maine. And been in college and not be able to go very far, because of the snow storms that came every couple of days. Jimmy remembered the old saying about being in closed of days in the cabin, and they called it, having Cabin Fever. Jimmy thought it wound be great maybe to play a round of golf. So, he pick up the telephone and called Bryan and asked him about playing golf Saturday morning. Bryan said O.K. but were was they going to play and he need a ride. Jimmy told him he'd have a ride for him and they pick him up at eight o'clock in the morning. Then he called Arthur at his home he said he'd come. All Jimmy needed was one more person, he thought LeRoy would be a good one to play golf. But he didn't have LeRoy number, so he find him on campus and ask him in person. Jimmy called around asking if they know were LeRoy was and finely someone said he was at the gym playing basketball. So Jimmy took a ride down to the gym to ask LeRoy about playing golf. When Jimmy when in the gym LeRoy was practices his shooting. Jimmy walked up to LeRoy and said ,"Not bad shooting LeRoy." Jimmy took the ball and tried a shoot, it when in the hoop. LeRoy, I came here to ask you if you'd like to play golf these Saturday with the guy." Jimmy stopped and looked at him. LeRoy couldn't believe Jimmy was asking him to play golf with him. "What do you mean, play golf with you, why? LeRoy asked. I'd like you to play with us because I'll bet you're a good golfer. Your good at all the other sports why not golf!" replied.

"Well, I can play, but I don't have any club." LeRoy said. "You're not a bad player? I get you so good golf clubs and I'll buy you lunch too, alright buddy?" Jimmy told him.

"Yeh!, O.K, I'll wants fried chicken and my girl friend would like a couple of lobster too.

"That fine with me anything you wont, but I expert a good game of golf LeRoy. You're good at most sport we'll see how good you are at my game golf. And I wont you to try to bet me, O.K?" Jimmy replied.

"Hell I can beat you any time any place, Jimmy". LeRoy said to him. LeRoy shook his head, it was alright. I'll pit you up Saturday, at Eight o'clock. LeRoy said fine.

It was another warm day in Maine. Jimmy pick up LeRoy, but Rachel didn't wont to go. Jimmy had rented a set of golf clubs for LeRoy at the pro shop and then they when on to the golf course five miles away, were they met Bryan and Arthur.

Jimmy on the first hole hit a long straight drive about three hundred yards, had a nice drive, the next short Jimmy did was chip on the green and the first put when in the hole and won the hole with Birdie., LeRoy had a nice drive that matched Jimmy but two putted to lose the hole. And by the third hole, Jimmy was up two hole on the pack But on the forth hole LeRoy had a supper long drive and one putted to won the hole with Eagle that tied the game with Jimmy After nine holes they was both tied with at forty four LeRoy hit hard and long drive to keep up with Jimmy. That was just what Jimmy wonted a good game but it was turning out to be a great game of golf and both player were at their best. The ninth and last hole Jimmy and LeRoy was on the green in two. LeRoy was away and putted first. LeRoy turned to Jimmy and said, " For a short white boy you play pretty good. Last change to beat me Jimmy. How everything going with your uncle will, Jimmy? You think your going to get a lot of money out of the will? "

Jimmy thought he's trying to get my mind off the game so he can beat me. but he replied back to LeRoy saying, "From what I know my uncle didn't have that much money to give away. most likely it will be a little something not much, it's the thought that counts, I gust?" Jimmy turn his attention back to the game. These was the last hole and they was tied who ever win the next hole won the game ."LeRoy, you played a good game today. I'm going to put the game away with these short. "And my uncle's will is just, fine LeRoy ."Jimmy said with a smile on his face. Then Jimmy turned his head to look at the last hole on the course, the hole was just twenty so feet away. he put his fingers around the handle of the put and looked the put over . It looked like it might turn just a little left at the end as the ball rounded down the green. Jimmy moved his arm slowly back and then smoothly hit the ball, it rounded straight to the hole. The ball started turning to the left a bite to much and hit the lip of the cup and slowly rounded in the cup with ping of the ball. Jimmy slowing pulled put the cub back and watched the ball round in the cup., Jimmy won!

LeRoy leaned forward and shook his hand, and said" Nice game, Jimmy." "Thanks I had a good time." Jimmy said it was a great game we'll have to play again some time and I'll give you a change to get back at me." .Jimmy had a big smile on his face he very well could have lost to him, but he didn't.

CHAPTER 4

Jimmy found the number of the lawyer in the telephone book. And dial the number. The phone rang a couple of time and then a voice with a slice down east at scent answered the phone and said "Hello, these is Attorney Wentworth office. What can I do for you? "It was female voice, most likely one of the lawyer secretary's

Jimmy said to her in a nice voice, "Hello, I'm Jimmy Bentely Orono Maine would like to speak to attorney Wentworth please, on a family matter. it's about the Orland will, I under stand he is the attorney for the late Mr. Orland." Jimmy waited for the girl to reply back to him. .

Then the female voice said "Yes, I'll see if he's free to talk to you, please wait a minute, she went to see if he would be free to talk to the young man.. A few minutes later, a deep voice of the Lawyer said "Hello, I'm Wentworth., What can I do for You? "Jimmy replied to the male voice on the telephone line, in a pleasant tone. " Hello, I'm Jimmy Bentely of Orono Maine I'm a student in college and I received a letter in the mail saying I was named in my uncle's will and to come to your office at the date on the letter., is that right?

"And what was his name on the letter for your uncle that was named?" the attorney asked.

Jimmy replied back to him My uncle's name was Orland." and he when on to say, "Do I have to be there for the reading of the will, sir?"

Wentworth had a very deep raff voice with a heavy down east act
–sent .when he answered Jimmy, "Ah, Well it would be good if you
attend your uncle's reading of the will. If you don't you might not get
what he left you young man. I was hoping you could tell me about the
set up of the will If you have a idea what I might be getting in the will
sir." Jimmy went on to say, and seeing if I must be there if you could
tell me the best place to wear I could stay wily I'm in town, and a good
place to eat wild I here in town, sir?"

"Ah, can't tell you anything about the Will young man, it is in a
sealed envelope, and I not opening it tell the day for the reading of the
will but Ah, I can tell you that there are two motels in town. And well,
that you could call one of them about a room, and have them save you
a room for the time you're hear." the lawyer when on to say, "It's going
to be a busy time of year to fine a room in town. And you asked me
about a restaurant. Oh, Yes ah, by the way I believe you do have to
attend the reading of the Orland's will. I don't live in town myself I live
in Calais, a few miles away.

Jimmy told the Lawyer in a nice voice, "I haven't be up that way
in a few years. I think I remember there was a nice restaurant right
in town, with real nice food, is it still there, sir?" Jimmy asked the
lawyer.

"Why yes I believe so, there are a couple nice restaurant in town."
Wentworth said in his riff down east voice "So, what are you going to
college for, young man?" Wentworth the lawyer asked. Jimmy?

"I wont to become a big time lawyer, and so I can help people that
need me help. "Jimmy replied. "Oh, that will be nice if you can do
that. I have to go now I have work to do young Wentworth now he
had a down east act-scent , but hell he didn't care around hear almost
every one had a little act- scent , he was well dressed and one of the few
lawyers around these part of the State, hell he smile to himself, call me
what you wont, you could say I'm a potato Lawyer and the big money
was in the drug dealer , they paid the best. Hell so if someone had
to be there lawyer, why not him he like the money. Wentworth turn
around in his chair what the hell was he doing handling so die man
will, there wasn't any money it figure job. Oh well all he had to do was
read the will and he'd charge them big time for doing so. he when back
to thinking about his work, no more thinking about a stooped will.

I'll see you the day of the reading of the will, I have to get back to work now. Good bye young Jimmy." Wentworth hung up the phone."

"Good bye, sir" Jimmy said, as he hear the lawyer hang up the phone Jimmy also hang up his phone. Jimmy looked in the phone book and found the number of one for the Motels in East Machias and dial the number a male voice answer the phone After a couple of rings. "Hello, these is the Randle Motel, what can I do for you?" the voice said. very flatly.

"Hi, these is Jimmy Bentely I like to rent a room for the night for August 11 for Monday these year. I'd like a single room if possible.

How much will it cost me?" Jimmy ask.

The voice on the phone thicken in tone and replied, "It's our a busy time of the year for use. you'll have summer rates to dial with. It will cost you one hundred forty dollars a night. How many nights are you planning to stay, he said bluntly ?" He said bluntly.

Jimmy thought to him self, August eleventh seem to be near the end of the summer section, the voice was lying to him but there wasn't much he could, go to a different motel, there was only one other motel in the area. Then he when on to say, "A couple of nights. That seemed a bite high, could you go down a bite?" Jimmy asked him. The voice on the phone posed a moment, then when on said, "Well, will you be alone? If so we could, and I don't know what the boss will say, but I could come down a bite to a single for a hundred and fifty for two night payment?" the voice over the phone said. "I'll pay by credit card." Jimmy didn't know if he could trust the voice on the phone but he'd take a change and give the man on the other end of the phone his numbers to his card. What did you say you name was?" Jimmy asked the voice on the phone."

The voice at the other end of the phone cleared his throat out and the didn't wont to give his name out but he did, "My name is Milton Fess." he told Jimmy. It was o.k. now so Jimmy told Milton the numbers on his credit card. then when on to tell Milton that he wonted the day of August eleventh as he had business in town. ".Milton took down the numbers and told Jimmy he'd save the room for the day of August eleven for him and then the Milton the manger at the motel he be looking forward to meeting Jimmy on August eleventh and then said thank you , that the room would be ready at that date, thank him and hang up the phone.

Now he'd have to fine someone that could fine he's ten year old car, he'd ask around, it the club and school to see if he could fine someone to fix his car. He thought he heard someone say about a man that did cars for extern money. Jimmy was in the dome room he got up and walked out in the hall. He'd ask around and to find the name of the man who fixed cars.

Jimmy asked a couple of guy in the hall, know one know of the man. So her when down stairs. They was Eddie and Vic. He asked them. They didn't know, but Eddie said he had heard of a man that when to so club. Jimmy That him and when on. He looked around the room, not a girl, he thought a guy would know one who fix car, much better. He seen Bill Morten, he bet he'd know. He was biker and like fast cars. Jimmy walked over to Bill and asked him if he know of anyone that fix cars. He told him about a man that went to the men club in Brewer.

Bill, was thinking, know what was his name? It's sort of a deferent name. It begun with a C. He tight to think. Clake, not clean, Clen... don.. Yes that was the name. Clendan. And he live in Brewer, so wear?

"You Know his last name", Bill or close to it? Jimmy said. "Know lets see. Let me thank so more, and it may come to me. Pool, something like that."

Jimmy thanked him and when to make a couple call to find out wear he might live. He called the Men Club. and Asked the male voice that answer the phone. The bar tender told Jimmy it mind be Clendan White. Jimmy looked the name up in the book and found it and dial the number. The phone rang a couple of time and then a man with a deep voice answer the phone and said, "Hello!"

Jimmy replied back, "Is these Clendan White, the man who make ex money fixing cars?"

Clendan answer in his deep voice, "Yes, I'm a mechanic who works on cars from time to time to get extra. what can I do for you?" Clendan was hopping it was more work for him. He was thinking about getting married again and need the money.

"Hi, these is Jimmy Bentely and I'm planning on going on a long tripe to Machias and wound like you to look over my ten year old Mustang. So I can make the tripe safely. I'm leaving in a couple of week. I'll pay you what it cost for the parts up front, if you with?" Jimmy told him.

"Ok, you bring your car to my house tomorrow and I'll take a look at it. If it needs to much work you'll have the rent a garage with a lift if need. I live at 214 Silver Road, in Brewer. I'll can see you around nine o'clock in tomorrow, if that alright with you?" Clendan said in a friendly voice.

"That will be fine, I'll be there tomorrow at nine o'clock in the morning. Tank Clendan." and Jimmy hang the phone up.

The next morning Jimmy was there with he's car and pulled in the drive way at ten minutes to nine .He got out for his car and walked up to the door and knotted on the door. After a short wild the door open, it was Clendan. It looked to Jimmy that he been drinking. They was empty beer bottle all over the living room and the door was open to the bed room, there was bottles in there too. It looked as thought Jimmy woke him up. He was only haft dress and seem haft a wake. "Is it nine already?" he ask Jimmy. Jimmy said yes with he's head. Clendan put his shirt on and they walked out the front door to take a look at Jimmy car. Clendan shook his head and said, " Doesn't look to bad to me. Now lets take a look and see what we can find wrong with it." About that time a car drove up in the drive way and a nice looking woman got out of the car, and waved to Clendan. "Hi, Clendan what are you doing?" the pretty girl said. Clendan was looking at Jimmy car, he looked up and said, "Hi, Cassie."

Clendan was looking Jimmy car over, he slide up the car to take a look at the under neigh of the car. Jimmy looked at the beautiful girl walking up to him. She was five foot four inches tall. Much shorter then her six foot boy friend, Clendan. She had a nice figure, around a hundred and twenty pounds. She had shoulder length brown hair with beautiful full face and a nice smile. He voice was soft as she spook to he. "Hi, I'm Cessie, Clendan friend." he put her hand out, and Jimmy shook her soft hand. Jimmy looked at her pretty big brown eyes and smile back at her and said. "Nice to meet you, my name is Jimmy Bentely and these is my car. Clendan is looking at. I'm going on a trip in a couple of week and I'd like my car in good condition of the trip. Clendan got out form under the car, and told Jimmy, "You'll need to replace the right ball joint. I think I can do it right hear. I've got a portable lift. I'll check the engine out he when and lifted the hood of the car. Then went inside the car and turned it on. It ran of a minute or two then he turned it off. And looked at Jimmy and said, the engine alright, good and tight. It will do just fine.

Clendan was a big guy at six foot six, not that good looking, with bad teeth and thinning gray hair. Jimmy thought Cessie was far to good looking to be going with a guy like Clendan. Yes he was a likable guy but he was a heave drinker and only work, once in a wild. Jimmy talked to Cessie a little bet and told her about Uncle Orland Will. She took Clendan almost every Friday and Saturday night to the Club to drink and dance a little. She hopped to meet Jimmy there so time and have a dance together. Jimmy said he'd like that. Clendan intervened, and said " We can pit up the parts tomorrow and I can put them on for you then.

The next day they went and pitch up the parts and Clendan put them on Jimmy car. Only took two and a half hours to do. Cessie and Jimmy talk together all the time. Jimmy liked her and, I think she liked him, but Clendan was her boy friend and that was it. Jimmy and Cessie became fiend that day. Jimmy wonted to ask her if she wound ride to Machias with him. But he didn't think Clendan wound like it, so he didn't ask her.

CHAPTER 5

Clendan had tuned up the engine and fix the front end of Jimmy car, he had the car in top cheap. The engine song quit just as a new car.

Jimmy had been up scent six o'clock getting ready for the trip down east for the will. He had dress, showed and shaved and packed a few things so he could stay over night and be at the reading on time. At seven O'clock he turned the key and the engine came to life. He put the car in gear and stepped on the peddle and was on his way to Machias. Jimmy stop in Ellworth and have breakfast room. Get a little some thing to eat and bed down of the night. He was hopping to see some of his cosine he hadn't seen in years. Jimmy hadn't seen Betty or Mary of mothers side of the family. And their was also Nancy and Gale. Jimmy stopped in Ellworth and had his breakfast at a local restaurant then went on he's way to Machias. He tuned the radio up a little. It would be his company on the trip. The music was a soft song at could put him to sleep he hoped it would change to a fast beat soon. Jimmy becoming up on the stitch of woods called the Franklin Woods. He drove on down the high way. It wasn't a bad strip of road. Jimmy remembered there was a crap turn just up a head. He'd have to slow down so he could made the turn safely. Jimmy couldn't stop thinking about what would happen tomorrow at the reading of the will. Funny, Jimmy's father didn't like Orland very much. Jimmy tried to think why. Well there was the time when they all stop in on aunt May and uncle Orland. Jimmy was Six years old. Jimmy's mother went to visit her sister May and Dad went too. We went up the steps and my mother knotted on the door. Aunt May came and the two sister hued and said hello to each other. And we all went in Aunt May house. Uncle Orland said Hi, to my father and they shook hands. May started talking about old time. my sister when up starts with her cousins. Jimmy stayed in the kitchen with his mother and father.

Uncle Orland said to my father, "You must be hungry, after that long trip?" to my father.

My father replied, "Well, a little. I'm shore the children are. "Uncle Orland, turned back to what he was cooking on the kitchen stove, a large peace of steak that had been in the pan. That he'd been cooking for so time, and it was almost done. Jimmy could smile the meat cooking and it smiled so good he could almost could tasked in his mouth. It had been hours before Jimmy had eaten and he was a bite hungry and his mouth watered as he could almost task the meat in his mouth My mother and her sister set at the big kitchen table, I set it the much smaller table and chair for the children, to the right of my mother .My father and uncle Orland stood up talking May's kitchen was much small compared to our. May kitchen was all white and looked very clean. It was a nice kitchen a bite small that's all. My sister and cousins were only stairs a little wild went, my Uncle Orland went to the stairs and hauled up the up stairs that it was going to be time to eat dinner in a couple of minutes. My aunt stood up and walked over to the cabinet in the kitchen and took out some cans of food to eat. May walked over to the kitchen table and handed them to my cousin to open the two large can of beans.

I keep my eye on uncle Orland who was cooking the tasty steak on the kitchen stove. My cousin opened the can beans and passed them to their mother aunt May, so his could cook the beans on the stove. I watched uncle Orland pick up the large goosey steak with a folk and fop it on his plate setting on the kitchen table. Orland went and pick up a large knife so he could cut the steak and set down at the table. Orland took the knife and cut a peace of the goosey steak and put a peace in his mouth. I thought I heard him make a sound as he chewed the peace of steak in his month .I thought I heard the sound of him as he chewed the steak. "Arrrrrre!" Orland said it was so good in his mouth.

Aunt May spook to me and told me to set down and have

something to eat. I set down, I was still watching uncle Orland eat the steak. Aunt May handed my a plate, I took it and set down to eat. I turned my head to see aunt May with a pot of something and place large spoon full of beans in my plate.

My eyes widen, beans! I thought to myself, I had been thinking I was going to get steak too? I looked up at uncle Orland who was still eating the steak. Orland ask my father if he was going to have something to eat too.

About that time my father inter upped him and said. "No thanks, I have to go down the road to his other bother in law Peter,

I'll be back in a couple of hours to pick the kids up then." He turned and lift to go to Peter, his other bother- i- law house.

I was still hungry I pick up the fork and eat the can beans. Jimmy witched his father leave Orland house, my father never went in Orland house again. I stayed with my mother why she visited with her sister. I was young and at first, I didn't know why uncle Orland eat a big goosey steak and every one else had can beans or cereal to eat. But now that I'm older and I think I know why Orland eat .the steak and no one else did? My father was greatly offended by it! And never when back to Orland's house again.

Know that I think about it, it's like the lion king that takes what ever he wants from the kill or the meal and the wife and children get what left over if anything! Uncle Orland thought of himself as the lion, the great white hunter. He eat first and they got what was left. I liked my uncle Orland, I don't thing I really under stood him, but he was good man. Uncle Orland house was a nice little house that was out in the country in a small little town. The closes house to Orland's house was a good three hundred yard away. On one side was his bother in law Peter and the other side fence was a cow field and his other bother in law Orland. .It was a pretty little house with a kitchen, living room and master bedroom and bathroom on the bottom floor and three bedrooms and bath on the scent floor. Jimmy had been up stairs only a couple of time and seen the rooms were small, but very clean. There was a one car garage just in back of the house off to the right. Jimmy never seen Orland park his car in there. I think he used it for thing he bought. And Jimmy seen a old car engine in the garage, which Orland must have been working on at one time.

I learned much later, that my father did go to his bother in law and had a nice dinner of meat and potato's with vegetables. My father and his other bother in law got along very well together. Unlike my father can beans, and think his going to like it. For what I know my father never when in side Orland's house again. When you come to my father house you eat very well. Roast beef, steak, chicken pork and fresh fish. nothing but the best. What he eats, you can have to eat too as his guest. My father would never give you anything out of a can. How dare you serve him can beans From then on, when ever we went down east my father dropped us off at Orland and when over to his other bother in law Peter's house. My mother would go visit her sister for a bite, but that was all. My father never razed his voice to Orland. They said Hi, to each other that was it from then on. At the time, I thought, that my father lived in the city and made far more money then uncle Orland did. My father could afford to eat well, and uncle Orland couldn't. That the time it was happing I didn't under stand why uncle Orland acted the way he did? But now that I'm a few years older I think I do under stand just a little bite.

Traffic was lit and the radio was still playing a soft tone. Jimmy keep his eye on the road but he was thing about who uncle Orland was and why so many people didn't like him as a man., Jimmy like uncle Orland and was trying to under stand him. Jimmy thought his uncle acted the way he did it was the old way. Uncle Orland was the bread winner and thought of himself as the king of the house hold.

The male lion, that eat first and the female and her cubs weighted and eat what was left if any thing was left. Uncle Orland thought of himself as the male lion, king of the house hold. I didn't think it was right to do that to his family but he did. I like my uncle he was a good man.

The music in the car that Jimmy was driving was playing a tone that he really liked. So, his thought went back to driving once again. There was a sharp turn up a head, so he slowed the car down to fifty five. Jimmy seen the sign and made the turn. His wheels almost when into the dirt, he turned hard the car when around the corner. He made it! Next time he'd go even slow. Jimmy had heard that to many people had die on that turn, it was going to get him. He drove on He be in Cherrifield I just a minute. He was not very far for Machias now. Maybe a half hour or so. He listened to the radio as he drove on to

Machias, to the Motel was just ahead. The roar for the most part was good and Jimmy speed along at sixty five and seventy.

According for what he could remember the Motel was just around the corner. Yes, Jimmy thought he could see the sign to the Motel. Machias seem to be a nice quit little town. He pulled the car in the Motel driveway and turned the engine off and got out of his car and walked to the office of the Motel. He signed in at the deck and was given keys to room fourteen. The room had two full size beds he took the one closes to the twenty three inch T V . Jimmy was a little tried. He thought he'd watch a little TV and get some sleep. Jimmy watched T V for a couple hours then he pulled the covers down on the bed and slide in bed. He turned T V off and tried to full a sleep. of was the big day he was going to have with the reading of Orland Will. and what cousin at the lawyer's office. But final he fell a sleep. His body was at rest and his mind twirled with thoughts. He sleep the first few minutes he didn't dream, then later he fell in deep sleep. In his dream he was walking in a large white building. I walked up the four white stairs and a man in black suit open the big white door. I walked in to a hallway. My feet sink down in the tick light brown carpet. I looked around, there was a door way to my right and one to my left,. and there was another door straight a head. A large man wearing a white glove neigh me forward. I moved on down the hall. The hand behind me pointed to the right for me to go though the door and turn way to the right. I moved on throw the door way. There was a row of chairs to my right and left. I could hear people talking, but it haze, and I couldn't see them, but I know they was there. The man behind me neigh me forward. I walked down the ill. I could hear a woman crying and other mooing. I walked on down the ill. It was so haze I couldn't see much, but then I seen a beautiful brown coffin, just in front of me. I moved closer and I could se there was some one in the coffin.

I could see a person in the coffin dress in woman clothe. I was pushed forward. I moved closer then I could see it was a beautiful black girl. But couldn't see her face. The man behind me touched me hands and told me to fold my hands. And touched my head, so I bounded my hand. And I thought Lord bless these girl, I didn't know hear name. I was push to move on I move on down, what appeared to be a line. I lifted my head and moved on down the line. I was stunned to see there was a another coffin. And these one was closed. A hand

made me stop, I did. With out asking, I bounded my head and folded
my hands. Then I was pushed, to go on down the line once more.
I could see another coffin and it to was closed.   I thought, Rest in
Peace, friend. After a moment, I when on down the line and there
was another coffin. I did the same to it. Then I moved on to the next
coffin. I folded my hands and started to bowed my hands, but the
hands in the black glove stopped me. and pulled my hands away. I
turned around, but I couldn't see his face. I stood there a moment, god
what going on I don't wont to be hear but the hand in the white glove
pointed to the coffin. I was looking at the coffin, what did he wont me
to see? The hand pointed down at a silver name plate on the coffin. It
was hard for me to see it. I moved closer. And read the name on the
plate. JIMMY BENTELY ! My eyes open wide, I was shocked to see
my name on the coffin.

Then Jimmy started to woke up and round over on his other side.
Then Jimmy could fell tinning in his body, what had I been dreaming?
Jimmy tied opening his eyes, he had been seriating. My god was that
a dream, it seem so real? Yes, he had been dreaming open Jimmy eyes
and. looked around he was still in the motel room ,god what a dream
. He was back in his room in the motel. Jimmy tried to remember the
dream. Wow!, he'd been dreaming about some girl that had died. He
couldn't remember only some of the dream, not all of it. He remembered
seen coffins. It seamed so real at the time. Boy, what a crazy dream he
just had. Why they died he didn't know, Jimmy hadn't had a dream
like that in a long time Well he need to get up and start getting ready.
He was going to have a big day a head. These was the day of reading
of uncle Orland Will. I'm away dreaming crazy things, but that one
took the cake! I headed eating scents yesterday. All I needed was a good
breakfast. He laid in bed of a couple of minutes or more then Jimmy
grabbed the remote and turned the T V on to the news. The weather
man told him the weather was going to be just fine for the next couple
of days. Jimmy thought he'd looked around the room to see if there was
something to make a cup of coffee, After a couple minutes he found
the coffee maker that was under the little cabin after a few minutes So
Jimmy made some coffee. HE was still thinking about the dream, It'
had been a long drive and by the time he when the bed he was very
tied and just wore-out, guess that was why he had that crazy dream
about a line of coffins in some strange house. Well people get tired

guess that was why he had that dream. well he had think to do .he'd get dress and shaved in a few minutes. And later go down town for some breakfast. It was only six o'clock in the morning he had plate of time. He'd watch T V and go down town in a few minute Jimmy hadn't been Down East in years. He'd only been to Machias maybe twice in his life. And eating at the some restauant, wear they had great food, for all kinds. He thought he'd drive down town and maybe walk around Machias a bite and look to town over. Then he'd go get something to eat in the restauant he always goes to when he's in town. Jimmy parked his car in front of the restauant and walked in the restauant. It was only seven thirty in the morning. He thought maybe he'd have eggs and bacon of breast fast, then he'd take a walk around the town and look at what little there was to see. Jimmy walked in the restauant. Off to his left was a breakfast bar and there was a couple of men setting and eating they breakfast at the bar. Jimmy thought he'd set at the back of the restauant and he'd be able to look out the window down at the river that went by the back of the restauant. Jimmy started to walk to the back of the restauant and a pretty youny waitress stopped him. She told him the back part wasn't open in the morning and he'd have to set in the front part of the restauant. The pretty little waitress was a very nice looking blond girl, about five foot two, with a nice finger and a slim waist with beautiful face with slim soft lips. She had nice round full breast and a nice smile. "Can I help you." she ask Jimmy in a soft light voice, Yes, I'll have some egg and ham with toast please." Jimmy thought she was very good looking and looked at her as he told her what he wonted to eat. She wrote it down on her note pad and when to get the food.

There are times when you're young, you see a girl and you think she is the most beautiful girl in the world. She started to walk away then she changed her mind and stopped to talk to Jimmy. Their eyes met and he looked into her beautiful face, and she looked back and smiled Jimmy could fall in love with a girl as beautiful as she was. His eyes drank in her beauty. She was young but very beautiful as well. Jimmy thought for the minutes she make him the most happiest man in the world. That she would be his every thing he wanted in the world. To be with her would be all he need. Jimmy looked into her face and thought she was so pretty and said to her. "Hi, my name is Jimmy Bentely, I drove up from Orono, I'm going to college to studying to be a lawyer and I'm going to graduate in a couple years.. I haven't been to Machias scents I was a kid. " he looked at her and smiled and she smiled back at him. Jimmy went on to say, I came up here because my uncle Orland die and lift me in his Will. So, I have to go to the reading of the will around noon time. She looked at me and smiled. Jimmy thought he could tell she like him.

And she said, "Thinks like that can be sad, people drying and all."

Jimmy replied back, "Yes they can, I didn't know him that well, but I liked him.

She turned to go get his ford and said to him " I'll get you food and be right back, Jimmy." she turned and walked away to get him to get the food tat he order.

She thought to herself, he was a nice looking college guy, and he seemed to be so nice. One day, she wound move out of these town, and get a life. Get married and have a couple of kids. She loved children. She didn't do so well in school she had a hard time and all. That's why she got a job as a waitress. Hey, it paid pretty good in the summer time, she made good money. And she got to meet people like Jimmy. A real nice guy, she know he was, she could tell so, by the way he acted. Good looking and all. She placed the food in front of him, on the table. Jimmy looked at her and said, "What is your name good looking?" she looked back then she said "I'm Lisa Adams, I was born in these town twenty years ago." Lisa's voice lower a bite, and she seem to be a bite sad, "I hope one day to be able to leave this town and start a new life." She looked at Jimmy and there was almost a tear in her eye.

Jimmy looked at her and could see she was hurting a bite, and he said. " I don't go out very muck my self. I have to study most of the time. And when I'm out studying, I'm working at the book store to make ends meet." Jimmy looked into her eyes and smiled. In me the town and what there is to do, I guess there isn't much, but I'd really like to spend some time with you and get to know you." He said very softly to her as she looked into his eyes. There he add, " I think you're very need I'd like to have you as a friend." Lisa smiled back at him, she was a bite surprised to hear him say he liked her. But Lisa like it. Then Jimmy said, We could watch a movie or something. Just get to now one anther that would be nice," Jimmy said. He could tell she like him. Then he when on to say. "You have a telephone number? What time do you get off from work Lisa?" Lisa looked at him, maybe she could, he seem like a real nice guy and she said. "I get of at five and there isn't much to do around hear , but I'd like to see the movie in town, Shadow of the Mind, I hear it's real good."

"Ok! shore anything you say, is fine with me. You wont the world, I'll give it you, Lisa." He was joking, he though, but she was so beautiful maybe he wasn't? She wrote her number down quietly and headed it to him. Then she went to get his breakfast, and waved as she left. She came back in a couple of minutes and Lisa brought his food, then she had to go and wait on other people in the restaunt. Jimmy eat his breakfast and waved to Lisa, and his lips said quietly, I'll be back at five to pit you up Lisa. and blow a kiss her way. She smiled and turned back to the people she had been waiting on.

After eating Jimmy got up and lift the restaunt and he had designed to take a walk and look and around the town. He turned left out of the restaunt and walked down the street. Just looking in the windows to see what he could see. Like a lot of small towns, Machias had a down town and the stores were close together. And there was the stores lined up right in front of the sidewalk, just out front of the stores and the road. Jimmy walked down the left side of the sidewalk then he crossed the road and to the other side of the side walk and keep up walking. There was a barbershop and verity story across the street. There was a lot of places that had closed. Jimmy walked on, there was a bar and a lot of noise coming from it. Jimmy wasn't brave enough to go in side. He didn't know what to expect. So he cross the road and started walking back on the other side of the street. There was a bar on the other side of the street also. But it was much more quieter then other one across the street. He walked on pushed the bar. His car was parked in front of the restaurant and he keep on walking. He thought he'd walk down and see if he could find were the office of the lawyer was. The reading of the Orland Will was at one o'clock in the afternoon. He wanted to be on time. There wasn't much to see only a few stores and a lot of business had closed. That was it. Jimmy knows why Lisa wanted to move out of town and maybe go to a bigger city like Bangor. She'd have a change to make something out of her live. There are times when you have to take a change in life to be happy, and one day she'd take that change. Jimmy was young, and he wanted to get a head in life as a lawyer. And help him make big money and have every thing he wonted, plus helping people that needed his help. Could Lisa, be in his live, maybe, at some point. She was a beautiful girl and one day he was going to get marriage, maybe it could be her? Jimmy was on the other side of the road from the restauant. He could see his car parked across the street in front of the restauant. He turn left on the sidewalk and started walking up the street. To were he thought the seen the sign of the lawyer office. Jimmy headed walked very far when he seen the sign. Alben Wentworth, Attorney at Law The sign shone him the office was on the scent floor. He'd wait and come back around twelve o'clock these after noon. Jimmy opens the door of the A. Wentworth Attorney office at twelve thirty that after noon and walked in the room on the scent floor. The room was full of people some he know like his pretty Nicole cousin and he thought he seen Jennifer way in the back of the room. The room was a large room so thirty by sixty feet with a hard wood floor and what appeared to be, thirty wooden chair on the right and left. Had another thirty chairs on that side too. With an ill going down the center of the room. At the front of the chairs was a large wooden desk and chair. Jimmy thought that were the lawyer would set and read Orland's Will. Jimmy walked on down the room were the desk was and seen his cousin Dale standing there token to a lady he didn't know. Dale seen Jimmy and stopped talking and turned to greet him. Jimmy put his hand out to shack hands with Dale, and said "Well it's be a wild scents I've seen you, Dale. How's thing going with you?" "Fine, Jim, I hear you going to be a big time lawyer one of these days?" Dale replied back to him. Jimmy looked around the room and said,

"Didn't know that many people in hear, I gust there from his side of the family?" There were two gray hair older lady, at looked like they was sister setting down in the chairs up front and a tall man, that looked like it might be Orland's bother. The seem to be more people then chairs. "Yeh!, Orland had a lot of family around hear. There a large family." Dale looked around the room, Jimmy cousin Nicole walked up to him and put he arms around him and said,

"Jimmy, It's be so long scents we seen you. You been hidden down in Bangor all these time and haven't came to see you're favorite cousin. You devil you." She kissed him on the cheek. Jimmy replied, " Yes, it has been a wild scenes I've been up hear to visit my family, I been going to college. Studying and all."

There were people moving all around him as they talked. There was a short little girl long side Nicole. She dropped her arm from around Jimmy and put her hand on the girls friends shoulder and said, " These is my friend Susan. She my sister in law, my husband Brad, couldn't be hear his working." Nicole, a nice looking mother of two kids. She still had a nice figure and her long blond hair. Her girl friend was much shorter and not quit as good looking. With brown hair and heavy finger, but looked nice just the same. Jimmy looked at her and didn't say anything.

"Jimmy change the subject, "Are there any other of my cousins around hear?" as he looked around the room.

"I think so, maybe we could fined a chair to set in why we can. It will be starting in few minutes." Dale said. Jimmy and Dale when to set down, but Nicole and Susan walked off to talk to some one else.

"Tell me Dale, who are some of these people. Like those two older lady over there and that old guy that looks like Orland, is it his bother?" Dale replied, " That lady over they. I think was Uncle Orland girl friend. He pointed to a older lady in her late sixty with gray hair. Her name is Silver Fox and those two lady (older) over there are Orland sister and that tall older man that Orland's cousin, Abdel Porter. These cousin Gale over their at the exit door. Jimmy always like cousin Gale. She was easy to talk to and likeable too. Jimmy got up and told Dale I'll see you in a minute I wont to talk to my cousin Gale. He got up and walked over to were Gale was standing. Jimmy walked up to her, and said "Hi, Gale, it's you're cousin, Jimmy how are you doing after all these years, it's so nice to see you. "She seemed surprised to see him. She said in a flat tone. "Oh, Hi, Jimmy my husband over there, I have to go. It's nice to see you." and she turned and walked off. Jimmy turned and when back to his set by Dale. " Guess I was wrong she's not so nice." A short fat man with a big round belly wearing a gray suit walked in the room and set down at the wooden deck

The lawyer set down at his desk and open the draw and then pulled out some papers and set them on the deck in front of him Wentworth looked around the room at the people that had attend the Reading. And said in loudly squeaky voice. "Good after noon people. We are gathering hear for the Reading of Orland Will. Orland died a year ago. He lived a long life and was a good, hard working man. He had a big ruff voice and said only what needed to be said. I know Orland little bite. He tried to make money many ways. Orland is not a rich man, but he made his mark on his life as a fair man.

Orland was born in Maine. Orland and his wife lived in Calais, Maine. And married his wife also living in the same town. Orland went to school in Calais and so did his wife May wear they met and got married. They moved to Eastport were Orland bough his home and lived there till he died late year. He and May had two daughter and later they adopted there grand-daughter and lived with them until she married and moved out at eighteen years old. Orland loved his granddaughter" Now for the reading of Orland Will." Wentworth the lawyer cleared his throw. And looked around the room. Then He pick up the paper and started to read it.

Wentworth spook in a loud raff voice. "Orland atuomoble, and he only drove Cadillac," he moved his finger on the paper in front of him and said, "Hear the Cadillac. goes to his daughter Ellen. The lawyer looked around the room and fond Ellen in the middle of the room. setting down in a chair. He waved to her to come up to the desk. Then Wentworth looked in the folder and pulled out a envelope with her name on it. Next it was Orland other daughter, Margo was the older daughter. "Margo, you're father left you the two trucks." He looked at her and waved her up. Margo husband work with Orland when he was alive in the trucking business. Wentworth handed her the envelope. "Next, know let me see." he folded the paper over and said, "Is Gale. Orland left you the furniture in the house on Perry road goes to His daughter Gale. Gale walked up and took the letter from the lawyer. Well we're moving right a long. To David White, Orland left the motor boat and trailer. Wentworth waved to a girl and told her to go get him a glass of water. She when to get him some water. Wentworth waited till the girl came back and took the water from her. And shook his head thanks. He took a drink of water. Know Orland had a big family and he like them all. Next, David Adams Orland's nephew he left him five thousand dollar.

The Lawyer waved for him to come and get the envelope. Orland 's and his wife jewelry will go to Orland nieces Nancy. That valued at five thousand dollars.

Jimmy was thinking to himself. What the hell, Jimmy thought to himself I'm going to be the late person in the room that is in Orland Will. Add end up getting his dog or the cat? Oh, well what very it is he had got to see his cousins and the few member of his mother side of the family And Jimmy's uncle had thought about him before he die., that was fine with Jimmy. Yes Jimmy remembered his uncle Orland as being a very tall man around six foot eight. Jimmy remembers seen him walk to his big Cadillac He took long lumbering strides. I guess it was because he was so tall.. When he walked he was a bite hunch over a little at the shoulders. Jimmy looked back at the lawyer as he pitted up more papers and said in a lower tone. The house going to Orland girl friend Silver Penn of many years .Ellen and Margo looked at Silver with disc believe. How come their father, give the house there lived in all there live, to a hoer like her?   Sillier was the biggest position. If looks could kill, Silver would be die now.   But the old rankled girl friend of Orland could see that well. And couldn't see the anger on there faces. Wentworth, the Lawyer could see the anger on there face and didn't like it. But there was nothing he could do to help them. So he put his thought back to the reading of Orland Will. "Know were getting down to near the end of the reading. There only a few left. Robin Orland granddaughter, Orland left a thousand dollars in cash. There was a few more people Jimmy didn't that was called up for a small amount of money.

Wentworth, the lawyer looked around the room. He didn't know what this young fellow looked like. And said loudly these are the late person on the list. Orland owned an old run down cabin on Black Lake. It's not worth much and ten areas of land witch the cabin is on around a small part of the lake. It goes to his nephew Jimmy Bentely.

It was hard for Jimmy to believe Uncle Orland had left him a cabin on Black Lake. I guess Uncle did care about him after all. Woo how what great thing uncle Orland had done for him. Jimmy had a big smile on his face. Boy, and his father said he wouldn't get much Woohow. Her won't to put his hand in the air and shout out, Great1, but he held back and just had a big smile on his.

Wentworth just looked at the young foul, and shook his head. If Orland give the kid anything at all. It couldn't be worth anything at all. Wentworth, wounded tell the kid, it might be best to turn down the cabin and give it back to the town.

People in the room had started to began to leave and were heading for the ext door

out of the building. Wentworth walked up to Jimmy and tried to tell him he could turn down the cabin. But Jimmy didn't lessen to the Lawyer. It must be worth a little bite of money and that would be just fine with him.

It wasn't that late were Jimmy left the lawyer office and he was beaming with joy. it was almost five o'clock and he walked over to the restaurant to meet the beautiful little waitress he'd just meet in the restaurant. As Jimmy walked to the restaurant Lisa was just coming out of the restaurant. Lisa seeing Jimmy and looked up and said, " Hi, Jimmy," she was glad to see him and could see thinks when well with the lawyer and she when on to say, " You look happy things when ok, I see."

Jimmy smiled back at her and said, "Yes I guess so, my uncle left my a hunting cabin by Black Lake. Way up in North Maine some wear." Jimmy put his arm around Lisa and he tweezed her shoulder just a little, and said, "The lawyer told me it wasn't worth very much but a little bite just ok with me." Jimmy's car was just out side the restaurant. And he pointed to his car and said told her, " These is my car, it's not mush but it works just fine. Can I take you some ware?" Jimmy when on the say you're the one who knows you're way around hear, I don't."

"Well, I asked you if we could go see a movie, is that alright?" Lisa replied. "But can you take me home to change my cloths first?" Lisa said with a smile. Jimmy looked into her beautiful face and said, " I think you've bewitched me. I've never feel like these with any other girl before. What have you done to me Lisa?" Jimmy said with a big smile on his face.

"Really, I bewitched you and what have you done to my?" she when on to say, "And what have you done to me?" Lisa said, " Taking me a way from my big time job and I've mostly lost all cares of money thank to you. And what are you going to say to that, Jimmy?"

Jimmy, know she was joking and he replied, "Oh, take you away from you're big job and you'll could have made millions?" He winked at her when he said that. "Well you never know!" she said, "I might have?" Lisa looked into his handsome face, and she moved closer to him. She could fell his warm body next to her. Lisa moved her face close to him and kissed his lips with the passing she felt for him.

Jimmy arms when around her beautiful body and they kissed long and hard. Jimmy looked into her pretty face and said, "I think we could go, so you can change you're cloths and we a can go have a drink and see a movie." They were still in front of the restaurant wear Lisa worked, and it would be best to move away if they was going to do more kissing. Her sweet body really tune him on. Lisa's father's house was ten miles up the road passed East Machias on route one. Jimmy started to get out of the car and then Lisa asked Jimmy if he didn't mind waiting in the can change her cloths and she be out in just a couple minutes. Lisa didn't wont to tell Jimmy right now that her father had been laid off from the closing of the mill and he had nothing to do all day but drink and by these time in the evening he'd be drunk and she didn't know what her father would think about Jimmy. And Lisa knowing her father would say the worn thing to Jimmy and dam it she didn't wont to lose Jimmy. Lisa didn't know when but the right time would came she'd have to tell Jimmy about her father and his drinking problem, but not right know. When Lisa was young she couldn't have asked for a better family. They laughed and played and when on trips together. Lisa couldn't have been more proud of her parents. But know that she was old and her father was out of a job. Her father shouted and shook his fist at her for every thing she did. Lisa worked to help the house hold out, but that wasn't enough. Lisa just wonted to go some wear and be happy, that was all. Just live a good life like other people did.

Lisa, reached over and kissed Jimmy on the cheek. .Jimmy waited in the car and she was back in just a few minutes. Lisa, open the door and slide in the front set of Jimmy's car. Jimmy turned and looked over at Lisa. when Lisa came back she was wearing a pink blouse and blue jean shorts. She looked so beautiful it was hard for Jimmy not to look at her. And Jimmy said to her, " You look so beautiful, you're not going to be cool are you?"

"I'll be just fine Jimmy, turn right down the road and the movie theater is just down the road a few miles." She looked at Jimmy and said, " Thank you, Jimmy for taking me to buy movie, I don't get out much, know that I'm working." Lisa moved as close to Jimmy as she could and took his right hand in her fingers and said as she pointed up the road, " The store is just up the road a little bite, Jimmy, I hope they have the movie I wont?"

Jimmy turned the wheel of his car and started down the road to wear Lisa wont him to go. They drove ten , twenty miles and then Lisa told Jimmy to turn left down a side road to the store wear they could rent a movie. He drove on down the road, and then after five miles of driving they came to a gas station and Lisa told Jimmy to turn in the station and he turned in the gas station. The car stopped and Lisa got out of his car and said, "Come lets go in and check out the movie Jimmy" Jimmy got out of his car and walked in the store with Lisa.

When Jimmy walked in the gas station he looked around it there was a small grouser store at the back part of the store and off to the left was a small disc-play of movie. Lisa walked over to the movies part of the store and started looking for the movie she wonted to see. After an few minutes she found the movie she wonted and then she when the counter to pay for the rented movie. The man behind the counter knows, and said to Lisa, " Lisa, I haven't seen you for a wild. What is a beautiful girl like you doing know days?" With out stopping went on to say, "And who is these nice looking man you're with?" "Oh, these is my friend, Jimmy, his a college guy going to school in Orono. He's a real smart guy and his studying to be a lawyer, and make big money some day soon." Lisa said. She turned and looked at Jimmy and said, " Jimmy, these is my friend Erik, he was the owns these fine store. Say, Hi, to him Jimmy." Jimmy said, " Hi, how are you doing?"

Erik, was a tall man well over six feet in his late fifty with big old looking brown eyes and a weather beating face with very large ruff hand. Erik reached over the counter and put his hand out to shake hands with Jimmy and said "Hi young fellow, I'm doing just fine. What brings you hear to our little town anyways young fellow?" Erik said to Jimmy.

Jimmy replied back to him "I'm hear on business, sir. I'll be going back to Bangor in the morning, I have to get back to my study, so I don't fall behind." and then Jimmy when on to say, " I haven't be up these way in years"

Lisa started going to the door and waved good bye to Erik as she did. As Jimmy seen Lisa walk to the door he said to Erik, "Well, I guess it's time to go." and he waved good bye to Erik as he walked out of the market with Lisa. Lisa had paid of the movie and had the movie in her right hand as she walked to the door with Jimmy .and opened the door of his car and Lisa slide in the front sear of the car. And Jimmy walked around and got in the other side of the car and said to Lisa, "So wear to now, girl friend?" And Lisa replied, " You're at the motel in town, right?

"Jimmy shook his head, yes. "Well you've have DVD player in you're motel, we can watch my movie in you're room." Lisa kissed him on the cheek as she said that. "You know better then I do, girl it's you're town." Jimmy stated. "So, come on big guy, let's go to you're play and have a little fun, honey." Lisa said with a smile on her face. " And spend some time together why we can. And watch my movie and get to now one another even best then we do now, honey." Lisa put her hand on the upper part of Jimmy leg with her warm hand. At first he pulled away then he looked into her eyes and could see the love in her eyes, and looked back at her to say , it was ok!

They drove down the road back to Jimmy's motel. It was starting to get late and there were only a few cars on the road. It only took a few minute and Jimmy pulled his car into the driveway of the motel. Jimmy stopped the car and got out and opening the door to let Lisa out of the car and they started walking to Jimmy's room in the motel. Lisa slide her arms around Jimmy's wrist and Kissed him on the lips.

Jimmy could fell her warm hot body press again his chest as they kissed. He moved her along to the door and he opened the door to his room and they when in his motel room. They stopped kissing and Lisa said to Jimmy. "I think I'm in love with you, Jimmy?"

Lisa's eyes were bright and a pretty blue and her face had a look as love on her face, as she smiled at him, with loving care.

Jimmy could feel her full round breast push again his hard hairy body as they kissed once more. He rapped his arms around Lisa's slim warm beautiful body. Her blond hair was again his face as they kissed. Jimmy put his arm under her shirt and could feel her warm soft back in his fingers. He kissed her once again and said to her in a soft caring voice, "You are so beautiful it's like a dream holding you in my arm. I can't believe so one so beautiful, could love a guy like me." Jimmy said to Lisa. "And I do love you, oh, so much Jimmy." Lisa said almost in a soft pant of passing. They moved over the couch and they set down on the couch ever so close they were almost one, and they could fell the wrath of each other person.

No these nothing wrong with two young people falling in love, it's nature. Was it because Jimmy came from bigger city and meet these little country girl Lisa and found the girl that he thought he loved in a little town like Machias and these girl was the girl he'd been looking for the girl of his dreams, Lisa. Was it in the big city things when so fast there was no time for true love. But now when Jimmy came to these slow moving little town you could slow down and find true love. You was so close to nature, the tree and fortress, the animals, and the flowers you could find true love so easy. And that what Jimmy found beautiful Lisa! Like the beauty of the human body, as a flower in the field, the wind blows and the seeds of life that are go in the wind, it's called nature. Jimmy had falling in love with beautiful Lisa and she had falling love with him, young Jimmy. Lisa had moved away from Jimmy and was slowly getting up an d going to the rest room.. Jimmy watched his beautiful young Lisa as she walked to out for the room. She wore Jimmy's white dress shirt, it came haft way down her pink little body. Jimmy watched her perfect little pink body move across the room , Jimmy thought she was the most beautiful girl in the world. She wasn't the most beautiful but at the time Jimmy was in love with her with your and he thought so. thought If only each one of us could be in love like that. Isn't that what we are put on the earth to love a multiple? And to enjoy the feeling that love bring, that a wonderful feeling of finding that special some one in your life.

Lisa turned around and looked back at Jimmy and said, " I'll be right back in just a minute sweet." and she closed the door the rest room. she was gone only a few minutes and came back and seat beside the man she loved , Jimmy.

Lisa placed the movie on the coffee stand. She wonted Jimmy, she didn't care about so movie, she was in love with the guy in her arm, Jimmy. And he was all she wonted him so much she could barely stand it! Lisa had waited twenty years for the right boy to come alone and now she though he had came in her life. Jimmy, the guy she loved had come to her finely. Jimmy un-butting her bra, it slipped away from her pink white flesh and the bra dropped down off her round breast. Jimmy moved his hand around to the front of her chest and his hands caressed her soft white breast ever so softly. Jimmy 's fingers found her soft tan nipples and his fingers fondle and squeezed her nipples and they started to harden just a little with passing that she had for him. They kiss long and hard and for a moment they said, nothing but just looked at each other with love on they minds.

Lisa looked into Jimmy's eyes and said, "What do you thing

Jimmy?" Jimmy looked at her, yes he wonted her more then anything, but he was a smart young man and he said, " You know I wont you, but I don't wont it to be a one night stand. " Jimmy, posed a scent and looked into her eyes and said, "So, why don't you call you're parents and tell them you're staying over night with a friend?" He kissed her softly on the lips, and when on to say, "You don't have to go in to work tell later in the day, do you? And I'll take you back home in the morning so you can change and get ready for work." Jimmy was holding her in his arms and looking into her eyes as he talked to her. some times when you're young and maybe a bite older your eyes see something so beautiful you can't stop thinking about her. You see her and right then you know she's the one for you! She's don't something to you know other girl has done. You can't stop thinking about her. She's turned on you're passing for her, you're sex drive go wild, you know you've falling in love with her.

Lisa wonted to say yes and she know what ever she did her father would be mad at her. And she really did love Jimmy and didn't wont to lose him. He was a smart college guy and what he just told her mint he really did care about her and he'd come back to her real some after he left to go back to school. .More of the boys that met her only wonted one thing and she know what that was, sex. Lisa, felt good about Jimmy, he really did love her. She looked around the room and seen the phone over by the stand and told Jimmy, " Of course I'll stay with you as long as you wont me too. Do you have something to so we can be save?" Jimmy shook his head yes. She kissed him and slide her pants off. For a minute she didn't know what to say then she said, " You really do love me and you are going to coming back for me aren't you?" Lisa moved over and kissed him then she set on his lap.

"Yes, I will come back for the girl I just fell in love with!" Jimmy told her. Lisa stood up and walked over to the phone and pitted it up and dialed the number of her parents. Lisa spoke into the phone after you got done dialing, " Hi, Mom I'm going to stay over with and friend place tonight and I'll see you after work tomorrow after noon. Her mother said something back and Lisa replied back, " Mom, I'm twenty years old I need time with friends from time to time and Dad going to have to under stand." she know he wouldn't. He'd hauler at her and maybe even hit and though her out of the house. But this was something she just had to do, no matter what! "Mom, I love you. I'll be alright, just tell Dad, I'm with friends for the night, please, thanks. She hand up the phone, and walked back to Jimmy and set down along side of him. And said to him, "It's all set I'm spending the night with you honey." She kissed him Lisa, stood up and un-butting her shorts and the shorts slide down her legs to the floor and she stepped out of them. Lisa stood in front of Jimmy with just her white panty and bra, and then she set in Jimmy's lap and kissed him.

Jimmy told her about his family and his father owned a small store in Bangor and his mother stayed at home taking care of the house and then he told Lisa about his sisters. Then it was time for Lisa to say something about her family. Lisa told Jimmy about her family and that her father was laid off from the mill and there were times he drunk to much. Lisa told Jimmy one day she wonted to move out of these small town and go to a bigger city like Bangor or even Boston some day. And she hopped some day that her and Jimmy could get married and have a couple of children one day.

After a couple hours of talking it was going on twelve o'clock at night Jimmy got up and with his hand pulled Lisa up too. They walked a couple feet to the large bed and Lisa slide under the sheets. And Jimmy took his pant and shirt off and slide in bed with beautiful Lisa. It was nice to have a warm shapely female body next to him, it felt really wonderful to have the girl he love next to him in bed. He kissed her. and told her he loved her and wonted her.

The next morning Jimmy woke up and Lisa was still sleeping, he kissed heron the face and her eyes opened. Lisa looked up and seen Jimmy's handsome face standing over her and she said "Good morning, lover, I had a grant night thanks to you honey."

"I did too, it's getting late you better get dress and I'll take you home so you can get ready to go to work at the restauant." Jimmy had been up of a wild and was already dress. Jimmy looked out the window and seen that it was raining out side. Jimmy pitted up the phone and called his parents in Bangor and told them he was on his way back to college and would be back soon, and then he told them he'd meet a nice girl and had Lisa say Hi to his mother.

Jimmy pulled his car into Lisa father house and they got out of the car and "You call me when you get to school please." Jimmy said he wound and that he loved her and wound sees her in a few weeks. They kissed and she when into her house and Jimmy drove off.

So times in life things happen, Jimmy had no idea he was going to meet the girl of his life, but he did. On the drive back to Orono Jimmy was thinking about having Lisa in his life. He smiled as he was driving, it wound make him happy. It wound put meaning into his live. Something to work hard for, a live with a beautiful girl like Lisa wound make him very happy. He could see in his mind that she wound fix in his live just fine, and wound give him something to be proud of in his life. A wonderful girl like Lisa. He drove on to Bangor to his parents home to tell them about the girl he just fell in lover with, Lisa. Jimmy new his mother wound be happy now in he found a girl that could be his wife one day And Jimmy know his dad wound do very thing he could to help Lisa if she moved in with the family for a short time. and god his sister wound love having another girl in the house. Jimmy keep driving on to the family house in Bangor traffic was getting a little heaver as he got closer the Bangor and all the shopping mall.

CHAPTER 6

When Jimmy got home, the first thing he did was to go on the computer and find were Black Lake was. He found the Lake it was way up north of Bangor and know doubt Jimmy thought on a dirt road some were. Acidly the Black Lake was a few miles before Fort Kent. From route eleven he could turn of by just past Wallagrass to the right.

Jimmy first told his room mate, Berry about the trip. Berry was all for going and asking other people. Jimmy would call Jill and ask her if she would with them and also tell Rachel about going. Jimmy thought it wound be nice to ask Clendan and his girl friend if Cessie about going to the lake with him. Clendan said he couldn't go but Cessie said she like to go. Then Jimmy called LeRoy and asked him. He said he'd go, if Rachel when. Jimmy when down to the restauant were Sarah was working. She told him she couldn't she had to work.

Then Jimmy call long distance to Machias and talked to Lisa. Jimmy thought she like him and he plead for her to go. Finely she said, " Yes, she go!" Jimmy asks LeRoy if he'd take his four wheel drive car. He said, "Yes. They all decided to go with Jimmy to Black Lake. take sleeping bags, food and something to drink and a radio and portable TV. And bring there cell phone. They all said yes, and it was going to be great fun. Jimmy, wasted not time. The next weekend at seven o'clock in the morning. Jimmy gas up the car it took just up a hundred dollars to full the car. He picked food and drink. Cola , whiskey, a case

of beer and water. Plus he put together a first aid kit. Jimmy and Berry
when to pit up Cessie and they was ready on they way to Black Lake.

Jimmy drove up route two on to Lnland Fall and then on to
Smyrma Mills. Then turn on to route 212 North to Knowles Corner,
and then turned just after going by Knowles Corner to route eleven all
the way to Wallagrass and a little ways past it to the right turn off on to
a dirt road to Black Lake.

Jimmy turned on to the dirt road on the way to the be Black lake.
For the very first few yard on the road , Jimmy could tell it was going
to be a ruff ride all the way to the cabin. There was a large hole after
hole on the dirt road. It best he could only go five miles a hour A haft
mile seem like five miles of smooth road. Each big hole the car sank
into, you hoped the old car would brake down. You could hear the
bang of the car as it hit the road. Dam! But you keep going on very
slowly, guess hopping you'd make it just a little further. LeRoy's four
wheeler wasn't doing much better. And yet there was times when the
four wheeler could have gone fast.

Lisa set up front with Jimmy driving the best he could. There
was a time when the car sunk into a big hole and stopped the car
from moving forward. Jimmy tide to back up, but was stuck big time.
Jimmy waved to LeRoy and their put the rope on Jimmy car, and
LeRoy back up and pulled Jimmy car out of the hole. Jimmy turned
hard to the left and went forward just missing the hole by inches. They
couture on down the dirt road at a snail pasha. The road had pot hole
after pot hole every couple of feet. As you looked down the road it
looked like you was driving into a tunnel surrounded by tree, that
amount tough the top of the car. Jimmy was driving almost haft a hour
bang after bang as it hit hole after hole. Suddenly the trees gave way
and the road widen just a little. and you could feel the air was cold as
though you was near water. Jimmy thought to himself the cabin can't
be far. Then as he turned right he could see the cabin by Black Lake.
Lisa, looked at Jimmy and said as she pointed to the cabin in front of
them. "That has to be you're cabin, Jimmy. God, I thought we wasn't
going to make it, with out breaking down." she stared at the cabin in
front of them. "It beautiful Jimmy, just a nice little cabin by the water.
Who! Bam it good!"

Both car doors open and they all got out for the car. LeRoy stopped
his car by a tree just a few feet away and they all jumped out of the

four wheel drive car. Rachel made a full turn around as his looked the
place over her arms out straight. Jill got out of the car and said, "Hell,
these isn't a bad place at all! LeRoy, slide his long legs out of his car.
And looked down the road at the cabin. I n his mind Jimmy was trying
to make a move on his girl friend and he didn't care much for Jimmy.
Hell the place is all right, know big deal! They all started unpacking
their cars. Jimmy went around back of the car and opened the truck
with the key. The truck popped up and Jimmy pulled four sleeping
bag out and Lisa helped pull out the chest of food. It was pretty big
for a little girl like her, but she got a good holed on it and took it out
with ease. She turned, and started to walk to the cabin. Barry pulled
out the cage of beer of the car. " I've got the most important thing.
Were do you would it Jimmy?" Berry asked him. "By the car is just
fine for now. Lets see what the cabin looks like inside. Jimmy walked
ahead of ever one else to the front door of the cabin. The Door wasn't
locked. Jimmy was very careful, were he walked, as not to fall thought
the old wooden floor. Lisa put the food down on the porch along side
Jimmy. He opened the door slowly. Jimmy and Lisa looked into the
cabin and seen a dirty dusty floor. As they walked into the cabin Lisa
thought she hear something moving around. She and Jimmy looked
around the cabin. Suddenly, something raced by them, and another
one and another one hiding under a piece of paper on the table, and
another one came from hiding in the wall on the floor every wear and
another one raced pasted them into the woods. So fast they couldn't
get a good look at any of them. Lisa fall in Jimmy arm for protection
and said to Jimmy "God, what was those thing? " Lisa curdled up in
his arm. Jimmy big strong chest protected her so she thought from
harm. They had raced by so quit you could tell what they were! The
creatures weren't rats, but they were the size of large one .rat or cat?
As they had ran by Jimmy and Lisa one bushed her leg almost cutting
her ankle. They raced out of the cabin so fast you couldn't tell what
they were. Could it was a rabbit or something like that., Jimmy didn't
know! But one of them bushed Rachel leg and bang against LeRoy leg.
As they had run past Cessie one of them nipped at her ankle cut her
leg. The blood slowly ran down her foot. Cessie howled in pain as it
cut her foot. Oh, what to hell, they was in the middle of the woods,
theirs to be bound to wild animals, But not like that, what ever it was?
Jimmy didn't like it. She sharp pain in her leg as it had cut her leg , as

it raced by her into the forest. Rachel turned to help Cessie as she had heard Cessie scream in pain. Jimmy eyes wading his body tennis. He looked around the cabin, he couldn't see anymore of the creatures in the cabin. LeRoy also turned and looked back were the creatures had ran into the woods he couldn't see them anymore .LeRoy big tall body tennis as he looked were the creatures had been. in the woods

Cessie cried out in pain "Wooh! What the hell was that." As things disc appeared into the woods behind them,. LeRoy grabbed her in his arms to protect her for the creatures that raced by. Dam! I thought I was going to like this place. Now I don't know if I'm going to?

Lisa was shaking a little bite as Jimmy and her walked in the cabin. Lisa didn't know if she warned to go in the cabin? But she was with Jimmy and she felt a little save with him, so she when in. She looked in every corner to see if she could see any more of the small creator. Lisa didn't see anything she felt much better now. After almost a hour, they all started to feel beater. What ever the creatures were, they hadn't came back and they were staying in the woods. And Lisa was starting to fell beating and Jill had stopped shaking and was felling a little beater. LeRoy was thinking about having something to eat. "Hey, How about something to eat, Rachel, I'm a growing boy. "LeRoy said.

Jimmy and Lisa when back in the cabin, it was only four o'clock and was still light. And they once again looked the cabin over. Lisa looked in every corner, to see if she could see any more of the creatures, she couldn't find anything. She feels much better Jimmy went and looked in the bedroom, nothing there. The place was very dirty and dusty. You know Jimmy we didn't bight a broom or mop with us. And I don't see one any were." Lisa said to Jimmy. The place was very dirty, hadn't been clean in years, no doubt There was a large dirty wooden table in the center of the room were one of the creature had been hiding. There was no other future in the room. No running water, no kitchen, and no bathroom. There was a second room straight a head of them and Jimmy opened the door. Most likely it was a bedroom but there was no bed in the room. On the right side of the room was a old fire place, witch hadn't been use in years. There was a wooden frame window, so dirty you could hardly see out of them. "The room was so dusty it was almost hard to breath. "It's going to take a month to clean these up" Jimmy said to Lisa. "Oh, it wont take that long, honey. Just need a little work and thing will be fine." Lisa looked at Jimmy and winked at him. She looked around the cabin to find anything to clean with .She couldn't find anything in side the cabin. But Cessie said, "I found a old bar of soap and a dirty rage. Well it's something to clean with, Lisa."

LeRoy and Rachel walked in the cabin and looked around. Jill and Cassie came after them. Cessie was still blooding form the bite.

"Jill and I are setting up the gas stove and Rachel is getting the food ready for cooking." LeRoy said with a smile on his face. He thought the danger was over. What ever they was had gone into the woods and they was save now. Jill was a city girl and right now that's wear, she wouldn't to be. Jill tried to get a hold of herself. She looked around the cabin. It was really dirty, maybe she could do some cleaning and take her mind off what happed. Jill said, " These place needs a little work I'd say. If you don't care LeRoy, I'll sleep in the car?" LeRoy shook his head Ok.

Cassie said, "Well we can clean it up a bit. I'll go with you Lisa, we don't know what's around here that might hurt us.." Jimmy and Lisa walked out side.

LeRoy, Looked at Rachel and said to her, "I'm so hungry I could eat a house, how the food coming.

Jimmy and Lisa were behind the cabin. Lisa put her arms around Jimmy's neck and kiss him hard on the lips. Jimmy put his arm around her also and they embraced, with a long hot kiss. After almost a minute Lisa pulled away and said to Jimmy in a soft voice. "I think I'm in love with you, Jimmy." she put her lips to his and they kiss once more. " Know I love you to Lisa." Jimmy replied to her. "I'm going to treat you real good to night honey." Lisa said. She kissed him once again. They walked back to the front of the cabin were ever body was hand and hand.

"Did you find to broom? " Jill asked. Lisa shook her head no. And looked at Jimmy, I think we for got to look. Lisa smiled at Jimmy. Lisa had on a pink shorts and a low cut white blouse. She was a beautiful girl with a nice figure. And Jimmy now it.

Rachel turned and looked into the woods and said "Did you hear that?" "What?" Some one answered. "It sounds like something is whistling, a animal of some kind making a noises. As the day went on, things were starting to look better Lisa and Jill had cleaned the cabin up a little bite Cessie was cooking hamburger and hot dogs. LeRoy went and got the radio out of his car and tuned the music on loud, to some rock sound. Rachel dance to the music. Her tall slim body with those long beautiful legs, moved to the beat of the music. Barry got the beer out and poured every body a drink in paper cups. Jimmy had Lisa in his arms with a drink of whiskey in his hand. Lisa had a drink of beer in her hand. Jill had a cup of beer as she was helping Cessie with the cooking. Jimmy and Lisa walked down to the lake and Lisa bent down and put her hand in the water. She looked up at Jimmy and said, "God, these water is cold, almost freeze." Jimmy put his hand on her back and bent down beside her and put his fingers in the water too. "You're right, it is cold. Maybe the water coming for a under ground spring, that's why it so cold. Tomorrow when the sun high it well warm it up a bite." Jimmy told her. "I don't think I wont to swim in that water. I don't see any fish and there aren't any birds around either." Lisa

There was a large bubble that had formed on the wall. an right then another one pooped up under neither that one and their was one more, and another one appeared on the walls .and in seconds hundreds of bubble pope in sight on the walls of the cabin.

Jimmy looked at Cessie in amazement and said, "Did you see that?" as he started to point at the wall.

Cessie looked at Jimmy, she seen what ever it was going on. So did LeRoy and Rachel. Jill turned to look at the wall had several bubble pope up on it. There was a sound as the circle like bubble pooped up on the wall. Jimmy had lauded his school papers on the old wooden table, when they moved in the cabin the other day. And now it seem there was something under the papers that was moved the papers as the papers rose up a inch or two. Jimmy eyes wading as he watched the far wall of the cabin change right in front of him in amazement. Was it real, the things came back, that was in the cabin or was these a new horror.

Cessie grab Jimmy arm with apprehensive. Jill seen the change in the wall ran to the other end of the room. Jill seeing the things appear on the wall went into panic of her life. Barry, seen what was going on moved away from the wall. Rachel ran to were Jimmy was at the front door. Lisa was turned and couldn't see the wall changing and was looked at Jimmy not knowing what was going on, but she was a alarmed at seen Jimmy face.. Big LeRoy was up and on his feet when he turned and seen the wall change.

The round bubbles on the wall burst open, and then another and another one and the creatures raced to the door. The strange looking creatures were hinging, unseen, in the wallpaper, in the wooden ceiling and in the very floor they were standing on inside the wood on the floor. As the creature rose like bubble in the Wall paper and appeared out of the ceiling and floor like magic. Suddenly were their seem to be nothing, there were hundreds of jelly looking spider like creatures all over the room, were Jimmy and his friends were in and racing for the cabin door.

For a scent, Jimmy thought of shutting the door, but then he thought, no to let them run out into the woods was the right thing to do.. He moved back from the door, pushing Cessie to the wall.

The creatures bust from the bubble on the wall and hit the floor and started racing for the door. They raced past Berry and Jill on their way to the door. These time all thought they ran supper fast Jimmy could see what than looked like. Jimmy and Cessie had never seen anything like them as they race by them. Jimmy couldn't get a good look, but as they ran past him, he thought they looked like round clear like jelly spiders with six legs. So of the invisible spiders were two inches a round and there was some that was six inches around. One, two, three ran out the door. And there was more to come all in scents of each other. One ran past LeRoy, then another and another one. LeRoy lifted his big size ten boot and came down hard on top of it. You could hear a squish of the jelly creature as it was being killed. The next creature as it ran by LeRoy nipped at his boot, and slash a tear in his boot. The scent one and last on in the cabin snipped at his heal. LeRoy razed his foot as the creature banged into his ankle and raced to the door. "What the Hell?" LeRoy hulled as it hit his ankle.

Then suddenly there were hundreds of creatures racing for the front door of the cabin.

LeRoy stomped his foot down hard, but these time he miss the creature by a couple of feet. They was lighting fast. The creature past Jimmy and out the door headed for the safety of the woods. As the last one raced out the door and no more seem to becoming out of the walls or were ever they was hiding. The drown thing seem to be able to hind under and in almost anything. I know it seem impossible, but one of them was hiding under a piece of paper on the wooden table. It seem impossible, but not for this thing. It can do, what no other animal could do. It can Hide any wear, any place it wonted to hide, under a piece of paper and you wouldn't know it was there.

Jimmy found his cell phone and dial the number to the college. There was no answer, It was Saturday and the office was closed tell Monday morning. "I'll try again later we really are in any danger." Jimmy, open the door and looked around the things were gone. LeRoy walked past him on his way to his car parked up the road by the tree. The whistling started up again, it became very loud and then it stopped. The creatures hadn't gone very far. They were watching the two legged being for the woods. They started whistling once again to each other. Jimmy and the other turned to look wear the noise was coming from as they hear the whistling of the creatures in the field. Jimmy couldn't see the creatures but he now they couldn't be far away. by the sound of the noise.

When LeRoy went up to this car he looked down and seen that he had a flat tire. As he got closer he could see the tire had been ripped apart, by some animal. know doubt they were the same creatures that were in the cabin a few minutes ago. LeRoy looked around, he know they couldn't be far away, and hiding, god know wear! Dam, he'd get them for what they did the his car! LeRoy was a big black man, know little creature was going to beat him. He'd never see anything like those thing before, he wonder wear on earth they came from? And why was these little cabin so far in the woods all by it self and not another cabin for miles around., LeRoy had no answer. But he know the little creatures were going to be another but treble for all of them

LeRoy looked out over the field wear the creatures were. What the hell are these thing that had just ran by him he had never seen anything like these in his life before a creature that can hide under a peace of paper, what the hell, he thought is going on? Berry moved over by Jimmy and said to him, "Jimmy what do you think about these thing at was in the cabin, I've never seen anything like this before! You think we're going to be save hear to night? " And Berry also looked out in the field were the noise was coming from. Jimmy replied, "I tried to call the college to see if they might have a idea of what might be going on but being Saturday the office is closed for the week end." Jimmy told Berry. Then he went on to say, "Hopefully they stay out in the field and leave us alone. I guess we'll just have to see what there going to do, if anything ,Berry." then he went on to say, " May have to have a look out to night just is case they attack us, we'll be ready to defend our self."

"Boy them dam thing sore scared the hell out of me. Well I guess we can finish un packing now. and we'll make the best of it." Jimmy said. Then he looked around to see if he could see the creatures in the field

CHAPTER 7

Jill started shaking in fear, she had came here to have fun with her friend and party and have a drink or two but these little things that had ran by her was horror able looking and she thought tey were so wicked little animal from hell. Jill didn't know why but she now they was out to harm them all maybe kill them. It was just the way they looked like nothing else on earth, one of a kind a natural kill. LeRoy couldn't have killed one of them. They hadn't hurt anyone at that time. but she know what's going to happen, there hinging around in the woods waiting for what to happen? The next morning the creatures had tore LeRoy car apart getting back at him for killing one of them. LeRoy couldn't have killed on of them and now they got back at him by destroying the tires on his car. And they also did the same to Jimmy's car parked by the cabin as well.

The dam thing destroyed LeRoy's tires, they wont to fight I'll kill every one for them, he thought as he looked around to find one of them. You wont a fight I'll fight he thought to himself, he had his shot gun he'd get those little creatures. He had came hear to have fun but he like fight as well. He held the gun in his hand and looked into the field were the creatures were hiding. "Dam little beast!" he said shouted out loud.

We must decide what to do? We have lost one of our children. The two legged beast has killed our child. We must do something! We can't let them go unpunished. They scare the flying things in the air with their loud noises. And the swimming things in the water are afraid of them too.

They have taking our home away for us. We must fight back to save our home and children. We have lived here to long to loose it now.

The whistling sound came from the woods once again. Like a wave of sounds or whistling sounds, the strange inhuman voices that came from the woods. The whistling sounds like a strange whistling voice says to it's children, be cram, it's going to be alright. The beast has come back after all these years. But we will be all right. Maybe they well not stay long and we can go back to our playing and a new beginning, once again. As we did before the beast came. We must make a plan, of what to do next.

We must decide what to do? We have lost one of our children. To the two legged beast, it has killed our child. We must do something? We can't let the beast go unpunished.

They shear the flying things, with their loud noise. The swing things swimming away for their life. They taking our home away from us and they have killed one of our children. We must fight back to save our home. We have lived here to long to lose it now. The whistling sound came from the woods, like a wave of inhuman voices.

We'll kill! We'll kill! We'll kill the beast. We'll Kill them all!

They started moving though the grass and the trees. They had decided what to do, to Kill! Kill, Kill them all! They moved to were the beast was slowly and carefully. They were good hides. They could hide any where they wonted too.

Lisa walked over to Jimmy and put her arms around his wrest, "What's going on honey?" Lisa asked Jimmy, as she got in between Jimmy and Cessie.

"LeRoy car has a flat tire, Lisa." Jimmy told her, he didn't wont to tell her how it became flat. He started walking to his car, along side the cabin. No flat tires, that was good. He open the door and took out the car keys. Jimmy turned the key. Nothing, no sound of the engine starting. Jimmy open the door and pulled the leaver to open the hood of the car. It pooped open. He walked to the front of the car and looked inside. Dam, the wires had been eating by some animal.

Jimmy took out his cell phone he'd call the Sheriff. He dialed the number, then the phone rang, and rang. Some one pitch up the phone it was a female voice answered " Sheriff Department how may I help you?" t he voice on the phone said

"These is Jimmy Bentely I'm at my cabin by Black Lake. My car was bent torn apart by some animal and my friends car has a flat tire. We need help. "You don't need the Sheriff to fix a tire, call a tow truck." the female voice said.

"I don't have a phone book. Can you give me the number, please?" Jimmy asked." I think we're in some danger, one of them tried to bite my friend in the foot. It cut his boot a couple of times." Jimmy said.

"Call the tow truck and I call the deputy Sheriff and see if he will check it out." then she hang up Jimmy called the garage a man answer and toll Jimmy it wound cost him a hundred dollars to go that far and he'd be there in a hour or two. Jimmy said "OK", and then he told the man wear the car was, and the man hang up the phone.

LeRoy was starting to change the tire and Jimmy walked up to LeRoy and said "Did you try the car to see if it would start?" LeRoy Looked at Jimmy puzzled and shook his head, No.

"Think you better check it out LeRoy." Jimmy told him. LeRoy dropped the tire wrench and got in the car. Took the key out and turned the key. No sound of the engine turning. The engine was die. Jimmy walked up to were LeRoy was and said, "They did the same to my car to, eat the wires." he posed and added, "I called the garage and the Sheriff. To ask if they wound help us. It's going to be a couple of hours before they come, LeRoy."

"We might as well make the best of it." Jimmy said he started to walk back to the cabin, when he thought he heard a sound of the grass moving in the bushes in the woods near them . Jimmy looked be hind him to see if he could see what it was he couldn't see anything, but he and LeRoy could hear the rashly of the bushes behind them. Jimmy body tens up with fear. He walked back to the cabin a bite faster. He turned Lisa around to walk with him back to the cabin.

Jill stood just inside the door, watching Jimmy and LeRoy with there cars. Cessie was just past the front steps a few feet. And Barry was along side Cessie watching what was going on with Jimmy and LeRoy with there cars. They could tell that something was wrong with there cars by the way they acted. They all thought it was best to stay close to the house for their safety

The whistling had stopped for a wild. But you could hear movement from the edge of the woods, all around the cabin.

Lisa put her arms around Jimmy once again this time more tightly then before. Jimmy looked at Cessie and said to her, " I called a tow truck to help us and I also called the Sheriff's department, and I told them about these thing around the cabin. The woman said they might send someone she didn't know.

"Why don't we get the food out and have a little breakfast. I know we have eggs and bacon, and I think we have some ham too. We can have a nice meal and thigh to tank our minds off all of these." Jimmy waved his hand around and pointed at the woods.

Jill and Berry came out of the cabin to help set up the food. And LeRoy and Rachel started setting up the gas grill. Cessie moved close to Jimmy, and Lisa was still holding on to Jimmy.

Lisa thought she was in love with him after last nights love making. She had never made love to anyone like that before. Lisa looked at him with love in her eyes Jimmy was getting the paper dishes and plate forks out and put on the table and Cessie said to Jimmy " What do you think about these thing?" she went on to say, "You know you've never seen anything like them before, Jimmy?" Cessie looked into his eyes as she asked him. Tomorrow you could try to call you're college. And if you can't get though, try calling the Machias college, it closer." Cessie went on to say, "We might have stumbled on to a new life from. Like nothing ever seen before, Jimmy. Maybe it could be study and reported on paper?" Cessie told him.

Jimmy looked into Cessie's eyes, Lisa's arms were still around his wrist. "I'll make so call as soon as I can. Do you have a cell phone, Cessie?"

"Dam, I left mine at home, But I bet Jill has one. I'll check with her and see." he said to him.

Jimmy lessoned to her as he set the up the table. He placed plate forks a spoon on the table and picked up the paper plates. Jimmy looked there was a bubble under the surfs of the table. Jimmy didn't have time to think. Suddenly, the bubble breast open and a clear jelly like creature jumped out of the bubble. creature as it ran passed

Cessie snapped at her finger, cutting it. Then raced to the safety of the woods.

Cessie, hauled in pain as blood flood down her hand to the ground. Jimmy seen that Cessie was hurt said, "Dam, are you alright, Cessie?"

"That Dam thing bite me." Her face showed that she was in pain.

"Come on, Cessie the First Aid kit is in the cabin." Jimmy escorted her to the cabin. Jill seen that Cessie was hurt and came running to her side. Jill had worked in a hospital once as a nurses ad and now a little about first aid.

Jimmy got the first Aid kite out. And Jill took Cessie hand and looked at it. The cut was a deep cut on her hand, Jill told Jimmy and really could be sighed, but we can stop the blooding of now." she told Jimmy.

"Jill these a butterfly band aid in the first aid kite, it well work just fine. He handed it to Jill so she could put the band-aid on Cessie finger. After a haft hour, maybe more they when back to cooking breakfast. Rachel helped Jill with the cooking and. Cessie set in a folding hair and Barry set along side of her. Lisa set close to Jimmy and they all eat breakfast together. There was a little talking no much, every one was thinking about Cessie being bite by creature and what was going to happen next.

After breakfast, Jimmy called the nearest Sheriff office around Fort Kent. The phone rang a couple times. Then a female voice answered. "Hello, this is Sheriff office. What can I do for you?" the female voice said.

Jimmy answered," Hello, These is Jimmy Bentely. I'm in my cabin by Black Lake. my friends and me ran into a little trouble, hear. My cars out working and my friend's car has a flat tire. And we can't fix it. We need help." Jimmy said.

The female voice replied, "We don't fix tires why don't you call a garage, young man? "Hear, I'll give you the number." the female dispatcher said.

"And my friend has been bite by so creature. We stopped the blooding but I think we're in danger." Jimmy said pleading.

"Ok, I'll see if we can send someone out to check on you. Wear are you located." the Female voice said.

Jimmy told her the cabin by black lake. It's the old Orland places.

Alice interrupted him and said, "You call the garage, I'll get you the number, the number I gave you and I'll see if I can send someone out to help you, Sir." Alice hang up the phone. The old Orland road yeh she heard about it. Seem there is a old cabin way down the road , it's the only cabin on the road. Boy there a man , old Orland the bought the run down cabin from the Army, why the army had the cabin in the first play she didn't know? Well Orland bought the cabin he had some dam idea he was going to have fisherman go to the cabin and fish and he'd build more cabin and sell them to the fishermen. Great idea but there was one thing wrong, no body ever seen a fish. That was one of many big ideas old Orland had that didn't work out! Alice didn't know much about the cabin she thought the Army owned it back in the fifty, she wasn't really shore but she thought the Army did so strange experiment at the cabin she didn't really know what. but Alice thought it might have kill most of the fish so she thought. From what she heard no one ever cot a fish after the Army left. Boy Orland lost on that deal with the Army, he thought he was going to make big money didn't make a cent on the deal.

CHAPTER 8

The female's voice over the radio said " Car fourteen, these is base, come on." Alice, held the mike in her hands. She'd worked as a dispatcher for almost ten years She'd never been married and she was going to be forty soon. Alice liked her work as a dispatcher, she was good at it. Sheriff Cleyton, had always used her good. The Sheriff was much older then she was, but she thought of him as the man she could some day marry. Alice now in her mind that it not going to happen. Alice headed told him, and him she loved him. There were times, she looked at him and thought he know. Alice wasn't ever pretty, most people thought she was plan looking. So, that was alright, she didn't care. Most of her friends had moved the a bigger city, like Bangor. But Alice was happy living in a small town like Fort Kent. There wasn't many man in the town, most were married. That was alright all she cared for Cleyton. Alice's work was her life. She didn't have much of a family around. Much of them had moved away to the big city for more money. She had a Aunt that lived close to her and a uncle that lived a few miles away, that was all. And she thought of the Sheriff, even thought he was a lot older then she was as the man in her life.

"Yes, Alice, what do you wont these time." the male voice said in a I don't care way. The displacer answer, I got a call about a youny man is broke down on one of the back roads. He told me his car has a flat tire. I told him to call a tow truck, we don't fix flat tire. And he told me there was so wild animal around the cabin and he was affair them.

The male voice replied, "A flat tire, Alice what the hell they can't fix a tire, what are they city boys?" Alice replied, " I think so, I told them you'd check on them, Burt."

"Ok! Alice I'll check on it in a bite." answered in a I don't care voice.

"Alice, wear is these boy car located?" Deputy Burt said.

"Burt, it's the old Orland cabin just off Route Eleven then turn left by Soldier Pond onto a duty road about two miles in. It's the only cabin on the lake, I think!"

God, dam, Alice, Burt thought to himself. "What do you wont me to pound the hell out of my carouser?" Then he went on to say "That don't make me happy, Alice." Burt said, un- happily.

She didn't reply, she just hang the phone up. Alice didn't think much of Burt, he was a loser, in Alice's mind. He wasn't very good looking, plan like her. And he didn't do a good job as Deputy. He didn't seem to care much about his job or anything else. In a small town like these it's hard to get good help. So, the Sheriff had a no good guy like, Burt to help him

Burt was thinking there was only one garage_the area, Porter's garage. I'll bite the kid called them. I'll check after I have lunch., Burt shook he is head just a little as he was thinking about those kids. What the hell, a flat tire, what next a cat in a tree. These was going to be a hell of a day. He put the car in gear, he'd go to lunch. Dam, that cabin has to be twenty miles off the main road away on a very bad dirt ruff road with how know how many pot holes on it. After a hour and a haft of having lunch, Burt got back in his courser and picked up phone and dialed the number of Rusty garage. The phone rang and rang. No answer. Burt thought to himself, well, Rusty must be on his way to fix the kid up. Well I'm glad I don't have to go down that dam duty road. He hang the phone up Burt thought of calling Alice, but changed his mind, I don't need to call that bitch. Rusty was in the garage fixing Emmon's old Ford. Rusty had been working on the engine almost all day. Rusty wonted to get it out of the garage today. He thought a haft hour and he'd be done. Then he thought he hear the phone rang in the office. Rusty Turned his head to look at the office. Dam it was the phone ranging, hell, they'll just have to call back. tomorrow He won't to get Emmon's car fixed, before five o'clock to night, he was going to close the garage at five o'clock.. Rusty had other car lined up to be fix., he didn't wont the have to work Sunday to get cot back up on his work. The phone stopped ranging. Good, he could go back to work on the old car. If, it were important they'd call back later. He turned back to the work on the car. Rusty's garage was the only place with in twenty miles of getting you car fix in the area. There were times he worked lone hours on car to keep up with the demanded. Rusty was married with two children. He was a very hard working person and well liked in the town. He might wear dirty cover all but, he had a nice home and family.

The call from the old Orland cabin had been the late call to the station so far. Know wonder they got a flat tire on a road like that Burt thought, you pound the hell out of you're car and tires.

Burt thought he was lucky to have a good job like he had. In a small town like these one. jobs were hard to fine. Burt had never been married. He wasn't the greatest looking guy in the world, but from time to time he had his girl friends. A few years back he was having a affair with a seventeen year old girl. She got pregnant by him and moved a way. Burt never married her. But from time to time he sent money to help out and pay for his son. Burt didn't get a change to se his son very offend. Once every six months at the most. That was fine with him. She was the one who moved away. Besides he found another girl. Right now it had been eight months and he didn't have a girl friend. It was alright anyways he only won't sex once in a wild, besides women are all bitches. Burt thought, Rusty must have fix the boys car by now. Hell, he'd just drive around till his time was up and he was off duty. Maybe he could check on that nice looking woman down the road and see if he could get to know her better. Maybe get closer, real close. He hadn't had sex in moths. It was about time. Burt wasn't one who liked sports. There wasn't much sports in the area anyways. He was five foot ten and a slim build of a hundred fifty pounds. Burt like playing poker, a card game and he also liked to look at girly magazines and taps of naked women. It made him feel like a king. But more times then not a pretty woman could us Burt, to do what ever she won't him to do. The radio came on. It was the dispatcher on the radio. "Come in Burt. "It was Alice voice at the other end of the call. " Burt did you check on the kids, on the Orland road to see if they was Ok?" Alice asked. Dam it, that bitch. Burt thought it over for minute. Rusty must answered the call by now, and fix the Dam flat tire. No need to call him, besides it was getting late in the day. Know body won't to go down that road at night why not. She'll never know, besides the kids are on they way back home by now. And I sore don't wont to go down that road to night. " Every thing fine, Alice the kids are Ok." Burt said with a smile on his face. "Ok, Burt," Alice said. "Thanks," and hang the mike up.

CHAPTER 9

Breakfast had been over for over a hour, and no word of the police or the wrecker. LeRoy had got the short gun out of his car. And had it by his side at the pick nick table. Jill was along side of him. Rachel and Cessie was in the cabin clean up a bite. .Jimmy walked down to the water and Lisa walked behind him. There was little beach by the water. What were was of it was very rocky. Jimmy bent down and put his hand in the water. Lisa beside him did the same.

The water was very cold, to cold it seemed. Lisa pulled her hand out of the water quietly and said, "God, these water cold. almost ice cold." Lisa said.

"I know, Lisa," Jimmy replied. "I think there must <u>be</u> a cold water spring under hear so wear. That was why the water so cold. Something distracted him, he turned to look around, he could hear something moving around behind them. He couldn't see anything, but he now there was something out there. He stood up and Lisa did too.

The wood was so thick, you couldn't see but a foot or two into it. There was a Out House not far from the woods. Thank God, Jimmy thought to bring the portable toilet and put it in the back room of the cabin. It was way to dangers to use the Out House with those things all around Jimmy. He didn't feel save were they were on the beach. There was to much moment around them. "Come on Lisa, we better get back to the cabin." Jimmy told her

Jimmy and Lisa stood up and started walking off to the beach. Lisa moved close to Jimmy and put her head on his shoulder. And looked into Jimmy's eyes, with love in her heart for him. Know wonder, they had made love like she'd ever had before with him. She know he was the man for her. "Lisa, I love you, But there is a time and place, and right now these isn't the time."

Jimmy went on to say, "Both LeRoy and my car are broke down, and Cessie was bite by some animal is **around the cabin, I think we"** **As they walked by a large boulder,** Jimmy could see something was worn. The top of the rock was moving. Jimmy eyes widen, what was going on. It was as though the top of the rock had turned to liquid He put his arm on Lisa 's shoulder. "Come on, we have to go." Jimmy said with a shaky voice. They had back on the grass. Suddenly like a horror able magic, one after another appeared on the surfs of the rock. Jimmy. cutting their flesh. Jimmy and Lisa started to run up the small hill with the creatures at their heals napping them as their ran up the hill.

"Whoo!, God, were going to die." Lisa shouted in Terror. Lisa's leg was bleeding from the bites of the jelly creatures.

"Come on!" Jimmy shouted as he pulled her up the small bank. Jimmy had on a cotton pants and a short sleeve shirt, But Lisa wore shorts and a blouse. They were tarring her flesh apart, with their clause. Lisa lost her balance and fell. Jimmy had hold of her arm as she started to fall, so he could pick her up. Then one of the jelly creature jumped on her back and So Jimmy let go of her to take the creature off her back. Jimmy took the creature off her back. But picking up by scooping the jelly like creature with his fingers from under it and throw it in the grass. Jimmy helped her up again and the started once again to work their way up the small hill. As they reached the grass they could start running of the cabin, to safety. They could see the cabin now and LeRoy was by the picnic table with Jill.

Lisa, screamed to, " LeRoy, help us thought thing are after us trying to kill us." Lisa and Jimmy reached the picnic table were LeRoy was with gun in hand. He couldn't see the creatures, they must have stopped chasing them. It was like the creatures had varnish into the thin air. And yet I know they was hiding un seen in the grass. LeRoy razed the shoot gun but he couldn't see the creature to shoot at them, so he lower the gun.

Jill washed away the blood from Lisa leg. and put a disinfected on the cuts. Then Jill rapped her leg with a bandage. Jimmy walked up to were, Cessie was standing and said to her. "Those things were waiting for us on a rocks. You can see them till they appear and attack you. I don't know how tey do it but they can hide and you can't see them tell the last minute and the they ready to jump on you. How can you fight something you can't see? We have to be careful till someone come to help us. "Jill was banding Lisa foot.

Lisa started work almost right after she graduate from high school. Most of her friends moved to the big city to go to college or get a job. But Lisa stand in town and work in the restraint down town. She be working there in the restraint when she meet Jimmy. He was so nice and good looking, she fell in love with him right then. Lisa thought Jimmy was the man she had been looking for all her life, he was the man she dream about.

Jimmy asked her out, and she said Yes. They had a wonderful time together and they drank together and had great sex together. He asked her to go to the cabin by Black Lake. Oh, she wound go any were with him, she wonted to go to be with him forever . They spent the night together making love, it was a wonderful night of love making. together .and getting to know each other and the feel of they warm body together was great. The best sex she ever had in her life and would ever have with Jimmy it was wonderful, they made love most of the night. She now she'd meet the man in he life. He was a young college man, studying to be a big time lawyer. And she know he'd be a wonderful husband and father to there children. Lisa had been waiting of a man like him. Lisa, know she was in love with him and he said he loved her. Then monster's little jelly spades that attack her, and the hold world of love, she was in came to a end in, in fear and panic of her live. What was so wonderful became a nightmare.

"There Lisa," Jill said, "You could be ok, now." she put the last peace of tape on the bandage. Jill was shaking fear. She had do a good with her first aid, but she wasn't a strong person in something like these. Jill walked uneasily back to put the first aid kite back in the cabin. Rachel walked with her. "You alright?" she asked her. Jill shook her head Yes.

Jimmy when over and so he could talk to Cessie, "Did you fine another cell phone, Cessie?" Jimmy asked her. " You have the only phone, Jill forgot her phone." Cessie replied. Jimmy pulled out his cell phone and dialed the number of the Sheriff office.

The phone Rang and rang and rang again answering machine click on, it was Alice's voice, "These line is for emergency calls only. Please leave you name, address and a number we can call you back and what the emergency is about, and we'll call you back. Thank you."

Jimmy told the machine that no body had came to help them, and when would they get help? And hang up the cell phone.

"I talked to a answering machine. "He told Cessie. Jimmy waved LeRoy over so they could all talk together. It was now going on three o'clock in the afternoon and no one had came to help them.

LeRoy was a tall powerful black man. He was good at basketball. He had a dream of being a Pro play. He's father had been a pro with the San Tone team. And Leroy thought he could be one day. If not he was going to be a gym teacher. He really didn't like Jimmy. Jimmy made moves on Rachel and LeRoy know she like Jimmy But dam it, Rachel was his girl. LeRoy cared for her and that why he didn't like that white boy. One day, Jimmy was going to be a big time lawyer and LeRoy was only going to be a teacher. At times Jimmy made him look bad in front of Rachel. That little white boy thought he was smarter then he was. LeRoy thought, right know with these little bugs. You step on them or shot them and kill them. You didn't need a plan. You kill a few of them and they stay away that all you need to do. You fight them! LeRoy walked over to wear Jimmy and Cessie were.

The Buzz started up again, it was coming from the woods once more. The two leg beast when in the water to kill the swing things. We were sunning our self on the when rock when it walked by. When it came back we changed it for the beach, onto the grass and back to the cabin. The swing thing are save now. It killed another one of our people...No, It didn't kill me. It throw me on the grass. I'm alright now...No matter, we must kill them all.

Jimmy turned to look into the woods, the sound of the whistling had started back up again. Jimmy wounded what it met if anything, that straight sound coming from the woods. No matter, he turned back to Cessie and LeRoy and said, "You know there a change that we might have to stay another night in the cabin?" he when on to say, "I think one of us could stay up wild the other sleep, to be save. What do you think?" Lisa and Jill came over to see what was going on and Berry came also Right know, LeRoy was thinking to himself, with these little bugs running around you stop them be by stepping on them or hitting them or maybe shooting them. Kill a few of them and they'll stay way.

Jimmy is making a big deal out of these. Siring every body about a few bugs. Just to make very one think he's a big short and the leader of the group. LeRoy walked over to wear Jimmy was with Cessie were talking. Jimmy waved him over and said, "LeRoy, Cessie and I was talking about what we can do about these thing around the cabin." Jimmy when on to say, "I thought we could have some one stay up and stand guard if we have to stay hear one more day and rest of the use an sleep thought we all could carry a weapon. all we had was a bate, a wooden board ,knife anything we could find to fight back at creatures. I called the Sheriff and got an answering machine, I left a message and tomorrow being day may not get the help we need from the garage till Monday. So, we have to think about taking care of our self tell help comes.

"I've got my weapon." LeRoy thumped the short gun on the floor of the cabin.

Rachel and Jill turned to see LeRoy with the gun Berry pitch up a knife and held it *tight in his hand. Berry always seemed to be in the back ground, watching and leasing to what, when on about the creatures around the cabin. And from time to time he would say what was our his mind about the matter. Berry was Jimmy's room mate in college and Berry came from a very well to do family in New York. And most likely was going the work for his father in New York city one day. Berry was told by his father and family as a young boy that words was power full. You can make people do what you wouldn't them to do, by saying the right thing. And his mother, once said, that money was power, people well do what you would them to do, if you have money you have power, you can give people do the . fighter for you, Berry was more like a book worm. Berry didn't care much of sports of any kind. He liked playing Chest and TV games. Berry was good with women. Maybe it was that he talked to them. And they learned to truest him.

Berry wasn't that good looking but he did OK with the woman. Barry moved up in the group and said, "I think we could try to fix one of the cars. And get the hell out of here. we could, but car has two flat tires and the wires in the engine. Maybe we could try to fix Jimmy car. He has the wires cut but in time we mint fix it.

Cessie looked at LeRoy and said, "I wish my boy friend was were he could fix the car in no time a all." she said and when on to say, "You thing we can call him?"

"I don't think so." Jimmy said but I can try. He dialed the number on his cell phone. A light came on . Battery Low. The phone didn't rang. Jimmy's phone was to far away, make the call. I'll program the phone, but it would work tell tomorrow.

The Whistling started up again. It seemed to be much louder now. Cessie looked at Jimmy and said, "Cricket make noise at night and bird at light of day.

But these things are making noise both, day and night. "The whistling became so loud it was hard to hear one talk.

LeRoy with his gun in hand, when to the window and looked out see if hecould see anything. Every thing looked OK, but you could still hear creatures moving around. It seem as though they was crawling under the cabin and then creatures was on the roof. Cessie was near Jimmy with her back to the wall. She to was affair of what was to come. Cessie held the bate, she was holding, so tying that her nettles were turning white with fright.

The whistling sounds of the creatures and the sounds of things moving all around when on for hour and haft . Then suddenly, it stopped, and it was quit, aerie quit, not a sound.

CHAPTER 10

Jimmy pulled out his cell phone. He'd try one more time to call the Sheriff. The light came on, Batters Low. The phone rang and rang again. The machine came on once again. Jimmy left a message that they need help and turned the cell phone off.

There had been a thunder and lighting storm a few hours ago at the Sheriff office and had knotted the phone line out for hours. Alice had been having lunch and heard the thunder off in the distance. It didn't rain at all wear she was so she didn't think much about it. So, she didn't know the phone was not working of hours. She had lunch and came back and checked the answering machine, there wasn't any thing on the machine. Alice lived up over the Sheriff office in a nice little apartment that she paid of. It was now six o'clock in the evening. Burt had not made a report out on the Youny man with the flat tire. And the Sheriff would be back on Monday and want to know wear the report was. Alice would call Burt and tell him she need the report on the flat tire.

Alice, know Burt was off duty at four o'clock and it was now five fifteen. Most likely Burt had gone out to eat lunch at one of his girl friends or when to the down town bar for a drink and something to eat. She wouldn't be able to get a hold of him until he when home. Knowing him, he didn't take his phone with him. Well Alice would call Burt at nine o'clock and hope he would be home by then. Burt came from a family were he was the youngest of six children. Burt father, when Burt was a young boy, walked out on his mother, and never came back again for another woman. Burt headed see his father in years. Burt could remember his father hurt him and told him he loved him. Burt father never played ball or anything made him bitter, because of his father leaving him. Burt couldn't trust anyone or truly love any one again. Burt was at the local bar, beer in hand, he was off duty who gave a dam, he didn't. He took a drink of beer, he hopped one day he could forget his father.

Alice when up stairs to her apartment, she was standing in her kitchen and thinking. There are times you don't feel quit right about something. But you don't know what it is. It's just a bad feeling in her head. Alice thought she'd make something to eat what she didn't know? The feeling didn't go away, she only had one call. It was the young man with a flat tire. So why was she having these feeling? Maybe the kid was in real trouble. She tried to think, what else did he say. Something about animal around the cabin could that be it? She needed to call Burt and have him check on them again. But wear could he be? She would try his home phone. Alice called, no answer. Now wear could she call, his girl friend? She was hungry she thought she start something to eat. Alice could cook up a steak and fry, that wouldn't that lone. She stated cooking the food up. After supper, she'd try to get a hold of Burt and have him make another check on the young man and his friends.

Alice cared for the Sheriff and thought as him as her friend. She knows he'd be back on Monday. She had missed him a lot when he was gone. The sheriff had lost his wife four years ago with heart decease she had been his ever thing, and his true love. And now she was gone, he missed her. But he know one day he'd have to move on with his life. Fine some one he could love. Frank thought a lot of Alice as a friend but right now he could love anyone till he let his wife go. Frank was a lot older then Alice but he didn't think she cared about that. In the Sheriff mind he thought one day she make him a good wife. If he called Alice now, She would think he didn't have a good time in Boston. Well maybe he'd wait till Monday morning and call her. Alice came home from the Sheriff office at Six o'clock in the evening. Frank, the Sheriff would call her then. That evening there had been a lighting storm and it had knotted out the phone line of hours. Alice, checked the answering machine one number came up, it looked like a cell phone number. Was it that young man calling back? She thought it was. Alice started to get nerves; it was the kid that called. They must be in trouble. It was going on ten o'clock at night. She call around and see if she could finned Burt. She called his home, no answer, then she call his girl friend that know him, he wasn't there. Alice called one of the local bars. The bar tender said he was there and would give him the phone. "Hello, these is Burt what can I do for you?" Burt said. "Burt, these is Alice, I need you to check on the kids at old man's Orland cabin and see if their alright?" Alice said. She when on to say. "I tried to call them and their phone arte not working." "I'll check it out first thing in the morning Alice. I've had a couple of drinks, I'll go tomorrow." Burt told her, he was a little drunk. Alice didn't like it but it would have to do. The Sheriff wasn't hear yet to help her. Alice hang the phone up, she hopped they would be alright till tomorrow morning, she try to get some sleep, then she went and turned the light out.

Burt heard the phone click as Alice hung the phone up. so Burt dropped his phone down and turned to order another drink, it was his sixth one. The bar tender handed him the bottle of Beer.

Lisa put her arm around Jimmy. The whistling had stopped for a moment. It was quit once more maybe to die quit. Lisa had never been so scared like these in her life. Her eyes were wide and her body was shaking with fear. She looked up at Jimmy, he was her straight, he was the man she could count on in a alarming situation. Jimmy was smart and could think his way out of a bad situation.

LeRoy moved away from the window, gun in hand. Rachel moved alone behind him. Berry walked over to were Jimmy was and said. "Do you think they'll attack use to night, Jimmy?"

Jimmy shook his head, No. Then said to Barry. "I don't know, But we could have some one start up to make shore, thing happen." Jimmy looked at Barry then Cessie and said. "I know that we drove them from the cabin. And the creatures have fought back ever scene. It seem that they are not a dam animal. I swear, they think. This was there home and we came and took it away from them. Like any animal they will try to protect their nest, and they'll fight to get it back."

"You're right, Jimmy that's just what happing. They fight us back!"

Barry said. "So what do you think we can do? Jimmy looked at Barry, he had a uneasy look on her face. All of us were frightened of what time we had still help came.. Ever Jimmy was dreading of what was to come. How long wound it be they had to keep fighting? Jimmy looked back at LeRoy, who now was looking out the door, and said, "I guess we stay here the night and if we have to fight, we will. Hopefully help will come in the morning. One of us will have to stay up wild the ours sleep." Jimmy looked around the room. Jill didn't look good, she was still shaking with fear. Jimmy went over and put his arm around her. and said to her, as Lisa let go of him. "Jill, we'll make it just have faith, in us. We'll make it babe!" Jimmy kissed her on the cheek and let her go. She stopped shake for a wild. Jimmy when back to Lisa and put his arms around her and said to her, "It going to be alright."

It now was going on eight thirty and no body had came to help them. Barry said to Jimmy, "I'll take first watch, if you don't mind?"

The sound started up again. It would be hard to sleep later on with that noise going on.

Rachel and Cessie made something to eat and they all eat a little, and then set and lay around. There was very little talk., know one now just what to say.   Final Rachel spoke up and said in her soft voice, " You know, if we don't come back on time to night someone will call the police and tell them to look for use. "Leroy looked at Rachel he didn't know what to say, he was a strong person but he had never been though anything like these,. little creature that tried to cut his body snapping at his lower body LeRoy had fort them off with easy, but there was so many could he fight them all off?

Jimmy looked at Lisa, she was so beautiful and he wonted things to go right but these hellish things had put a end to it and now they may have to fight for there lives?

As it got later in the day the whistling came back and then it would stop At ten o'clock, at night there was no moonlight, it was pitch black and cloudy

It made thing ever more uneasy in the cabin. It would be very hard to sleep at all that night. Jimmy looked at Lisa she was so beautiful he wound take care of her and see nothing happened to her the girl he loved.

LeRoy didn't wont to, but he gave his gun to Berry and laid down to try to get some sleep. Rachel laid down beside LeRoy in the corner and closed her eyes. Jill slide in the sleeping bag and in a few minutes was fast asleep. She was existed with fright. Cessie also feel asleep in her sleeping bag. Jimmy had Lisa along side of him and Lisa feel asleep soon after would. Jimmy lifted his head he could hear moment out side the cabin and Berry looked out the window. It was black out side you couldn't see anything, but you could hear something moving around. Berry held the gun tied in his hand ready to shoot, if need be. Jimmy pitch up the bat and held it firmly in his hand. Were these the time they were going to attack. Berry looked back at Jimmy Jimmy's were large with fright, ready to fight back if need be. They waited and waited nothing just the movement in the three. Jimmy tried to close his eyes and sleep and do the best he could to rest and it was hard to do that at these time when you didn't know what might happen at any time. A hour passed, two hours pass nothing happen, just a lot of noise at times, coming from the deep woods.. At twelve o'clock Jimmy took over as look out. Berry handed him the gun. Jimmy didn't get much sleep, but he was alright of now. to do his watch Jimmy took the gun from Berry. You could see Barry was tired and needed a little sleep. He got in his sleeping bag an d tired to get some sleep. Every one was asleep but Jimmy he walked over to the window and looked out it. He couldn't see anything but he could hear sound out side the cabin. It seemed to be the longest night of his life, just waiting for something to happen. All he could hear was the whistling from time to time, from the creatures. Jimmy thought about his father who had wonted him about going to the cabin. But no, all her thought about was the money. And how much to cabin would bring. Dam, he was supposed to be smart. All the time he was just a dam fool. If he was going to be a lawyer he'd better wake up or he could get every one killed, Jimmy now he put himself in one hell of a jam. He'd be lucky if he made it out alive. He turned and looked out the window, nothing going on, good. Maybe they be save in the cabin? There are times when you have a feeling maybe a scene, call it what you wont! Something isn't quit right, that something is going to happen. He turned and walked over to here LeRoy was sleeping with Rachel buy his side. Jim said to him. "Time to get up. It's you're turn to do the watch, LeRoy."

LeRoy pushed away from Jimmy and turned over in the sleeping bag. Jimmy repeated what he said once again, "Time to get up LeRoy, it's you're watch, big guy." LeRoy opened his eyes and looked at the face of Jimmy and said, "Yeah, Ok!" And he moved to get up from the floor.

They were deep in the woods of Maine, and they were in real

trouble with the creatures out side the cabin. Jimmy handed the gun
to LeRoy. Jimmy couldn't sleep, her had to much on his mind. He
put his friends in danger, no one else. It was now five o'clock Monday
morning, hopefully someone would come and help them. Jimmy
know his mother would call the police because he hadn't came back
on time. He thought help was coming they just had to hold off a little
longer, that was all. Jimmy would try to get some sleep. He closed his
eyes and tried to sleep. He fell asleep finely, Jimmy hadn't sleep for
a long time he need the rest. Jill was a city girl she didn't now much
about wild animals. And these creatures out side the cabin biting ever
one, she didn't under stand what was going on. Hell you'd have beast
running around in the city. Jill came because Jimmy was her friend,
maybe one day Jimmy would look at her and see that she really like
him and maybe she loved him. Jill came with him to the cabin and
thought it would be fun. It wasn't! She did never been so scared in her
life. Jill thought of her self as a strong, but now she was a frightened
little girl. She never thought she could be this terrified in her life. She
had been so afraid she shook with fear. Jill never thought anyone could
be that afraid. Jill closed her eyes and sleep. But now she seen death
every were she looked. The Devil beast (the creatures) was waiting to
kill them all. Jill was at the point of existing she fell asleep. Jill dreamed
of her family. She dreamed, her little sister was with her and Jill was
tilling her that his loved her so much, and she may never see her sister
again. Jill was going to be an angel, and would be with her sister always
in heaven. And Jill would watch out from her all the time tell the end
of time. Her sister held Jill around the neck and said, Don't leave me,
Jill. And Jill replied, Maybe, I wouldn't? Jill was in deep sleep, witch
she need so badly. .Jill when off to college to study nursing she would
have like to go on and become a Doctor but her family didn't have
much money and it would cost way two much so become a RN. was
the next best thing.

Cessie was up at six o'clock and Lisa shortly after wounds. It
seemed quit no noise, that was good. LeRoy and Rachel was up and
out side the cabin Jill and Jimmy were still sleeping.

So, Cessie and Lisa started breakfast for every body. It seemed quit
so they cook out side and hope every thing wound be alright. They
had plant of food to eat. Cessie started the fire and Lisa got the food
ready to cook. LeRoy, walked over to the picket table, gun in hand. He

looked the area over. Every thing looked ok. LeRoy could use a little breakfast he was hurry. He was a big black man and hadn't eating for a few hours. Berry brought the food over to Cessie so she could cook it. Lisa brought the hamburger and the bums over and set them on the table. "Well it lest we'll eat good. I just wish thoughts dam little thing would go way, so we could have a good time for once."

Suddenly, on the pit nick table appeared one of the jelly creature, with a pop! As the creatures popped in sight Cessie and Jill as they jump back in fear of being hurt by the beast . Lisa, screamed in panic, as she put her hands to her face.

LeRoy hearing Lisa scream, turned to see the jelly beast on the table. He swung the gun across the table noting the jelly beast on the grass.

It fell to the grass, but this time it didn't run. The jelly beast ran back at LeRoy leg and snapped at he's he'll. LeRoy seen the jelly spider move to his leg moved his leg quietly, to avoid being bit by the beast. " God, Dam!" LeRoy shouted. He lifted his big foot to stomp on the beast. But it moved quietly out of the way to avoid being killed. Scent and third jelly spider popped in sight on the table .LeRoy looked down to see the spider appear and came back swing the gun across the table one more time. The Jelly creature fell to the ground and ran into the woods. LeRoy aimed the gun, but didn't fire, he pulled the gun back to his shoulder.

Jimmy set on the steps of the cabin, as he seen what was going on he rose up to help if need. Jimmy had sleep only two hours and was at the point of exposing. He wasn't thinking clearly, so he shook his head to clear his thought. Berry was much better and turned to help if needed, LeRoy seem to have every thing in hand, it the moment. LeRoy turned back to face Cessie and said, " There, them dam thing won't bought use know."

LeRoy looked around every thing looked Ok, there was no moment any wear. And this creatures was very hard to see at time, it was almost invisible at time. As it popped into sight to attack you, giving a person little time to defend ones self. LeRoy walked around the cooking area, it seem save for a moment. So he said to Cessie and Jill. "I'm hurry, girls, how about cooking so food up?" He held the gun in hand as he talked to the girls. LeRoy was thinking to himself he had never been in anything like these in his life. His mother was so proud of him when LeRoy when to college. LeRoy came for a family of seven and was the middle child. LeRoy had play basket ball all his life, he was good, a star in high school and was one of the best ones in college. LeRoy won a clanship so he could go to college. LeRoy was a smart guy when he wonted to be. He was hopping to become a pro ball player one day he knew the changes were again him. Oh, he was a tall boy at six feet eight inches but in the pros there were tall and taller guy all the time There were guy seven foot something and made him look small., hard to think a six feet he would be one of the smaller player, and he wasn't that good of a shop. LeRoy could rebound a little but would it be good enough? Right know his life was in danger by these little creatures and he'd have to battle to stay alive. Leroy liked battling with people, Jimmy was at good sport but in basket ball LeRoy ruled .those dam little things were out to kill him and that way his dream, he'd have to fight like never before. He'd fight them off just like every thing in his life, one big fight to get a head. but these was for his life! Leroy thought to himself he was a big black man he could fight and win! A chill when down his spine and his eyes widen a little, he had no choose he must fight

Cessie moved over and put a couple hamburgers on the hot grill and also a couple hot dogs. The food scissile as it hit the grill. Lisa put the large iron fry pan on the grill and put a couple of eggs and bacon in the pan. Jill set up the picket table and chairs. "You're going to eat a little aren't you, Jimmy?" Lisa, asked him. He shook his head Ok and got up and walked over to the table. Jimmy thought he'd have a little something to eat and go back and get a little sleep after breakfast. He wasn't thinking very clearly now.

Suddenly there was noise coming for the near by woods. LeRoy and Berry looked to were the noise was coming from in the woods. They could hear moment, but couldn't see anything, so they went on turned back to their breakfast. The girls did a great job of cooking the food, it taste good. LeRoy had a smile on his face as he eat the food. Jimmy had one egg and a slice of bread and butter. Then he went back to the cabin to get a little more sleep. LeRoy had a hamburger and three eggs and bacon. Berry had a couple eggs and bread and the girls had eggs and bacon also. There was a little noise from the woods as the creatures moved around, but you couldn't see them. There had been not much happing from the jelly cheaters. Maybe they only chatter at night? As night fell the air got much colder and there was a chill to the air. The tempter must have downed ten degrees.

Berry didn't know LeRoy that well maybe it was time to talk to him. Berry looked around, very thing seem Ok it the moment. He looked at Cessie and then at LeRoy and said to them, " We're not out of danger quit yet, but very minute those thing stay away, it means we are that much closer to getting help.

Lisa went in the cabin so she could be with Jimmy, the man she'd fell in love with. She wonted to be with him, to put her warm body next to the man she loved. Lisa walked in the cabin, Jimmy was sound asleep, she lauded down beside him on the floor and put her arms around his wrist, she truly loved that man.

LeRoy replied to Berry, "Yeh! you're right, those dam thing seem to wont to fight, for some reason. Well, I can fight back as well, Berry."

CHAPTER 11

Burt was up at six o'clock , he head was pounding from all the beer he drank the night before. Boy it's going to be one hell of a day. He really didn't do very much, he drank beer and talked to a girl friend . Now what was her name, Sue Ann, a big tit girl with blond hair. She kissed him and put her tough in his mouth. I think she wonted to screw him but he was to drank to do sex. Burt remember getting in his car and driving home around two o'clock in the morning. He couldn't remember were he left the girl, Oh he didn't give a fuck anyways. She was a dam hoer.

He slide out of he bed, his feet hit the cold floor of his one room apartment hell he need was a bed to sleep in any way. Burt pulled his pants up around his waist and batten them. He put his gun belt on over the pants and his shirt was hanging on the chair in front of him, he slide that on too

.Now he was ready for work. He took a choom out of his pocket and bushed his hair. His head was still fogged up. He tried to think, now what did, Alice ask him to do? Oh, Yeh! Check on those dam kids with the flat tire. He'd have to go up that dirt road of a good ten miles and hope the car could take the beating with out breaking down. He'd ask the Sheriff if he could use the four wheel drive car and out he's car. And then he'd have to make a report out about the flat tire, Oh boy, that was just great! Well today was Monday and the Sheriff would be back from his vacation and Alice and her big mouth would tell the Sheriff every thing, and kids in the cabin by black lake with there flat tire. Burt looked bad in the Sheriff eyes. Dam bite, he thought to himself. Burt turned the key to the car and the engine came to life with a rough. Burt put the car in drive and stepped on the accelerator, the car moved forward. Burt was a little hurry he hadn't eating scent yesterday. He'd stop in and get a little something to eat and then be on his way to the Sheriff office down the road.

The Sheriff open the door to the office, Alice was behind her deck as away. He missed her, she looked so nice in her pants and white blouse, she really was a beautiful, he looked at her pretty face with her big brown eyes, He walked over to his deck. There were a couple of papers on the deck and to days newspaper. He pitted up the papers and looked at them. A couple calls about a lost cat and one about a cow in the Main road. And then there was the call about a couple of men having trouble with a animal.

Alice looked at the Sheriff as he was looking over the papers, and Alice said to the Sheriff, "I asked Burt to check on the college boys up at Black Lake again these morning to see if they were alright. I haven't heard from him yet He could be reporting in any time now, Sheriff." She had a uneasy tone to her voice.

The Sheriff looked up to see Alice nervous look on her face and replied back the Alice, "You think the young men are in a bite of trouble, Alice?" Alice didn't wont to up set the Sheriff, seen he had left her in charge over the week end, and then these thing with the young men came up. She did asked Burt to check on them and then it see if they called back. So she told the Sheriff, " Alice didn't wont to up set the Sheriff, seem he had left her in charge over the week end, and then these thing with the young men a came up. She'd asked Burt to check on them and then it seem they called back. So she told the Sheriff, " Sheriff, I received a call about some young people who's car had a flat tire and they said some animal was around the their car and they thought they might be in so danger. So I told Burt to check on them at the old Orland road at Black Lake, Burt said he would. And later that night I got a call from the same telephone number. When I picked up the phone I didn't get a answer. I tried to call back but I couldn't get thought. *I think the cell phone was out of time,* we'd been having trouble with the phone line do to a storm that night for a couple of hours. I just have a un -easy felling about the call. I just think something wrong. Sheriff, I don't know what it's just a feeling, Cleyton." She looked into his eyes with a where'd look on her face. as she told the Sheriff about the young kids at Black Lake. "I then asked Burt to check on them again today to see if they were alright." Alice said to the Sheriff.

The Sheriff could tell Alice was up set about the people at Black Lake so he said to her, "I think you could call Burt right now and tell him to be on his way to Black Lake to check on those kids, Alice." The Sheriff walked over to were Alice was it her deck.

The Sheriff, office was small. Just the Sheriff deck and Alice deck plusa table behind Alice deck with the radio on it, there were no lock up in the room. Alice pitted up the mike, with her finger turned the radio on. You could ear the hiss of the radio as it came on. Alice talked into the radio, "Burt, come up in!" She said into the radio. She turned up the radio, "Burt come in!" repeated her self. No answer, she tried again, and again.

Burt was at the restauant and had just order his breakfast when he heard his hand radio when off. It was Alice on the radio, asking him to report in for duty. He pitted the radio out of his pocket and turned it on, "Yes, Alice what do you wont now." he said in a flat un -caring tone to his voice.

Allis's voice came over the radio. "Burt" she said, " The Sheriff, Cleyton wont you to check on the people at Black Lake as soon a possible.

"Burt replied back to Alice," I'm going too Alice, just as soon as I can. But I'm going to need to take the four wheel auto, I don't think these car can that the pounding on that dam road, Alice?"

"Ok, Burt I'll ask the Sheriff if you can use the car." She told him. The Sheriff was leasing to them talk and shook his head Ok.

"The Sheriff said Ok, Burt, it well be at the station. Burt you need to get a move on, and check on these kids at the Lake."

"I'm going to, Alice." Burt replied.

"How long is it going to be before you're at the station, Burt?" She asked him.

"About a hour, Alice." he replied "Make it a haft hour, Burt. "Alice said strongly.

" Ok!, Alice I'll been in as soon as I can." Burt told Alice in charm voice. The waitress brought Burt's food to him, pancakes and bacon.

And placed it in front of him. "Thank, but I have to go Betty he said to the waitress .Can you put it in a boggy bag, so I can eat it later?"

The waitress left quietly as to box and bag up Burt's breakfast. She came back in just a couple minutes with Burt's food boxed and ready to go. Burt took the foods from the waitress and walked slowly out of the restauant.

Burt turned the key and the engine rowed to life. He put the car in guar and the car sprig forward. Burt was on his way to report in to the Sheriff office and pit up the four wheel auto, so he could safely go down the old Orland road to Black Lake. Burt was thinking to himself, Why hurry the dam kids most likely have already go by now. But the Sheriff was back and Alice no doubt has told him every thing about the kids at the lake and add a little more to story to make Burt look bad in the Sheriff eyes. He stepped on the excel or and make the car go a little faster. Hell if that what they wonted him to do, by God he'd do it, he'd go down that dam dart road to see if those kids were there.

CHAPTER 12

June was up at six o'clock in the morning and had designed to make her husband breakfast. She was out in the kitchen when she thought she heard her husband moving around up stairs. Howard her husband didn't have to be to work till eight thirty to open the store. And he'd have plate of time to have breakfast. June took a large fry pan out of the cabinet and placed it on the stove. She could hear Howard walking down the stairs so she turned to greet him, as he walked in the kitchen. " Hi, honey." she said. "Did you hear if Jimmy, did he call yet?" Howard looked at June pretty face she had a concerned looked on her face. He could tell she was worried about Jimmy, he hadn't call when he said he would. Howard went over and checked the answering machine. Jimmy didn't leave a message. He looked back at June and said, "No June I didn't hear from Jimmy. I'm shore he must be Ok. I'll try to call him on his cell phone in a couple of minutes." Howard said he tried to be cram and not up set June any more then she was already troubled. June took a pan out of the carbide and placed it on the stove, then she turned back to her husband and said, "Howard, I think you could try to call Jimmy now." Howard set down at the table and looked back at June as she was talking to him and said, "Ok, June I'll try to call him now, if it well make you field any better. He stood up and walked over to were the telephone was in the kitchen. Howard pitted up the phone and tried to thing of Jimmy's phone number. He dialed the numbers the phone rang, and rang. A voice came on the line and said , Jimmy cell phone was out of service and to leave a message. Dam, Howard thought to himself and then he turned back to June and said "I think Jimmy's phone out of time or maybe it's to far away to reach Bangor."

June hearing that said to Howard, "So what do we do now, Howard, call the police and have them check on him?"

"Maybe that the thing to do now, June. I'll call a friend of mine who's a detective and ask him what to do, first. I know Ned, well be more then welling to help us. June can you get me the phone book, I have to look up his number. I know he'll know who to call to check on our son June."

June handed Howard the phone and he dialed the number of his friend the detective. The phone rang and rang again, "Hello, this is Ned Fairwell." the voice at the other end said. Howard told his friend about not hearing for his son and asked Ned if he would help. Ned said yes and asked wear was his son the last. time he heard from him. Howard told him they went to Orland cabin by Black Lake and Ned asked wear was Black Lake located? Howard told him it was twenty maybe thirty miles south of fort Kent. Just off route eleven and five miles North of Eagle Lake. Ned wrote down what Howard said. And thought to himself that was a hundred eighty miles from Bangor, boy that was way up North of Bangor almost to Canada. Ned would have to look up the number of then nearest law enforcement office and give them a call. It had been over thirty hours scent any one had talked to Jimmy. Ned could ask the office to make a check in the area for them to see if they were alright. He now the office won't turn him down, they check on the kids. After talking to Howard Ned would have to make a couple calls to find the right deptment Ned told him he would do what he could to find out were his son was and thank him and hang up the phone. Ned pitted the phone up once more then he dial the number to his Bangor office and asked the deptment operator to find the right number to the closes sheriff office to Fort Kent. The operator told him the numbers and ask if he wonted her to dial the numbers for him. Ned said No he'd call, thank her and hang up. Then he dialed the number that he was give. The phone rang and rang once more then a female voice, that of Alice answer and said, "Hello these is the Sheriff office, how can I help you." Ned told her his name and he was a Bangor police detective for the deptment. And he'd like to speak to the Sheriff. She told him to wait and she get the Sheriff. Can I ask what it is about? Alice wasn't shore she wouldn't to hear what the detective was going to say next. Alice's body tens up a bite as she waited for Ned to reply. She didn't wont to hear what she thought he was going to say next. Alice looked around the small room the Sheriff was a few feet away at his deck looking at so papers.

He looked up to see Alice with a concern look on her face and wondered what was on her mind as she looked around the room.

Alice could see the small room of the Sheriff office, these was a small town not much happen in these area. It had been a quit nice little town and know something was going to happen to put a end to the peace, she just know it! Her voice tighten up she could hardly talk as she told Cleyton the Sheriff he had a call from a detective in Bangor. "Cleyton, there a call for you on line one from Bangor." The Sheriff pitted the phone up quietly and said, "Hello, these is Sheriff Cleyton, What can I do for you?" she didn't wont to hear what he was going to say.

Ned deep clear voice said calmly, "These is Ned Fairwell of the Bangor police deptment. I'm calling to ask you to check on a young man and his friends that were going to Orland cabin by Black Lake. His family hasn't heard from him in forty eight hours." Ned add a couple hours so it would seem more important to the Sheriff. "His name is Jimmy Bentely, his a college boy and so is his fiends. They went to the cabin for the week end and he never called home to let his family know he was alright. So, they asked me to call and ask you to check on them." Ned said calmly to the Sheriff.

"You said Jimmy Bentely?" The Sheriff asked.

"Yes!" answer the detective. Cleyton voice was business like as he said. "It seem as though we heard from them Saturday and it was reported that they had car problems, we have a note to check on them as soon as possible today detective. I've been told me deputy is been told to check on them as some as he can. He's on he's way to pit up a four wheel drive car so he can make it down the road alright. If you leave you're number I'll call you in a couple hours and let you know what my deputy find out about the young people." the Sheriff told Ned.

Ned said, said "Ok!" and give him his number and hang up the phone. Cleyton wrote the number down that the detective gave him and looked back at Alice, who was alright watching him on the phone.

"Alice you better give Burt a call and tell him I when him her a quit as he can make it. Tell him to put the siren and make double time getting hear. I need to know what going on with these kids down at Black Lake.

Alice pick up the mike and said to the Sheriff, "You don't think something wrong with those kids do you, Cleyton?"

"I don't know, just make the call and get Burt on the move." Cleyton waved to her to get going with the call.

Alice spoke into the mike, "Burt, the Sheriff wont you to put the siren on and make double time getting and to the lake to check on the kids. We just got a call from Bangor to check on the people at Back Lake, It's important Burt, out" she let go of the button on the mike.

Burt replied back to her, "Ok! Alice I'll turn on the siren and speed up, I'll be there in a couple minutes, Alice Out."

"Ok, Burt I'll have the four wheel drive car out front of the station, when you get hear." she replied back to him. "Thank, Alice, out."

Alice let go of the mike, and turned to look at the Sheriff and said to him, "If you watch the phone I'll go get the four wheel drive and drive it around front Cleyton." She gives the Sheriff a little smile that she cared for him.

The Sheriff seen her smile, but he was more concern about what was going on at the time. His face had a business look on it, he was deep in thought at the time. "Yes, Alice I'll man the phone, be sides I think I'll call Harold and till him I need him for back up at the station." He turned around and pitted up the phone and started dialing Harold number.

Alice waved good bye to the Sheriff and started to walk out the door to get the car ready for Burt when he came in the station yard.

Now the Sheriff could here the sound of the siren of Burt's carouser not far from the station. Alice checked the gas gage, it was haft fuel'. It would have to do; Burt was almost to the station now. She turned the key and the engine rowed as the car started. She put the car in gear and speed around front of the building with a screech of the tier.

A scent later Burt Pulled in beside her and open the door of the car. Alice pasted Burt the keys to the other carouser. It's important Burt, the Sheriff thinks some thing might have happen to the kids.

Burt shook his head Ok and took the keys from Alice and got in the carouser and turned the key and speed off.

CHAPTER 13

"There June, Ned said he'd make some calls and let us now as some as he could." Howard went back to the table to eat his breakfast. Howard really didn't wont to eat any more he'd lost his appetite some time ago to eat breakfast. All he could think of was if Jimmy was alright. He'd know some. He still didn't wont June to be to upset, so he'd eat a little breakfast to try to remain cram.

"So, what do we do now Howard." June said with a very shake key voice, she was greatly up set about out hearing from Jimmy. It wasn't like him not to call to let her know they was alright. So the phone ran out of time he mush be able to get to a phone and call home. June thought she know something was wrong, but she didn't know what? She just had an any uneasy felling in her head. Howard turned to look at his wife beautiful face. She had a worried on she face. He moved closer and put his arms around her and said to her softly,

"I guess we'll just have to say a prayer and wait and hope for the best June." he kiss her softly on the lips and held her tie. " I've none Ned a long time June we went to college together. He'll find out what going on with the kids at Black Lake. He kissed her one more time.

"June I have to open the store in a little wild and Ill stay there and make shore every thing alright and come home as soon as I can, June. He let go of her and   started to walk to the bedroom to get ready for working the store. June didn't wont Howard to go but he when anyways.

Howard got his clothes out of the closet and put them on the bed; He'd go in and open the store and then put Addy in charge of the store tell he got back a few hours later. Addy was youny but a smart boy, and he'd do a good job for a few hours. Howard slid his pants on and buttoned his shirt; he'd be to work in just a few minutes to open the store. June came in the room and said, "I'll call you if I hear anything Howard. "She kissed his cheek.

"I'll most likely be back before anyone calls June." he replied. "If you hear anything you give me a call and let me know." Howard didn't like not know what was going on with his son but something had to be hold him up from call him and he didn't like it at all. But what could he do but wait a hope for the best. Howard looked back at his wife June he know she was up set too.

June knew her son, when he said he'd call he always did, but these time something was worn he didn't call. she know her husband Howard didn't like the idea that Jimmy had gone to old Orland cabin by the lake, God knows what he'd meet up with at the cabin. The cabin so she heard was deep in the Maine woods and if his car brought down it wound be miles away from help. Or he might have meet up with a wild animal and god know what might have happened if he did. Jimmy was a smart youny man but he was a city boy and didn't know much about taking care of himself in the heart of the woods. June wound pray nothing happing to him but someone had to go and see that he was all right. June some not think of anything but her son's safety at the moment.

CHAPTER 14

LeRoy was the first one up and pitch up his gun and walked over to the front door of the cabin. He pocked his head out the door. It all seem quit not a sound to be heard. The air smelled fresh and clean, so LeRoy walked out on the steps and looked around, nothing to be seen. He had his gun in hand and walked off the steps and took a walk around the cabin, there was nothing going on it was save of now. LeRoy walked back on the steps of the cabin. He thought later in the day he'd try to fix one of the cars. He wasn't the best merchant in the world but he new a little bite about fixing car. And it would give him something to do. About that timer he heard a sound be hide him, he turned to see Rachel in the doorway. She had woke up shortly after he did and walked out to see what LeRoy was doing. Rachel seen her big black boy friend with the gun in his hand and she smiled and said "Hello, LeRoy what's going ?" LeRoy looked around and seen Rachel , she was a very beautiful girl and he know he loved her. LeRoy told her he planned on trying to fix one of the cars later in the day. Jimmy had only a couple hours of sleep, but by eight o'clock he felt much better. He was young and strong and need only a little sleep and he was ready to start another day.

Jimmy walked over to were, Lisa and Cessie was and set down in the chair. He looked at Lisa, she was young and beautiful with her soft white skin and slim full finger. He had made love to her just the other night. He wished thing was better so he could spend more time with her, but with these creatures running around biting every body. Jimmy had to stay in focus with what was going on around them.

Jimmy took Lisa's hand and stood up pulling her with him and said, "Come on lets take a walk around a little bite. Jimmy put his arms around her. Lisa said, "Yes!", she thought he really did love her and maybe one day they'd get married and have a couple beautiful baby together. But for right now just to be together and make love and get to know one another was Ok with her for right now. But Jimmy was in college and that must come first right now. One day Jimmy would be a big time lawyer and make a lot of money for her and the family they was going to have. Lisa held on to Jimmy waist: he was the man she loved. Yeh, and one day Jimmy have to meet her mother and father. Oh her mother would like Jimmy and be happy for her, but what would her father do? Would be fly in a rage and try to kill the man she loved , Jimmy or wound he give Jimmy a change and talk to him and find out like she know Jimmy was a wonderful man. And her father could be glad to have him as a son –in law. Lisa wished her father would be the nice man he could be, but why he was still drinking she know better. He be the mean cruel man he always was when he was drinking. And it seamed now he was that was all the time. Lisa could remember when she was young he was kind and loveable to her. And now he had no job all he did was drink and hate people.

Jimmy, could feel Lisa squashing his waist, and know Lisa had falling in love with him. That was ok with him because he loved her a little bit too, but right now they had walked a little ways from the safety of the cabin. Jimmy looked back and could see Berry talking to LeRoy; and Jimmy thought he could hear, Berry give his opinion to LeRoy, about what to do about the problem they were in with the creatures. And LeRoy, said something about a fight with the creatures. That wasn't what Jimmy wonted to hear: he thought they could be quit and peaceful and wait tell help came from town. Those thing may not attack if they all remained cram. Jimmy had never faced anything like these before. Most likely no body had ever see any thing like those almost invisible creatures, that popped out of no wear to attack them. Jimmy bet the Earth had never seen any thing like those jelly like invisible creatures before. Most likely these creatures was a new strange living form of life, or just maybe they came from outer space?

Jimmy took Lisa hand once more and started walking to the shore of the lake with Lisa by his side. Jimmy hopped things would go better these time. They walked slowly along the grass trying not to bother the jelly spiders as they made there way to the water.

Lisa wasn't sore she wonted to walk along the grass near the water, but she did because she wonted to be with Jimmy, the man she loved with all her heart. She'd do anything for him at this point. Her love was strong for him.

Jimmy watch very carefully wear they was walking, he didn't wont anything to happen these time. Jimmy and Lisa walked down on the beach Jimmy sneakers sank in the sand as he walked along the sanded beach. Jimmy held on to Lisa hand as they walk on the beach. Jimmy looked towards the water, it looked so peaceful but he knew there was danger all around. Jimmy stopped and put his arm around Lisa's shoulders Jimmy looked back over his shoulder to see LeRoy walking away from Berry with Rachel by his side. Berry started walking back to Cessie by the picnic table.

Dam, these place could be so nice, it could be peaceful place to be, it had a great view the tree, the water looked so nice even if the water was ices cold it looked great. It could be peaceful the way it looked but it was a place of hell.

Jimmy looked to his right to the coast line he could see something that looked like form, what the hell was it these was a lake not the sea., you don't have foam in lake? What as it some strange fangs that the creature had done to the lake? Jimmy was a smart guy but he didn't have time to figure it out right now. Jimmy turned and stopped and checked his cell phone it still wouldn't call out. They walked on down the sore line. He seen the rock wear they had seen the jelly like creatures were and walked around them slowly. They didn't appear these time maybe he was right. If they showed the creatures they weren't going to hurt him maybe the creatures would leave them along?

Lisa looked at Jimmy the man she was in love with and took his hand, she thought he was the best looking guy in the world; she had a tingling feeling come over her and Lisa said to Jimmy in her soft sexy voice, "Jimmy, you must be tied couldn't we go back to the cabin and you could get some rest." She stopped walking and looked up into Jimmy's face and poised and went on to say, "After I make love to you in the sleeping bag, and it well be fun, honey. Then you'll need the sleep after that work out honey." She had a big smile on her face as she said that to him.

Jimmy looked down at her and seen she was smiling at him in a loving way. Even being in great danger wasn't going to stop the love she had for him. Jimmy did love Lisa but right now he had to think about them being in a very dangers place. He didn't wont anything to happen to her, their would be plant of time latter to make love with out being in so much danger as they was now.

Maybe that was the thing to do go back to the cabin, they were walking in a very dangers place at the moment. He took her hand and they turned and started walking back to the cabin; they wont that far away from the cabin at these point.

Jimmy looked around, the water was a few feet away from were they were at these time. It wound have been nice if Lisa and he could have been on the beach, but they was to much danger all around them. Jimmy looked closer at the water. There was something wrong with the water. Jimmy stopped a scent to see what was going on with the water in the lake. There was a white firm on top of the water. Jimmy thought to himself, it wasn't foam, it was a white coating of so kind of thin firm that stacked several feet from the beach, All around the water. Jimmy didn't have time to set any longer, but he'd make a note in his head of the strange looking firm on the water. They started walking again. Jimmy could see the rock in front of them the one that had the creatures on it when they first went down the path

Suddenly he could see the creatures once again on the rock. There was maybe two or more jelly creatures that popped into sigh as he was watching them. Maybe they were sunning themselves to keep warm on the rock in front of him. As the creatures turned to look at them, Jimmy body tines up in with fear of what was to come. He could fell something moving in the grass beside they feet. Jimmy and Lisa started running to the cabin grounds.

Jimmy could see LeRoy and Rachel coming out of the cabin; LeRoy was saying something the Rachel about fix one of the cars so they could get out of these hells place.

As Jimmy, looked around he could see the jelly creatures on the rock once again in front of them. He stopped walking for a moment to try to get a better look at the creatures on the rock. They was hard to see, but as some of them were on the rock the light seem to be better and Jimmy thought he could get a better look at them. Jimmy could see three jelly creatures on the large rock in front of them. The one closes to him, he thought he could see them much better and he could see that the creature had a six inch rounded top body and flat base with four maybe six legs. Four long round skinny legs and two short legs on the body and a two and haft inch rounded head witch was also clear looking. Jimmy could see right throw it. He could see no eyes, and you couldn't see any body parts, like the heart or lungs or anything. else. You could see right throw it to what was on the anther side of the beast. It was Clear like a piece of jelly might be with no color to it. Jimmy held on to Lisa soft little hand. Lisa seeing the creature wonted to keep on running to the cabin, but Jimmy held her back so he could get a better look at the creatures on the rock in front of them. It also had a one and haft inch sires like mouth that could ripe you're flesh apart in a scent.

Jimmy thought he heard movement in the grass around them. Lisa pulled on Jimmy's arm for him to get moving back to the cabin were they might be save? So they turned around, and slowly started walking back to the cabin that wasn't that far way.. All the wild they could fell and hear moment all around them as they walked slowly back to the cabin. Then one of the jelly creature snipped at Lisa's leg then they started running to the cabin as fast as they could, all the time the creatures trying to cut they legs with their claws. Lisa and Jimmy reached the bring of the shore line and the creatures popped up from hiding in the grass to snapped at their legs and lower body. Jimmy helped Lisa get up the band and once again they started running the cabin. Lisa looked at Jimmy with fear in her eyes and Jimmy said to her, "We've got only a few feet to go and we'll be save, Lisa." Lisa eyes were wide with panic as she held on to Jimmy hand, but they keep on running to the cabin together. Jimmy could see LeRoy came out of the cabin still caring the short gun in his hand. LeRoy told Berry he was going to try to fix Jimmy's car with part from his car. Rachel was close to his side as they walked down the steps of the cabin to Jimmy car along side the cabin. Then he sore Lisa and Jimmy running to the cabin in fear of they lives. So he turned to help them LeRoy with his gun in hand watching them run towards him to the cabin. and if they needed help he'd be ready to help them if needed. Lisa ran up to wear Leroy was standing and Jimmy right behind her. Jimmy said to LeRoy

we tried to walk on the beach and them dam things started attacking us
so we started running. Guess they don't like us near the water?" Jimmy
added he was almost out of breath The creatures stopped chasing them
as they got near the cabin. Jimmy held Lisa in his arms to comfort her
and said "I'm sorry Lisa it was a foolish thing to do go walking on the
beach when I know the creatures were still around and out to hurt us.
Are you all right, sweety?" They walked over to the picnic table were
Berry and Cessie were standing watching them and listing to the music
on the radio. Berry looked at Jimmy his room mate in college and said,
"Are you all right, that wasn't a very smart thing to do Jimmy, thought
creatures are out to hurt us!"

Ever in great danger as the young people at the cabin were in
they tried to keep busy doing something to pass the time tell they was
rescued. Cessie was use to cleaning up to keep busy, so she clean the
cabin up and pitted up after every one else to keep busy. Jill turned
back to her nursing and cooking to keep her mind off the danger she
was in and Lisa thought of the Jimmy and being married to him to and
raise a family with him and how happy the y would be. Jimmy know
he'd invited his friend to the cabin for a party and they met the little
creatures in the cabin and all around that was out to hurt him and he
was felling a powerless to do anything to get them out of the danger
they were in at to moment. He could have planned better what to take
with them. Dam only one cell phone and it was low on battery power.
He knew his mother would call for help when he didn't turn up on
time. Dam he know better Jimmy try to think of something to help
them get out of hear quieter. But right now it seamed to just set and
wait for help to come, was the best thing to do right now.

LeRoy was the type of man that needed to keep busy doing
something like maybe he could try to fix one of the car LeRoy thought
to himself, about fix Jimmy's old Mustang. He could try, and just
maybe he could get it to work for a little wild. long e-huff so they
could get to hell away from the cabin, and them dam creatures? LeRoy
turned to Rachel and said, " I need you to come with me and help so
I can try to fix Jimmy car. I'll need someone to hold my gun and tools
why I fix his car. Let me take a look at his car first and then we'll go get
my tools out LeRoy opened the hood of the Mustang he could see all
the wirer were ripped and torn apart by the cheaters. The motor was
duty old but just maybe he could get it to working using part from he's

car. Hell he'd try what harm would it do? LeRoy could try to put what wirer he could back on the motor. Him big hands moved slowly as he twisted the wires together.

Jimmy and Lisa walked in the yard of the cabin: they were save for now.

Jimmy heart was pounding with fear. Lisa was shaking so bad she could hardly stand up. Thank God, Jimmy thought we made it. They stepped out of the deep grass on to the dart ground near the cabin. Jimmy could see Berry and Cessie was talking by the fire place and LeRoy had the open the hood of Jimmy car. Rachel was beside LeRoy holding the short gun in her hand.

LeRoy thought to himself, what wires he couldn't twist together maybe he could tape together? LeRoy worked for several minutes on the wiring. Rachel handed him the wrench and turned to see Jimmy was back from his walk with Lisa. Rachel thought Lisa was nothing but just a young school girl with a crash on Jimmy. And didn't know a thing about life, she marry him in a minute and didn't know a thing about how to be a wife.

Rachel was a woman that could please Jimmy with her slim beautiful body. He wouldn't need anything if he was with her, she could take care of him just fine. She stared at Jimmy as when into the cabin with Lisa. It could be her with Jimmy not at little girl right out of high school, Lisa what did she know. It wasn't easy for Rachel being a black girl in a State like these with almost ever one in the State was white Their was a few black girl in the State but not many, she was out number by fifty to one. Rachel know she was a nice looking black girl but Jimmy didn't seem to care, was it because he was so in to his college studies that he didn't care to have a girl friend but Lisa made he way into his heart. Lisa though herself at Jimmy offering sex for friendship and I'll beat if the solute got herself parent wound like it .She'd have Jimmy trapped in a reliance ship he couldn't get out of and Lisa win him over. Rachel thought she was the one for Jimmy, she could make him happy and always love him not like little Lisa. Rachel thought she was in love with Jimmy. In her mind she could see herself being married to Jimmy and she wound be so happy and so wound Jimmy. At times Rachel tried hard to get his attention. Oh, Jimmy told her that he thought she was pretty, but he dated Lisa a white girl out her. Rachel came from a nice black family. Her mother wasn't as tall as her and deeply believed in the Lord God. as her way to live. Rachel's father was working black man and they lived in a nice house in Brunswick, Maine. Rachel had two older bothers and one younger bother. She was the only girl in the family. Maybe that was why she acted the way she was? But there was times when being a black girl wasn't enough. Rachel was good at sports as she was a tall, strong black girl ,but she wonted more. From time to time Rachel had nightmare of coming from a black family and dreamed of her grandfather being on a slave ship and being whip by a white man .many years ago. How could they do that to him? Well what had happen happened she couldn't change it! Thank God things change for the good. But she still was that little black girl in love with a white boy named Jimmy. And at times he didn't care enough about her. Why didn't he look at her as a met and a girl he could marry one day.

LeRoy work on Jimmy's car for a few minutes and did all he could with no tools. LeRoy opened the truck of Jimmy's car and looked for tools. He couldn't see any tools. Then he looked in side the car, no tools that he could use. Well he'd have to go and get the tools out of his car. He pulled his big body out of Jimmy's car and started to say something to Rachel. When seen a creatures appear on top of Jimmy's car only a few inches from there head. He acted fast and swung the gun across the top of the car. Knotting off the Jelly creature. "Dam, get away from hear!" he shouted to the thing at was flying in the air at the time. His black face had a lighter color to it he was mad.

Rachel, pulled back as she seen the thing on the roof of the car go flying in the air. Rachel body tens with fear. Rechel hell back a steam, she moved her hands to her face. the creature hit the ground with a thump. It squealed in pain and ran off into the woods.

LeRoy staying his body by pulling back his shoulder to his full height .He know, he was powerful and could kill the little creatures.

Dam!, he still had to go and get the tools out of his car so he could fix the Jimmy's Mustang. So, they all could get to hell away from these dam place.

Lisa was close to Jimmy her arm were around his waist as they open ed the door to the cabin. Lisa's warm body against his hard body; she looked up at Jimmy's handsome face with love on her mind. "You think we'll be out of here today, I don't wont to lose my job, Jimmy?

Jimmy looked down at her beautiful face and said, " It wont

be long and some body will come and come to help us. I know my mother will call the police when she don't hear from us. I think it will be a couple more hours for us to wait that all, Lisa. He moved close to his bed row and un button his pants, they fell to the floor. Lisa looked into Jimmy eyes and know what he was thinking, she smiled back and thought the same thing as Jimmy did she wonted to make love with him also, and show him she really love him Lisa more her hands to her shorts and she un-buttoned them and took her short off and then Lisa took her blouse also and she bent down and slide in the sleeping bag with Jimmy. There was know one else in the cabin they was alone time. Jimmy pulled Lisa under pants down over her but ex. Lisa skin was so soft ,Jimmy became aroused. His private part became bigger and bigger till it was over ten inches long. Lisa, put her arms around Jimmy and he put his strong arms around her. There was little room to move around in the sleeping bag. Lisa wonted to put her legs around Jimmy's hips but there was no room to do so. So, they just held one another and kissed and made love. Jimmy's body warmed up, Jimmy kissed her hard and long, his tongue went in Lisa mouth. Lisa body was warm up and Lisa's soft pink round full breast that toughed Jimmy's chest and she kissed him long and hard. Jimmy must know then that she did love really love him. The sleeping bag rounded back and forth as they made love in side the sleeping bag, Jimmy could feel her soft sweet body in his arms and Lisa was young and beautiful. They made love long time. Lisa healed him in her arms, he was man she would love forever.

LeRoy, looked down at Rachel's tall slim body, she was beautiful, but right needed to try to fix Jimmy's car and then he'd try and see if Rachel would make love to him. He know she care a lot for him and it was time she showed him she cared for him, as he know she did. He was a big good looking black guy ,take all any girl need. He was all man and more. LeRoy lifted his big shoulder up and let his big chest out, he was a powerful black man nobody mess with. "Rachel, we have go get the tools out of my car and you have to go help my with every thing." He put his arm around her and she pulled back a little as he did so.

Rachel carried for LeRoy but she was in love with Jimmy. He didn't push her like LeRoy did. Jimmy was honest in his felling for her. Rachel know Jimmy cared for her, even thought he didn't say so. She could tell by the way he looked at her and the way he acted, that he carried for her a great deal. And one day they would be together. And she could make love to the man she truly loved, Jimmy. the pretty little white boy!

LeRoy, toughed Rachel shoulder, letting her know that he wonted her to come with him to help him with Jimmy car. LeRoy walked brassily toward LeRoy's own car that was parked under the large maple tree. Rachel, trying to keep up with LeRoy long legged steps as he walked to the car. It didn't take long, his LeRoy's car was only about a hundred feet away and in a let then a minutes they were near LeRoy's poor beet up car. He stopped short of the car and looked it over. The poor car had three flat tires and broken wind shell. LeRoy know that the wiring on the motor was torn apart by the creatures. He moved closer and opened the hood of the car. The wires were ever wear in the engine of his car. Jimmy car parked near the cabin wasn't much better but LeRoy thought he could fix Jimmy car much quieter then his car. It was going to take time to pull what wires he could out so he could fix Jimmy 's car. Hope that it would be enough to get Jimmy's old Mustang started. LeRoy was going to try anyway, he handed Rachel the short gun and open the hood of his car. Dam, it was a mess in there. Oh well, it was time to get started working on the car. He pulled back and when to open the door of driver side door, t opened with a pop. The branches of the near by tree was almost toughing the roof of LeRoy car.

Rachel was holding the gun in her left hand and LeRoy started to get in driver side door of the car. He pushed the front set down and clamed inside the back seat. of his car, the tools were on the floor in the back set in a metal box. LeRoy reached his long arm and put his hand on the handle of the metal box.

Rachel laid the short gun again the side of the LeRoy's car as LeRoy was trying to get the tools out of the back seat of the car. Rachel turned and looked back at the cabin. She couldn't see Jimmy or Lisa. They must be inside the cabin and that bitch. "What! What the hell!" she shouted.

Suddenly, something heave hit the top of her head. It was digging into her hair and cutting her flesh! Another dropped on her head. She screamed in pain. "AaaRrreee! LeRoy, help me, No, stop!" she howled in pain as the creatures were slashing at her flesh and blood started to pour out of the wound, Rachel screamed in horrible pain.

Suddenly Cessie and Berry heard Rachel screaming for help. They turned their heads to see what she was screaming about. Then they could see that Rachel was being attack by the creatures and they were all over her face and upper body. That the same time LeRoy heard Rachel howl in pain turned his head to see Rachel putting her hands to her face. As those dam creatures were all over her head. They were attacking her face ripping at her flesh!

LeRoy heard, them and seen Rachel scream for help. He dropped the tool box and started to move out of the back set of his car. "What wrong Rachel,?" LeRoy shouted, but he know the creatures wear back and attacking her. and then seen them little beast trying to kill Rachel .LeRoy was trying his best to get out of the back set of the car as fast as he could ,but he was a big guy and it took time.

"Help me, their killing me!" she shouted. Rechel twisted and turn trying to throw the creatures that had falling from the tree on her head as they were slashing and cutting her beautiful black skin. Rachel screamed in horror as the creatures cut her flesh. She whaled in pain "God, help me!" she shouted. LeRoy tried his best to get out of his car but he was so big and the back seat was so small it seemed to take for ever by for he made his way out of the back seat of his car. Rachel twisted and turn trying to throw the creatures off but there was way to many on her upper body to do much good. She screamed in pain as she fell back wounds.

Cessie was the closes one to hear Rachel scream in pain. Her brown eyes widen hearing the scream, she looked to Berry who was only a few feet away from Cessie. " God, something wrong go get Jimmy we've got to help them." Cessie said to Berry. "Jimmy, we need you, Rachel and LeRoy are in terrible!" Berry shouted as loud as he could.

"I'm going!" Berry replied back to Cessie. He got up quietly and started walking brassily to the cabin. As Berry did he shouted to Jimmy once again, "Jimmy, Rachel and LeRoy are in big terrible we need you help."

Jimmy had Lisa in his arms, they had been making love for the last few minutes. His pennies was deep in side Lisa soft beautiful body when he heard Berry shouting for help. Jimmy pulled his pennies out of Lisa and got out of the sleeping bag. Jimmy had no pants on he was nuked from the waist down.

He pulled his pants on and grabbed the baseball bat along side the bedding on the floor, and started running to the door. "I'm coming, what wrong Berry?" Jimmy shouted back as he when out the door.

Berry was at the top of the steps, his face was red from running to the cabin. His left hand was pointing to were LeRoy's car was a hundred feet away.

"Their attacking them,!" Berry said his voice sounded of alarm. We have to help them quietly, they kill them!"

Jimmy looked towards were Berry was pointing, God, he could see Rachel and. the jelly things were all over her face and there was some on her long black legs. Rachel back off from the car, trying to pull the viruses, clewing, biting jelly like creatures off her. Rachel's hands tried to grab the jelly creature. But her fingers sank into the body of the jelly creatures. Rachel screamed in agony,

"GET OFF ME!"

LeRoy pulled his big black body out of his car. The viruses, clewing jelly creatures pounced on LeRoy's back and head as he got out of the his car. They tore at his shirt and his flesh on his back. The feeling of great pain race to his head

"Dam, Rachel I'm coming!" LeRoy shouted. Were was his gun; it was hard to see. The creatures were jumping on his face now. He swung his long black arm around trying to find the short gun on the ground, then his finger felt the cold feeling of the metal of the gun. He pulled the gun to him. LeRoy finger felt the tiger. He lowed the short gun but Rachel was to close to him . So he swung the gun around in the air, hitting two of the creatures on the ground by Rachel feet. LeRoy shook his head throwing some of the jelly creatures off him. It was hard to see with the creatures jumping on him. LeRoy wonted to help Rachel but he was busy fighting off the creatures that was attacking his body and he couldn't see Rachel as she have moved away for him to try to get away from the creatures that were attack her. The creatures were falling from the tree so fast that it was almost like they were raining down on LeRoy's face and he couldn't see Rachel any more. LeRoy shouted out, "Rachel were are you, I can't see you ?" But Rachel was being attack by the creatures as well and didn't have time to answer him. Rachel had hopped by moving away from under the tree she could get away from the creatures, but there were thousands of creatures in the grass and they were also attacking her legs and lower body. Rachel was blooding from a gash on the neck very badly and had several cuts on her face and legs also. And she was starting to get weak from the loss of blood. Rachel wonted to run but she was to weak to run any more. She thought she heard LeRoy shout her name but she was losing the fight with the creatures they had hurt her badly and slowed down and then fell to the ground. with a thud. "Oooh!" She mood in pain. "Rachel!" LeRoy shouted one more time. He couldn't see her or hear her any more. LeRoy moved away from his car and twisting and turning to throw the creatures off him as he moved. LeRoy still held on to his short gun as he moved away from the tree were the creatures had jumped on his head. He looked around as he moved trying to see were Rachel was so he could help her in time. Then LeRoy seen her, the creatures were all over her upper body and she was in big treble with the creatures cutting her body as she tried to get away. LeRoy yelled to Rachel so she could hear him. "I'm coming to help you, Rachel, I'll be there soon. "It was still hard for him to see Rachel as blood was flowing down his face. But he was doing his best to keep a eye on her.

"Grab a weapon and fallow me!" Jimmy shouted to Berry. Jimmy started swinging the bat back and forth near the ground., knotting the creatures in the air to the side with a thud.

There were so many clear jelly creatures on the grass it gave a look that it had turning the green grass with a white coat, as they were thousands of them all around Rachel and LeRoy.. And in front of Jimmy and Berry the creatures were trying to stop him from helping their friends. As Jimmy tried to move forward the creatures in circled him from all side not letting him move forward as he wonted to do to help LeRoy fight off the creatures. .Berry had picked up a large piece of wood in his hand as a weapon. Berry was right behind Jimmy, ready to help fight. Jill had gone back in the cabin, and was in the back room of the cabin when she heard the commotion going o Cessie grab a smaller piece of wood, " I'm coming they need all the help they you can get. to fight off the creatures.

Lisa put her shorts on and butted her blouse and rush to the cabin door. She heard Rachel screaming and Jimmy shouting something about a weapon; everything was in a up wore. What the hell was going on ? God! The creatures were attacking them. Lisa mind was in a spin., what was she to do? She stepped off the steps; they all had weapon in their hands. Lisa looked around to find something to fight with. She pitched up a small piece of iron .pipe and held it tight in her hand. "What do you wont me to do? "

Lisa shouted to Jimmy.

Jimmy was busy fighting off the creatures trying to make a path to LeRoy and Rachel, her didn't have time to talk. Jill meet Lisa at the door and looked over her shoulder to see what was going on. She started to shake with fear. "NO! it can't be?" Jill cried out loud.

Cessie heard Lisa shout and turned to see Jill and Lisa in short. Her beautiful white legs exposed to be ripped apart. "Lisa go put you're long pants on so you won't get hurt." Cessie shouted back at her. Jill had been in the back room sleeping and came running out, she had jean and a blouse on, "What going on?" she said she ran for the first aid kit. God they was going to need her help.

They were fighting the jelly creatures. "God they killing me!" Rachel screamed as loud as she could. Jill heard her screaming and grab a big knife and held it in her right hand and in the other hand she had the first aid kit. Jill was trying to keep a clear head, and she needed to stop shaking, they would need her. She walked to the picnic table and laid her first aid kit on the table.

Rachel tried to run, but the clear jelly creatures jumped from the grass at her long black legs, bighting and slicing her flesh. She hallowed in pain, she was in horrible pain, Rachel was staring to get weak as the blood pour out of her wounds, she fell down on the grass, her body hit hard, "Oooh!", Rachel's eyes almost closed, but falling helped to knot off some of the creatures from her body. She had to get up, if she didn't she would die! Rachel was so weak it was hard to say awake. But she was going to get up. Rachel stood up and started walking away from the tree that the creatures were falling out of tree on her head. GOD, she wonted to live, she had so much to live for, Rachel so dam she didn't give up. Rachel had moved away from the LeRoy's car that was under the tree. The beast were still biting her but she keep moving forward.

LeRoy had also stepped away from the car that was under the tree, wear the creatures was jumping on his back, ripping and biting him. Her keep swing his arm around knotting the creatures off him. LeRoy found the gun on the ground with his hand and pitched it up and his fingers held his short gun tidily in his right hand as he swing around. LeRoy wonted to help Rachel, but she had moved to far away from him to help her. His finger was on the tiger now. LeRoy lowered the gun and fired. several of the jelly creatures were blown apart and pieces of they body with flying in the air.

Jill was going to have to do the best she could. She'd need more cloth for bandages. Jill looked down at Lisa and said, " Lisa stay hear and help me." Things were happing so fast it was hard for Jill to think. " You can't help them, help me. Their going to need use, Lisa." Jill told her.

Lisa turned and looked back at Jill, maybe Jill needed her more. Jill told Lisa what she needed. and to go back in the cabin to get them and come back as some as she could to help Jill with the people that got hurt.

Rachel was still fighting for her life. The slimy jelly creatures stick to Rachel's hair and body . The creatures tore at her flesh and blood was running down her face. Her long back beautiful legs were been tore a part by the clauses of the jelly creatures. Blood poured down her long black legs from the cuts. Rachel screamed in terror' "Ooooh, HELP ME!." But the creatures keep cutting into her flesh, trying to kill her. Rachel was losing a lot of blood. The jelly creatures tore at her round full breast, Blood ran down her black belly. "HELP ME, Oh GOD, their kill me." Rachel screamed in horror able pain.

LeRoy, twisted and turned trying to throw the creatures off his back. Blood ran down his big black body as he tried to fight them off of him. He won't to help

Rachel, but it was hard for him to see her. Rachel had back away from the car to get away from the falling creatures, and LeRoy couldn't see her that good anymore.

Jimmy shouted to LeRoy, "We're coming LeRoy just hold you on for a few minutes." He and Berry was knotting the creature to the side, but it took time Jimmy's bat hit another jelly creature and it went flying in the air and hit the ground with a "Thud!" They were making their way to Rachel and LeRoy, but it was slow work, there was so many of the creatures that had popped up out of the grass and what was green grass was almost white with the terrible creatures .coming out of it to stop them from helping Rachel and LeRoy. Jimmy notes that if you stayed out from under the tree, the creatures on the grass could only jump a foot or two. And the creatures were biting their pants not they flesh as they made their way down the road to help

LeRoy and Rachel. Jimmy could see as long as they didn't get under the tree; wear the creatures could fall on their head they was much saver for harm. Jimmy and Berry keep swinging their weapons down at the jelly creatures knotting them to the side.

Rachel's mind was spinning, she was losing straight fast, her body was getting weak from the lose of blood. She knows she couldn't keep going on like these much longer. I don't wont to die she said to herself. She keep on moving slowly down the road away from the car. She was bleeding from several places on her body. Rachel was at the point she couldn't feel the terrible pain anymore. She keep moving on; she didn't know but the creatures had nearly tore her right ear off and blood was pouring down her neck. I DON'T WONT TO DIE. She said to herself. Jimmy shouted, "Rachel, were are you going ? Come back so we can help you!"

She was slowly walking away from the car, but she was going down the road away from the cabin and the help that Jimmy and Berry was trying to bring to them. Jimmy keep on shouting to her and so did Berry and Cessie for her to turn around so they could help her, but she keep moving away from them, she couldn't hear them any more, her ear was gone from her head.

LeRoy shouted to her to turn around and come back to a saver place, she keep on moving step by step away from them. If only Rachel thought if she could keep moving away from the tree that the creatures had jump on her from she might be safe but the creatures held on and more jump on poor Rachel 's body as she tried to move away. Rachel was getting so weak she fell to her bloody knees. Rachel was so very weak it took all her straight to get up to her feet, but she did and started moving forward.

The creatures were on head her head back and face biting and ripping slacking a her flesh Rachel was getting so weak she couldn't fight back anymore

Jimmy shouted "Rachel, were coming hold on we'll be there in a minute

LeRoy, looked at Rachel just a few feet away. She was covered in blood. He started to run to her, long legs took big long steps. He was near her in a few seconds. Rachel was so weak she stopped walking. Now she was cover in killer jelly creatures. Rachel now was bleeding from several places on her body. She thought she heard LeRoy shout,

No come back. But she couldn't see anymore. The creatures had cut her eyes out, blood poured from her eyes socket, she was blind. She started to walk once again. She couldn't feel any pain now, she was in shock.

"Rachel, Come back." They shouted at her. Rachel couldn't hear anymore. She took a step and started to fall forward. Her eyes round back in her head, her eyes closed, and she hit the ground, she was die.

"NO, R.ACHEL NO!" LeRoy cried ,he had move close enough that he could see that Rachel was die. Her body was torn apart by the creatures, her eyes stared straight ahead and Rachel mouth was open and life less looking. A tear was in LeRoy's eye but those dam thing wound let him alone long enough to cry right now. He had to keep fighting to keep the creatures off him. Dam, there was nothing he could do to save her she already die, LeRoy turned and started back to the cabin.

"LeRoy, help her!" they shouted at him. With tears in his eyes LeRoy said , "I can't, Rachel is die!"

"Oh, God No." cried Cessie. The creatures have killed Rachel.

Berry turned to Cessie and said, "We have go now Cessie, we've got to get back to the cabin it's not safe hear." Cessie's arms was getting tied , she had been swinging at the creatures of a few minutes now. She was trying to hold back the tears, it was hard she loved her friend Rachel and now she was gone.

LeRoy pulled the tiger of the gun, it went off with a BANG1 A couple of the creatures were blown apart by the blast of the gun. Jimmy was behind LeRoy and notes that the creatures were starting to back off a bite. There was fewer of the beast to hit now, thank god, Jimmy thought as he moved slowly back to the cabin. Maybe it was because the creatures had made their first kill of poor Rachel. And the beast wear feasting on n her poor body that gave Jimmy and his friends more time to get back to the cabin. What ever it was they was back at the cabin and were save of the moment.

Rachel black body lay on the grass and the jelly like creatures were feasting on her body. Jimmy didn't wont to look at what was happening to poor Rachel body he turned away and said, " LeRoy we have to go back to the cabin it's not save hear we'll come and get her body when it's saver." LeRoy turned around and his eyes had waded with fear. He couldn't help her anymore. LeRoy, lose the one he loved. A tear ran down his black face.

Jimmy looked down were Rachel lay the creatures were starting to pull back and the grass was turning green once again. They'd wait and go get poor Rachel body as soon as they could as long as the creatures stayed back from them. Jimmy asked Jill if they had a sheet to put Rachel body in so they could bring her back to the cabin. Jill said she'd get a sheet for him and be right back. The creatures had pulled back now that they had kill Poor Rachel why I don't know but they did and they when deeper into the woods now that they had killed Rachel. And suddenly it was quiet, maybe too quiet? You couldn't hear the birds or animals, it was eerie not to hear a thing and you knew those hellish thing was only a few feet away and could attack at any time.

LeRoy lead the way with his gun in hand and Jimmy and Berry close behind. the girls stayed by the cabin Jimmy rapped poor Rachel's body in the sheet and Berry and him took her back to the cabin and put her body in Jimmy old broaching down car tell help came. Jill couldn't help herself she started crying and so did Cessie and Lisa. Tears rounded down LeRoy cheek He'd lost the one girl in the world he truly loved, Rachel.

Jimmy looked out were the creatures had been it was still very quiet you couldn't hear the birds or the animals in the woods. They all were thinking about what had happened to poor Rachel and how she died. Jimmy was thinking about you go though your life thinking you know to morrow will came things will be fine.

Then something happen horribly like Rachel being killed by the creatures and all your dream stop. Well you be the next person to die? Rachel wasn't support to die , she was a young beautiful girl with her whole live ahead of her. And then the creatures came and took her life away from her. Jimmy could still see Rachel's torn body laying a few feet a away and bloody body killed by the creatures. You look and see Rachel life's body laying on the ground. and you think you graduated from high school and when on to college and one day you wound become a lawyer too. You had it all planned out then something like these the killing of Rachel by the creatures and it all changes. And you stair out in space and wonder is you're life gone to end like Rachel and are these little beast going to kill all of us. Do you turn right or left or wait to be the next one to die?

It's like time stopped and all my planned are on hold as well.

Lisa was in Jimmy arms, he could fell her warm body against his chest and he looked down at her beautiful face. Could he fight the creatures and stop those creatures from killing again or wait for help to come? There is no answer, you don't know, so you look back at poor Rachel's body. You have to be strong what ever happen. Jimmy was the one who asked them to come to the cabin, but know he didn't now the creatures were at the cabin but he could have been more careful about going. Know he r raced to the cabin like a fool and now Rachel was die and now they was in big treble with the creatures wonting to kill them. His mother wound call the police and in time they wound come to rescue them they just had to stay away from the creatures if they could till help came.

CHAPTER 15

Cessie was greeted by Lisa as she reached the cabin grounds. Lisa grabbed Cessie arm and pulled her closer and gave her a little huge and said to he sobbing voice, "Thank God you made it back." Lisa eyes widened, she had a tears in her eyes. Lisa was standing by the barber-Q and the fire was out, but the radio was still playing.

Jill was standing by the table getting things ready to help with the cuts. Jill looked up to see Cessie, LeRoy and Jimmy come in the camp grounds. Jill could see that LeRoy needed the most help. Her was bleeding badly from the cuts on his back. Lisa could see LeRoy needed the most help, he was in pain as his back was cut in several places. LeRoy had fought hard, but dam it, he couldn't save poor Rachel. The pain race thought his back, he wiped in pain his nesh bent. Lisa held his arm and helped LeRoy to the first aid table were Jill was ready to help him. Lisa turned and put her arms around Berry and kissed him softly on the cheek and said, " I'm glad you made it."

LeRoy shirt was covered in blood, Jill cut his shirt off to real the many cuts on his back. Jill wash it the best she could and started to put a disinfections. LeRoy jumped a bite as she applied the disinfections to his back. Then she would stick the wound up if she could, if not she use a super glue to keep the flesh in place. Jill was shaking a little, the creatures had killed, Rachel, She was doing the best she could to tend to her nursing. LeRoy needed her help, she had to tend to him first, so she told Lisa, I need you're help, Lisa, well you come over hear, please?"

But Lisa was young and had never see anything like these before in her life. Poor, Rachel had been killed by the creatures. Lisa started crying, she was torn apart by the cheaters. The creatures had jumped all over Rachel's body, tearing and ripping at her flesh till the creatures killed her. Lisa keep on crying and bent down and started balling uncontrollable. Rachel had became her friend, that was not right to die like that. Lisa didn't know many black girl, there was only a few were Lisa liver. Add Rachel was just a very like able caring girl. It didn't mike any different what color she was she was, Rachel was a sweet, wonderful girl, and now his was gone. Rachel was Lisa friend, and all wise wound be.

Cessie heard Jill asking for help and replied, "I'm coming to help you

Jill. "Cessie had been swing her weapon to keep the creatures away for some time, her arm hurt, it seemed to her. as thought it had been hours of fight off the creatures. Cessie was tired mental and physically wore out. Cessie stumble as she tried to go help Jill. She had LeRoy blood all over her, from the fight with the creatures.

Jill looked at Cessie trying to walk over to her to help her, Cessie as almost at the braking point. And Jill asked her "Are you alright Cessie?" Cessie tied eyes looked back at Jill. Lisa was still crying and Cessie was shaking with fear but she said she was alright. Jill know better, Cessie had done more then her part in fighting off the creatures.

"Cessie, why don't you help Lisa I'll be alright." Jill told Cessie.

Jimmy was turned around looking out the window to were they had been fighting for they life. He held the bat tightly in his hands, as the bat was dripping with the white Oosh and slime dripped down the bat from the creatures her hit with the weapon, knotting them out of the path he'd made so he could help LeRoy.

"Jimmy, I'm going to help Jill for a moment with, LeRoy; is that ok with you?"

Berry asked Jimmy as he walked carefully over to were Jill was bandage LeRoy back. Jimmy said as his heart was pounding nervously, he keep looking out for the creatures to advice on them.

Jimmy's body was tense, like a warrior might be in battle ready to fight.

The creatures had killed poor Rachel and wound kill again if giving a change. He eyes was full and the adrenalin was rushing though his body. It was like a nightmare Jimmy and his friends were fighting for their life and help hadn't came yet and maybe they never come.

We need to move in side the cabin maybe it well be saver there?" Jimmy told Berry. Berry was already helping Jill with the cuts on LeRoy back, he turned and looked back at Jimmy and said, "It well just be a minute Jimmy, she almost done."

"Make it fast I don't know how long we have before they attack again?" Jimmy replied back to Berry.

It wasn't the best of bandage but Jill was done for now. "Well that going to have to do for now LeRoy. I guess we better go back to the cabin. She turned and looked back at the cabin it was only a few feet away they could make it safely. Jill helped LeRoy and they started back to the cabin. Jimmy stepped back a couple of sets, he keep his eye on the creatures. The creatures were started to make a little noise now and the creatures were moving around in the woods. The chatter was get louder and louder now.

The hair on the back of Jimmy neck stood up it, the noise was making Jimmy very nerve. Jimmy thought it was only a matter of minutes and the creatures were going to attack. He moved back slowly looking from side to side, Jimmy held the bat in both hands.

Cessie was in side the cabin now, and Lisa with in the cabin next. LeRoy and Jill were only a couple steps away with Jimmy not far behind. As Jimmy with though the cabin door, He thought he heard the jelly creatures stop their chattering, it was quit once again. Jimmy stopped at the door the noise had stopped for now. He open the door yet there was not a sound to be heard, it really was quit. You couldn't hear a bird cheep or a animal moving around it was to quit. Jimmy shut the door and locked it. Cessie went into the back room and laded down on a sleeping bag. She was tired, very tired she needed to get so rest. Cessie laded down and close her eyes, She needed a little rest.

Lisa had stopped crying but she was still shaking with fear. How could these happen, it was suppose to be so fun and it turned into get horror. GOD NO!, Lisa thought to herself.

Jill helped LeRoy set down and placed the short gun by his side as he set in the middle of the floor on a bed roll, and Berry stood by Jill, he had the weapon in his right hand. "Jimmy what do you thing going to happen now the creatures have attack us?"

"I don't know, but those thing aren't going to stop. That I know, they wont to kill us that I know. You thing someone wound be on their way to help us know."

CHAPTER 16

Burt had been speeding along, he had turned the siren off and had slowed down a bite, when up in front of him there was a couple cars that had came together cussed a accident. Burt put the siren on and slowed the cruiser to stop along side the two cars in the accident. Burt pitted up the mike and talked into it, " Alice, these is Burt, I've came up on a accident just before the turn off to road to the cabin. I'm going to be hear for a few minutes. I'm checking to see if anyone is hurt" Burt getting out of the cruiser, I'll call you back as soon as I know how bad it is Alice."

"Ok, Burt, let me know as soon as you can, Out!" Alice replied back to Burt." Alice turned to Sheriff, and said," We have a problem. Burt as came across a accident on the main road just before the turn off to the cabin. You think we could call of Sheriff?" The Sheriff looked at Alice, Dam, he thought to himself. "Yes I think we better, Alice. "Who do we have that close to the seen, Alice?" He put his gun belt on I'll go, but you could call up Harold. Tell him to meet me at the turn off to Orland camp road." Sheriff Cleyton headed for the door. I'll let you know what going on soon Alice." the Sheriff went out the door on his way to the accident: the door slammed behind him.

Burt walked over to the crash sigh, he could see that the front car was hit from behind and both cars were messed up pretty bad. " Is anybody hurt?" Burt asked. The man in the front car said that his girl friend was hurt. Burt could see that her head was bleeding. He when back to the police cruiser and pick up the mike, "Alice, come in! Were going to need a ambulance, we have a woman with a head injury."

"How bad is it Burt?" Alice replied, The Sheriff is on his way to the seen Burt; he called up Harold to help out. Stay on the seen, Burt we'll seen help to go to the old Orland's cabin.

"Ok Alice, I'm going to make a report out on the accident, and I'll get back to soon, over and out.

Alice turned back to the mike and picked up her coffee. It was going to be a long day, she need to keep sharp and on the ball.

CHAPTER 17

We have killed one of the beast, it fells good, doesn't it? The big beast run with fear in they eyes. We must kill them all and free our home of the beast once and for all. But we have lost so many why don't we just let them go and run in fear. We have won the battle isn't that effort. No, we much drive them away forever. So no more beast ever come back to our home! So what do we do now?

We kill one by one until they are all gone forever. That what we do! We must go and kill, kill them all!

The noise became big and big as we all shouted we must kill the beast! We have to kill the noise box, it scars the children, we must stop it.

Jimmy was passing like a lion back and forth on the cabin floor. Ever so often he looked out the window to see if the creatures were advising.

LeRoy started to lay down on his right side as his back was on fire with pain.

Jimmy seen him start to lay down said, " LeRoy I may need you don't get to comfy. Jill looked at Jimmy, she didn't like what he said and she replied,

"Jimmy he needs some rest he's hurt bad. Can't you give him a brake, for a minute?" Jill snapped at Jimmy." He need a little rest, dam it!" Maybe she couldn't have said what she said, they all was tired. But LeRoy had been cut several time in the back. And dam it well you stop pushing ever body, you're making me nerves.

Jimmy stop for a minute, he looked all around the room. Cessie was in the back room by herself and Lisa had all most stopped crying. She was curled up in a ball by the back room door and LeRoy and Jill was in the center of the room with Berry looking out the front window. Jimmy, know Jill was up set but he needed ever man and woman to help out when the creatures started fighting again. The creatures had stopped chattering for now. Jimmy didn't know if that was good or bad, at this point it didn't make much different. What was going to happen was going to happen, he twisted to bat in his hands nervously.

Cessie looked up as she started to lay down for some rest and as she did she thought she seen something on the ceiling.

"Jimmy, why didn't you-----" She stopped, they all heard Cessie screaming.

The Jelly creatures popped into sigh on the sealing above Cessie's head and another one pop up on the wall in the back of the cabin. And what looked like a clear wall suddenly appear, from no were, hundred of killer jelly creatures ready to attack Cessie. She screamed for her life! "NO, No, help me!

" NO, GET OFF OF ME! LeRoy help me." Cessie screamed. "Ooooh, no!" As she looked up she could see the horrible jelly creatures appeared on the sealing a top her head. "Nooo!" Cessie screamed as they hit her shoulder. and another and another fell from the sealing. The creatures started appearing on the wall. and also the jelly spiders appeared out of now out of no wear appeared on the floor. The creatures were all around her. Cessie screamed, "GOD, Help Me!"

Cessie started to lie down when something fell on her shoulder, and then another and another killer spider fell on Cessie. Now she was trying to get out of the sleeping bag, but the creatures were jumping on her and Cessie couldn't get out of the bed. She scream for help as the creatures tore at her body and blood poured out of the woos. Large gashes from the creature's claws were on Cessie's neck. The pain was to muck for her Cessie all most passed out and she fell back in the bed.

Jimmy, and Jill turned when Cessie screamed they looked to the door were Cessie was in the room. One of the jelly creatures slashed at her flesh. Blood poured out of the wound. Cessie SCREAMED she was in horrible pain. She tried to pull of the jelly spiders with his hands. Her fingers sunk in the body of the jelly creatures your fingers, the jelly creature just slipped though her finger and she felt the Ooozs of the creature go though her fingers. As she grabbed the jelly spider she scooped it up in her hand, she felt the Oooz of the slimy jelly in her fingers. Cessie pulled hard and scooped one of the creatures off. But they was several more on her head and shoulder now slashing and biting her. Cessie screamed in pain, "Ooh God no!" Cessie fall then she got back on her feet as blood poured from cuts on her head. She back to her feet and Cessie started running for the door for help. Cessie was trying to run but creatures had hurt her real bad and she stumble fell to the floor.

As she fell more jelly creatures jumped on her body. Cessie screamed as the creatures tore at her flesh. Blood started to run out from several woo and dripped to the floor.

Jimmy turned as he heard Cessie and he raced to the door were Cessie had gone to get some rest. "LeRoy grab you're gun." and without stopping he said, " Berry I need you too!" Jimmy shouted.

Cessie was laying on the floor and she was covered with the jelly creatures. Cessie was bleeding from her head badly; Jimmy grabbed her right arm and tried to pull her out of the room filled with jelly creatures

Were did they come from the window was closed and the door was closed? Jimmy pulled her out of the room, no time to think just fight.

LeRoy walked to the door, he was hurting but he did the best he could, LeRoy had his shot gun in right hand. He seen the room filled with jelly creatures, on the floor, sealing and walls. They must have been hundred of them in the room. Jimmy was pulling Cessie out of the room and Berry was helping him, LeRoy moved along side Jimmy and lowed the gun and pulled the tiger. Boom! the gun when off and several jelly spiders flow in the air. But they still was hundreds more still in the room, wonting to kill and hurt them. As Jimmy pulled Cessie out of the back room filled with jelly creatures,

Berry slammed the door shut. Jill rushed over to help Cessie, she still had some jelly creatures on her, so Berry and Jill frankly trying to pull the jelly creatures off Cessie, bleeding body. Berry scooped the last jelly creature off Cessie and throw it against the wall with a Bang!

Jill look down at Cessie, she was hurt bad. Cessie had a large wound on her neck. It looked deep and might have severed the vain. Blood was pouring out of the wound. Cessie needed to be stitched up and quietly. So Jill said to Lisa, " Help me put Cessie on the table."

Lisa looked at Jill and started to help her put Cessie on the table when suddenly, a jelly creature appeared on the table. Snapping at Jill hand, then another one appeared on the table. Lisa screamed for help. " No, it can't be?" But it was, there were creatures all over the table. Jill pulled poor Cessie body away from the table. " God, no!" Jill screamed, she turned and looked at Jimmy as he knotted one of the jelly creatures off the picnic table.

There was bubble that appear on the walls of the cabin and on the sealing there was bubble appearing all over the place in the cabin with a pop of horror! Pop,Pop,popthe bubble became jelly monster. The jelly monsters creatures fell from the sealing trying to land on they heads. There was bubble like creatures appearing now on the floor, trying to cut their feet. But there was to many of them to fight off. Jimmy was swing the bat as fast as he could at the jelly like monster creatures, but was so many of them he couldn't hit them quiet effect to do much good. Jimmy moved back and said," We've got to go, there's to many of them to fight off." Jimmy told Jill as they all moved back away from the jelly creatures "Come on we have to go there is to many to fight off.!"

LeRoy pulled the tiger of the gun and it when off with a boom!

Jelly creatures were blown to peaces and flow in the air. But now their was thousands of creatures that had appeared in the cabin ready to harm the kids. They had no choose they had to run from there life's.

Berry was swinging his weapon as fast as he could to fight off the creatures. His pants were torn in several places and his leg was bleeding from a cut by the jelly creature.

LeRoy pants was torn also and his shirt was torn to pieces by the creatures. Jimmy was un-hurt, he was wearing cowboy boots and jeans and a dress shirt that was torn, but he was still in good shape to fight.

Jill and Lisa pulled Cessie body out of the cabin as they were on the wooden pouch of the cabin.

Jimmy slammed the front door shout with a, Bang! But know they had to face the jelly creatures that was out side the cabin.

The area around the picnic table seem to be free of the jelly monsters for the moment and the radio was still playing loudly music no one wonted to care about hearing right now but they left it on anyways. All they could think about right now was staying alive.

Cessie eyes were closed and her face looked a little gray, Jill didn't like the way Cessie eyes being close and she said to Cessie in a caring voice, moving. Cessie, come on come back," pleaded to her, " You can't die?"

Lisa looked down at Cessie mushiness body. It was a night-mare,

she couldn't die too. Lisa wonted to cry they all was fighting for their life, they didn't have time to think only run and fight. Lisa was bleeding from several cuts on her leg, as she had been cut by the creatures a few time and her blouse was torn in a couple places.

Jill didn't wont to say it, but she had to. " Cessie gone, she die!" she started sobbed, almost crying out loud . Jill was also bleeding from several cuts on her legs. but she didn't think of pain, Cessie had just been killed by the monsters jelly creatures and Jill had to think of ways to just staying alive. Jill didn't wont to just leave poor Cessie body on the porch, but she wasn't strong e -huff to pick Cessie die body up. Jill touched Cessie die body, good bye Cessie my friend I'll never forget you, I love you she sobbed So Jill started to go of the porch and leave Cessie behind. If only she was stronger! She looked at Jimmy with tears in she eyes. Jill started down the steps of the cabin. She touched Lisa on the shoulder to let her know it was time to leave.

Cessie still warm once beautiful body lay on the cold deck of the cabin. Jimmy looked back and seen poor Cessie die body laying on the porch of cabin. Jill looked into Jimmy brown eyes and he handed Jill the wooden bat, it had grow and slim all over the head of the bat. Jill had tears in her eyes because of Cessie died.

Jimmy walked quietly over to wear Cessie lay and reached down and pitched up Cessie limp warm body and put her over his shoulder. Jimmy couldn't leave Cessie body on the cold deck of the cabin. He lifted Cessie body up and started walking as fast as he could the cooking area wear it seem there was no jelly creatures at the moment. The radio was still playing some song no one cared for music right now they was fighting for they life but LeRoy thought they better leave it on he could fight better with it on.

LeRoy aimed the short gun and pulled the tiger with a Bang! jelly creature was blow apart as the gun went off. Berry and Lisa made they way to the pith net table Jill cleared the table off so Jimmy could lay Cessie body on the table. LeRoy was along side Jimmy with the gun helping him make his way to the picnic area, Jimmy placed the body of Cessie on the picnic table softly. Then he took the bat from Jill and shook his head Ok! Berry looked at Jimmy and ask him, "Jimmy what was we going to do now ? We're not safe in the cabin any more were do we go now? " Jimmy turned and looked at Berry and looked around for a safe place to go. then he said, I'm don't know Berry right now I guess we stay right hear and see what the creatures are going to do. and do our best to fight them off.

The world is not fair poor Cessie lost her life to the creatures just like Rachel did. Both girls had so much to live for but it was taking by the horrible creatures. Cessie had graduated from Bangor High ten years ago and married shortly after. the marriage lasted only two years and ended in devoice. Cessie became prizefight the first couple of month with a girl baby. She named the girl Megan. Cessie razed the child by herself she came from a single parent herself her mother razed her as well. Cessie worked as a hair designer to bring in money for years she word for a local shop in town. Most people thought she could have her our shop she was that good, one for the best but she never did. Cessie dated many guy and had sex with most of them She met Clendon at the Bird Nest Club he was a tall nice looking guy and he told her about his devoice with his x wife and who it change him Yes it was his felt he had came out of the Army and he had a lot on his mind, so he told Cessie he drank to for get what happening to him. And he stopped for a wild and cleaned him self up joined the Club and met many girls then he met Cessie a single mother. Clendon didn't care much for dancing. Clendon mostly drank beer and talked about any thing the girl wonted him to talk about. Clendon was a big tall guy and girls liked that about him. Cessie was in love with being in love. She always thought the guy she was with at time was the right man in her life, and then she found out he wasn't the right man after a few month of being with him. Cessie had been with Clendon only a few month when she met Jimmy and ask him if she could go to his cabin in the woods with other friends, Cessie hell she'd love to go. Clendon had ask her to marry him and like a fool she said yes, but know she wasn't shore if she wonted too. Clendon lived to drink, he had his income from the Army and he work a little on old car's like Jimmy for extra money that was good enough for him but it wasn't good enough for Cessie she like new thing a nice home and new clothes to wear and nice jewelry to wear. .Most of the time Clendon was dirty and un shaving. and didn't car about things like that. As long as he had a few beer in the frig he was doing fine, to hell with the rest of the dam world.

Jimmy really didn't know her it well, but he like her, Cessie was a few years older then he was with a nice full finger and a beautiful face and smile. She was a warm and nice person to talk to about most anything. Jimmy wound miss her, Cessie had became a friend to him and all the kids at the cabin. Cessie was nice mother to her daughter and now her daughter was alone. It wasn't fair, that her life was taking by those creatures. Cessie never did anything to hurt them and they killed her. Jimmy had a tear in his eye. Jimmy looked to were Cessie body lay, and thought she is my friend now and forever. I will miss you and never for get you, you was a wonderful warm lady. tears round down Jimmy's face. He was sorry to have ask her to come with him to these hellish place with creatures for hell that wound kill her. I'm sorry, Cessie, I love you. Jimmy thought, he put his hands to his face as tears round down his face.

CHAPTER 18

"Alice!" It was Sheriff Cleyton, he waited for Alice to answered.

"Yes, Chief?" she replied.

"You better send a ambulance and fire truck to the seen on route eleven, we most likely will need them. Out!" Sheriff Cleyton said, as he was approaching the accident. The Sheriff could see it wasn't take bad of a accident, but some people had been hurt in the accident and need attention." he started to slow the carouser down a he approach the accident; Cleyton turned the siren off and pulled in behind Burt carouser. "Alice, I'm going to seen Burt with the four wheel driver carouser down the Orland road as soon as I get set hear." He went on to say, " Alice why don't you try and see if you can contact the young man over the phone." the Sheriff waited a scent and went on to say, " Maybe you can get though these time, Alice. I have to go now, Alice, out."

"Will do, Sheriff, out." Alice replied, the Sheriff had already signed off. Alice put the mike down and got up from the deck and proceeded to walk over to were her deck was so her could look up the number of the young man that called from the old Orland cabin. There was a large address wheel on her deck, she flipped though the papers trying to find the young man number. She remembered, trying again and again to contact the young Mr. Bentely and couldn't get though. The Sheriff ask her to try again and dam that what she was going to do, try. She hopped this time she'd get though. Alice moved the papers around trying to find the number of his cell phone. There it is, she said to herself as she found the number.

Just then the door open and a middle aged lady walked in the office. She wore a blue and brown house dress with old faded white sneakers on her feet.

She looked like a town person from not to far away. Alice looked over at the woman; she found the number and had the paper in her hand

"Hi, Alice." the lady said as she know her name.

Alice, really didn't know the lady, but she though she was a local lady lived in the town. Alice eyes indicated to the woman these was a office, not a meeting place to talk thinks over.

The lady walked over to were Alice's deck was and said, "I heard all that noise of the sirens out side and thought I could come over to see what going on. And if I could help?" Alice wasn't much on friend ship, these was a law office. Her eyes showed it.

"Ever thing fine, these is a place of business, What can I do for you?" Alice asked sternly; Alice picked up the phone so she could dial the cell number,

"I just live down the road a short ways. I've know the Sheriff for years," The lady was a clean looking woman with a faded blue and white house dress and a old but clean sneakers on her feet. She had short gray hair and she wore reading glass on round reeds face. She didn't mean any harm, she just came to see what the office looked like and if she could help. And maybe just talk girl with Alice; she lived alone and at time just got lonely and wonted to talk to someone. Alice dialed the number to Jimmy cell phone, and got a busy signal just like last time she tried to call. Alice tried again and again, she just

wasn't getting though. the cell phone might be turned off or the young man 's cell phone was to far away, Black Lake was in a very isolated place deep in the woods of Maine. It was to hard to get signal though the mountain and deep woods of that part of north Maine. Alice had disused look on her face, it was hopples. But the Sheriff said to keep on trying and that was what she was going to do. She dialed the number one more time, and got a busy signal. Dam she said to herself. She started dialing one more time. As she was dialing Alice looked up and seen the woman still in the office watching ever move.

The town lady could see that Alice was trying to call a number and couldn't get though. She put her hands on the Alice deck and looked Alice in the eye and said, "Are you sore I can't help you? Maybe you could try something different to reach the person you're trying to call

Alice didn't really hear what the woman said at first and she said, " I think you better leave, lady I have work to do!"

The lady didn't move, she had been watching Alice very closing and was leasing to very word Alice said. The woman moved her right hand and said to "I have a nephew who is in the Coast Guard, I'm sore they would be welling to help in any matter." The lady had a big smile on her face, she was glad to be of help.

Alice looked at her, what is it going to take to get read of you, lady. "I have work to do you'll have to go now." Just then the phone rang, Alice pitched up the phone and said, "Sheriff office what can I do to help you?"

The voice on the other end of the phone was a female sounded like a lady in her fifty. Alice thought she reacquired the voice as the lady in Sinclair on the main road. Alice couldn't remember her name but Alice now her husband wasn't a very well man. And he had been in and out of the hospital for year with heart problems. The lady alarming voice said, "My husband is having chest pains, I think he going to need a ambulance." She said it very quietly. Alice was use to people calling, who were very up set and talked to fast.

"Ok, tell me you're name and address and the color of the house or number. And please try to slow down so I can under stand you. the lady on the phone told her the address and Alice called the closes ambulance Alice pitched up the other phone on her table and called the ambulance and told them are told wear go to help the man and hang the phone up. Alice told the lady on the phone there was a ambulance on the way and if she need her to call back and hang that phone up. Alice looked up from her deck and the lady was still there.

"Well what do you think, you wont me to give you the number so you can call the Coast Guard?" The lady had a disturbing look on her face.

Alice wonted to tell the woman to get the hell out of her Office, but maybe the Coast Guard could help. Alice looked at the lady, she seem like a nice person, "Ok give me the number of the Coast Guard and I'll think it over Lady, what harm would it do?" The lady rout down the number on a pace of paper and handed it to Alice. Alice took the paper with the number on it. Alice had a address wheel on her deck, she'd look it up and see if they was the same number. the Coast Guard would have a stronger signal and maybe they could get throw to the young man's cell phone. It was wreath a try.

Alice still had the felling something was terribly wrong at Orland cabin. It was in a deep part of the Maine woods, in a very isolated place called Black Lake. Alice moved her hand to the address wheel to look up the number. Alice found it, and it was different then the number the lady had given her.

"Why is this different from the number I have in the book, Lady?" Alice said to the woman in front of her, very flatly. Alice looked at her for answer.

"I think you have the number to the main office, I have the number to the Land and Shore rescue deptment." The lady said honestly. The phone rang, Alice pitch it up. And told the person on the end of the line the Sheriff was out on a case and wood be back in a couple of hours, and hang up the phone. Alice walked over the deck were the radio was and pitched up the mike and pushed the button on the mike, "Sheriff come in!."

"Yes Alice, what going on?" The sheriff said, I'm at the seen now." But there a lady here that know someone in the Coast Guard and thinks they might be able to get though with a stronger signal, What do you think Sheriff?"

The Sheriff wonted to say no way, but their was a person leaning the conversing. Alice I can have them get involved officially. But if you think they can help un officially go ahead and try, Alice. I've got to get going out."

"Ok Chief, out." Alice said the Sheriff had already hang up. Well the Sheriff said what ever she thought was all right with him. Know it was up to her. Was she going to call the Coast Guard or not? Alice looked at the lady in front for her. The lady seemed to be a alright person and Alice still had that terrible felling something wasn't right. She pitched up the phone; "So what number is the best?" Alice asked the lady.

The one I gave you is the best, it will get you though top the rescue team much quieter." the lady said very confidently. That was alright with her, Alice was starting to believe the woman was right. She dial the number the lady gave her. the phone hang once then twice.

"Coast Guard, what can I do for you?" the voice at the other end of the phone said.

"Hi, these is the Sheriff office, and I have a request for you. We having a hard time trying to get a hull of some young people on Black Lake, we though maybe the Coast Guard might be able to help?" Alice told the male voice at the other end of the line.

"Well I don't know, well try tell me more about the contact and what is it?"

A group of youny people are in a cabin by Black Lake, and the forest around the cabin are so deep we can't make contact. The report came in that the young man car was brooking down and so animal was attacking them." Alice told the Coast Guard office.

"And what are they using for a signal?" the Coast Guard office said.

Alice could have known better. " Oh I'm sorry the number I have seem to be a cell phone number." If he could have seen her, Alice face turned a little red with imbursement. "A cell phone, I don't know? Let me check." the Coast Guard office turned and looked around for help. There were three other Coast Guard people in the room at the time. He told them the stitching and that the young college kids at Black Lake might be in trouble at that location and a almost unreachable location. He needed so ideas on what to do next from his fellow Guard men.

Alice weight on the telephone line for what might have been a minute, then the young man voice came back. "Miss, we might be able to help, I don't know, it's a chance. We don't have a chopper in the area at the moment, but we could call one for the military chopper on maneuver at Limestone, they might be able to go up and try to get in contact with the kids

"There's no base there anymore, but we know there is two of a chopper from Brunswick in that area at the moment that may help. I'll give them a call and see what they can do for you." the officer told Alice.

"Thank you officer." Alice said and was thinking about anything might help at these point, and hang the phone up. She turned and looked back at the lady in the room and said to her, "Well, I did it maybe that will help I don't know, she pitch up the pen and wrote it in the log book. I hope the Chief going to like it? She thought to herself.

Office Dunning of the Coast Guard picked up the telephone and turned to Office Ryan in the room with him and said, "I just got a call from the Sheriff office in town they ask us we could check on a couple college kids on Black Lake, they maybe in treble. Any ideas what we can do sir to help? " Office Ryan lessoned to him and then walked over to the map and tried to fined Black Lake on the map. He placed his finger on the location of the lake. It was deep in the Maine woods not far from Fort-Kent. We don't have anything that far in land are there any maneuvers going on in the area? Office Ells hear what was being said and started looking it up on the computer. "The Army has two chopper in the area doing training runs sir." the young office answered. " Ok, Ellis thanks lets give them a call and see what we can do." Dunning already had the phone in his hand and he looked the number up and dialed the number as the two offices watch him do so. The phone rang a couple time then a voice answered 'Hello, Office Downing here."

"Hello, these is Office Dunning of the Coast Guard we received a call from the Sheriff office a few minutes ago about some college kids that was at a cabin by Black Lake that they might be in so treble and need someone to check on them. We called you because you're the close one to them and we were hope you could do a fly over to check on the kid? "

Office Downing leaned to what told him and replied, "Well, yes we could do a fly over what's the low casting. By the way we're flying the Apache helicopters and it only holes two people, but we can do a fly over and see what going on if anything, Office. We going to have to fell up before we can go it well that a little time. By the way what is the train of the place the ids are at office? "

"We don't really know office Downing but I can guess it's deep in the woods by a lake office, the Sheriff said they received ma call a few hours ago. I think it was a cell phone, does that help you office?"

Can I reach you at these codeines office?" Officer Downing ask. He replied "Yes!" Ok, Dunning we're on our way, call you when we hear something officer, out "Downing hung the phone up Then Downing turned around a shouted to the offices in the room, men we have a job to do lets get the chopper ready to fly gentlemen." then Downing went on to say, "Frank and Mel fueled up the chopper we have work to do " Then the first officer and head pilot said "We're going to a place called black Lake there is a lot of thick woods around the cabin so I'm told we take a look and see what going on. See if we can contact the kids and make our report. Watch out for the tree on the way in gentlemen ," the paper came out of the copy machine and he handed one to each of them and said His the location of the cabin by Black Lake we'll go as soon as the chopper fueled up good lock men." the They all got up and ran to the helicopters to get them ready to fly.

Officer Frankland and Mel want to hook up the fuel line to the chopper and the pilots when to check out the choppers to see if any thing was in need of fixing. With in a few minutes the helicopters was fueled up and the pilots had checked out the chopper and didn't fine anything wore the them. Rainbow and his co-pilot got in the first chopper and Gene and officer Frankland got seated in then next chopper. officer Rainbow got the chip broad out and they started going though the check lest. Then Rainbow flitted a couple switches and the big propeller started to go around It would take a little over a hour to get to Black Lake from were they was at the base and a few minutes to find the lake. The chopper rose in the air and started moving forward they was on their way to find out what was going on at the lake and report back to base then the base wound call the Sheriff office as soon as they found out what was going on .

CHAPTER 19

"Now what do we do?" Berry said. They all were back up around the pit net table, with poor Cessie's body on the table.

Jimmy looked at Berry, Jimmy's face was tense with fright, LeRoy held the short gun tightly in his hand, he was starring straight forward. Jill was alongside of Berry and she was shaking baddy. Lisa was next to LeRoy with the gun and she was in shock with fear.

Jimmy said strongly, "We need to light the fire and use it as a weapon so we can fight creatures off. Who has a lighter?" Jimmy asked.

They all looked at each other no one smoothed but Cessie! Berry spook up first and said, "Cessie the only one that smoked, she might have a light in her pocket?" Jimmy moved over to Cessie's body and put his right hand in her front pocket, her body was still warm. His finger worked it way in her pocket tell he felt the plastic light in her tight fitting jeans.

Jimmy pulled the lighter out of poor Cessie pocket. LeRoy and Berry was looking out and seen far away thought they could see the field of grass was being covered with the clear jelly creatures and was waiting for them .in the field out far away. It looking like the jelly creatures had pulled back a bit, the creatures once had a line surrounding them as lose as it once point as twenty feet away and seem to be good sixty or more feet away for them now, just because you couldn't see the creatures didn't mean they wasn't there. If the creatures could hidden under the wall paper in the cabin and on a wooden table and you couldn't see until they pope into the air and was ready to attach you shore now you couldn't be shore if the creatures had gone or was they just hidden once again in the wood? So, just be course you couldn't see the clear jelly creatures on the grass, they still could be hidden there or had they just melted into the grass, then the ground? And was invisible once again? To LeRoy it was like the line of the jelly creatures had pulled back and had disappearing into the grass.

Berry was a bit more un sure of the creatures, he didn't believe that the creatures had pulled back, and if they did it wouldn't be for long. and the creatures wound be back to attack them once again.

Jimmy had Cessie's lighter in his hand, he turned around and was about to light the grill from behind Lisa. First he turned the gas on and with his finger flexed the light, he moved the flame of the lighter close to the burner and puff the fire filled the burner of the grill.

Adrenalin filled Jimmy's body, there was a over welling scene of regency to get ready of another attack by the creatures. Would it by scents minutes or hours before the jelly creatures would attack? But Jimmy, know they wound attack at so point in time. Jimmy was thinking they needed to be ready to defend them self or they would all die! The fire seemed to be the better defense at these point. in time If they could make touches of fire it could keep away the creatures from attacking them. They needed time to fight off the creature before the town people came rescuer them and help them get away. to safety

Pilot Rainbow lifted his arm over his head and with his finger pointed his finger down and said, " The lake could be down there, but witch one of the lakes is Black Lake Don I'm take the chopper down to take a look and see if we can fine the lake were the kids. are it. " the co-pilot answered him according to map Rainbow Black Lake is one of the smaller lakes around here. The long lake is near the road is Eagle lake and the other one is Square lake just to the east. Black Lake is fifty or so miles to the west of Eagle Lake Rainbow." Thanks Don, chopper two we're turning twenty degrees in ten seconds to the left, out." the helicopters turned slowly in the air on they way to Black Lake.

"Ok, Rainbow I'll try and see if I can make radio or telephone contact in a minute. then Don went on to report to the other chopper, " Chopper two were going down under a thousand feet to see if we can find the kids, Gene."

"Do you wont us to fallow you, chopper one?" replied the other pilot in the second chopper. then Don answered back, " Yes follow a few hundred yard away chopper two. We're going down now." The Apache was a fast ship maybe to fast for these job, but it could be done. It's was going to be a little harder to see but they could do it. The chopper swooped down to take a look and Don got on the radio and tried to may contact with the kids. The chopper started to dive down then it it pitched up turbulence and then the chopper started shacking and Rainbow pulled up on the stick Then Rainbow said in the mike " Chopper two pull up to the right. I just ran into heavy turbulences chopper two. We'll go up and come a little slow next time. I have know idea what happened there was strange winds around the lake that all I know right, that all I know , over chopper two." Chopper one pulled off to the left as it went by the lake. Boy, chopper two that some heavy wind down there, can you get a fix on the kids, Don?" Rainbow asked his co-pilot. Don answered him, " I think I can in a minute or two Captain." Don replied. The chopper when down these time a little slower and the strange wind wasn't quit as bad as the first time. The pilot Rainbow was the first to take a look at the location wear he thought the kids might be. There was a small wooden cabin close to the shore of the like it had to be the right one he hopped. As the chopper came in as low as he dare there was not enough open land for the chopper to land. Rainbow pulled the chopper back up and the helicopter rose in the air and scooped a way. Then Rainbow said in to the mike, " Chopper two I thought I see a body laying on the dirt road I think the kids are in real treble Chopper two " then he when on to say, "Don did you get a signal for the kids? Weigh a minute I can in a minute Rainbow."

LeRoy turned and looked at Jimmy and said, "What the hell are you doing?" Jimmy looked back at him and replied back, " I lit the grill so we could use it to make touches, so we had something to fight back with." Jimmy looked around of something to be used to make a touch with. The cabin had all sorts of thing that could be used to make a touch with, but it was to dangers to go in side to get anything. There were things out side the cabin that might be o f help. And in Jimmy's car, that been parked by the side the cabin had so of Jimmy's cloths that could be use to make a touch.

"I don't need no dam touch," LeRoy lifted his gun up so Jimmy could see it. "I've got my weapon."

Rachel poor die body was still laying on the wooden table, blood was dripping from her body on the grass, it made Jill and Lisa very uneasy. Jill was shaking, she was terrified of what was going on around her and Lisa tried not to look in the direction of the body of Rachel she was also terrified.

Berry was looking at the girl and could see the body on the table was up setting the girls. He moved closer to Rachel body and said to guys "You wont to help me and we'll move her body on the ground for now."

LeRoy turned and seeing Berry trying to move the body, he when over to help, Berry move the body off the table in front of the girls.

As Berry and LeRoy lay Rachel's body on the ground, Jimmy moved over and told them what he thought they could do next, "I think we need to go back so we can ma touches for ever body. Fire is the best weapon we can get for now." Jimmy said.

"I don't know, Jimmy we'll have to walk back in were the creatures are waiting. We barely made it out of the cabin and to safety the first time. God, two of our girl friends have all ready died." Berry replied back to Jimmy. "I don't think we could go, we could start here and wait for help to come."

LeRoy and the girls were leasing to what Jimmy said about going back so they could find something to make a touch with to fight off the creatures.

LeRoy thought Berry was a very smart person and if he didn't like going back then maybe they couldn't go. Jill really didn't know what to do. She now, Berry was smart, but Jimmy was also very smart too? Lisa was in love with Jimmy and what ever he said was alright with her. Jimmy took the first step away from the picnic area.

Suddenly, what appeared to be free of the creatures was no any longer .It was felled with jelly creatures. As they were popping up out of the grass one after another, ten, twenty, hundreds at a time out of the grass. The grass was becoming filled with the jelly monsters, hundred, thousands of them filling the grass, turning it into a place of horror! A slimy Oooz of the jelly monsters. The creatures ready to snap at Jimmy legs ripping his flesh.

Jimmy swing the bat he was holding again and again, knocking the creature in the air, trying to clear the path to the cabin were his car was parked.

The creature jumped at Jimmy's leg trying to hurt him. One for the creatures jumped as far as his waist, other tore at his pants trying to cut his flesh. Maybe he was going mad, he thought he heard the sound of his phone rang. He was way to busy to answer the phone trying to fight off the creatures. It keep on ringing.

Jimmy let go of the weapon with his right hand and reached into his pants pocket to get his cell phone that was still ringing in his pocket. Jimmy pushed the talk button , and he heard the voice of a young man say, " Coast Guard, come in!" said in a strong voice.

God, Jimmy wasn't dreaming it was the voice of the Coast Guard. Jimmy quietly replied, " These is Jimmy Bentely, two people in our party have already killed and we are being attack by strange creatures that wont to kill us. I don't know how long we can hold them off before we are all killed.

Just then one of the jelly creature jumped up add bite Jimmy's hand, blood poured out of the cut and Jimmy dropped the cell phone.

The youny Coast Guard office heard the phone drop and Jimmy hollow with pain. Then he heard the sound of screaming for help. And the young Coast Guard officer said, hoping that Jimmy might hear him. " Help is on the way, we'll be there in a few minutes, hang in there, out" the office turned to the soldier behind him said, " There in real trouble, call the Sheriff Office back and ask them how soon that they be there to help the people at Black Lake. And I'm going to call; the Base and ask if we can respond too?"

The phone rang in the Sheriff office, Alice picked up the phone and answered it then she heard the voice at the other end say, " Coast Guard, we contacted the people at Black Lake and they told me that two of the people at the lake have already been killed and they are afraid that they all may die if not rescued soon."

Oh God, I know it, she thought to herself. They really are in danger, I had that feeling something was wrong, I was right, they need help fast.

After hearing what the young man said from the Coast Guard, she thanked him, and then picked up the mike and called the Sheriff,

The Sheriff's receiver in his pocket rang; Cleyton, Sheriff pushed the button. It was Alice's voice that said, "Sheriff, the Coast Guard called they got in contact with the people at Black Lake, and was told there are two people die and the rest are in grave danger." Alice didn't wait, she when on to say, " Have you sent anyone from the accordant scene down the Lake road to help the kids yet?" The Sheriff hearing what Alice just said replied, " Burt on his way to the scene, Alice. He'll be there in a few minutes."

"Tell him to make it fast, the kids are in real trouble, Cleyton." Alice said.

"Ok, Alice I'll tell him, out Alice." the Sheriff turned the phone off. The Sheriff turned around and looked at Burt and said, "Burt you better going down the road to Black Lake and put you're short gun in the front seat. reports is that there is so wild animals around the cabin and they have already killed two people. Be careful Burt, I'll be down to help you in a couple of minutes.

Burt waved to the Sheriff and got in his cruiser and turned the key and started the engine, "I'm on my way Chief." He stepped on the gas and the cruiser started on down the road to Black Lake.

LeRoy seeing Jimmy being attack by the Jelly creatures watched carefully When the cell phone rang, Jimmy stopped swing the weapon so he could answer the phone. Then the jelly creatures had a change to jump on Jimmy and they did. They jumped on his legs and one jumped on his hand were he held the cell phone. As the creature slashed Jimmy's wrist it choused a large cut on his hand were he held the cell phone. Pain rushed though his hand and feeling the pain of the cut Jimmy's fingers opened up and he dropped the cell phone once more on the ground with a thud. Jimmy when back to fighting the creatures off his body by swinging his arms with the weapon in it. Jimmy was being over welled by the attacking creatures. Seeing that LeRoy lifted the gun up getting ready to firer the gun. LeRoy took a step in the directing of Jimmy so he could help him fight off the beast. And LeRoy told Jimmy, " I'm coming to help you Jimmy, dam it. LeRoy waved Berry to stay with the girl and he'd go to help Jimmy himself.

Berry didn't really wont to but he need to stay and protest the girls from harm. Berry had his weapon in his hand ready to fight off the creatures if need be.

LeRoy didn't wont to hit Jimmy with the short gun blast, so he waited until he was save out range, then he pulled the tiger of the gun and the gun when off with a bang, creatures around Jimmy were blown a part around him, clearing the path, so he could move on to his car by the cabin. Jimmy had a couple of small cuts on him, but for the most part was alright. Jimmy was shore he could make it to his car witch was only a few feet away now.

Berry watched Jimmy and LeRoy fight there way though the creatures to the cabin. Berry stood in front of the wooden bench and Jill and Lisa were on the other side of the bench were Cessie's body lay again the bench on the beside bench.

Lisa was very up set as she watched Jimmy fighting his way to the cabin. Lisa hands were waving in the air for Jimmy to come back to her and be save.

She was losing control of herself, she had tried to do her best but she was at the point of losing total control. Lisa shouted again and again for Jimmy to come back and out leave her as her hands were waving around she hit the radio and knotted it on the grass. As it hit the ground with a thud, the batters round out on to the ground and the music stopped.

CHAPTER 20

Burt turned the cruiser down the dirt road to the cabin to Black Lake.
Burt stepped on the gas and the cruiser speed up to forty miles per hour.
Then the front wheel of the cruiser hit a large hole in the road, the car
pulled to the right and Burt quietly turned the wheel of the cruiser to
the left. The wheel hit a scent hole and Burt put his foot on the brake
slowing the car to a almost stop. Dam, Burt though to himself, I've
never been on a road these bad ever in my life so bad. He moved the
cruiser slowly down the road not going much more the five miles a
hour. Whenever he could he'd speed up, but he didn't see a brake in
the road to speed up for a wild and may not on these road. The cruiser
hit pothole after pothole shaking the cruiser front end. Burt had both
hands on the wheel as he hit the pot holes one after another. It was
going to take time to get to the cabin at this rate.

Burt wonted to call Alice and tell her it was going to take time to
get to the cabin at this rate but he didn't dare take his hands off the
wheel to do so.

Jimmy could see the cabin in front of him and it was only a few
feet away from him now. He'd pulled the last of the jelly spiders off
him and only had a few small cut on his body, he was going to make it
to the car and get the things he needed to fight off the creatures. Berry
looked around as he heard the chattering of the creatures in the woods,
the line of the jelly creatures seem to be coming closer to them, why
Berry though was the creatures advancing on them now? Berry, lifted

his weapon getting ready to fight. He turned his head to look back at Jill and Lisa. Lisa was losing control, but Berry couldn't do anything at the time.

Jill was looking forward and could see and hear the creatures were advancing towards them. Jill also could hear that Lisa, who had been so strong with Jimmy by he side but now he wasn't there she was along and the creatures were there to kill her and end her dreams and now she was starting losing control. "Lisa," Jill shouted, "Pull you're self to gather, we need you're help."

But now Lisa had lost control of her self and didn't hear Jill any more, she had knotted the radio by swing her hands around .and it hit the ground hard braking the radio.

Jill moved around the table by Berry so she could help him fight the creatures off. Jill lifted her weapon so she could help fight off the creatures.

Lisa had been under pressure and she didn't think she could take anymore. She had left the town that she grow up in and the place were her family and the people she loved and the place she worked in to go off with a young college man named Jimmy. He was a good and nice looking man and the first time she seen him Lisa fell in love with him. And when he asked her to go off with him for the weekend to a cabin by Black Lake, she didn't wont to say no, because she was afraid she may never see him again, so Lisa said yes she'd go with him to the cabin that Jimmy had just inherited from his uncle Orland that had die a year ago.

Jimmy had never see the cabin until the other day they all arrived at the poor run down cabin. Jimmy was planning to have a party at the cabin with Lisa and his friends. But the little beast appeared and killed two of Jimmy friends and ever thing turned into a night-mare. Lisa didn't wont to die she was two young to die. She wonted to live, but she didn't know what to do to save her life? The jelly monster were all around her. Lisa tried to move back but the monster were every place and they was coming closer. Lisa hands were shaking so bad she couldn't hold a weapon. She wonted to run but there was no place to run.

LeRoy pulled the tiger to the short gun and it when off with a bang. He was trying his best to keep the jelly monster from attacking Jimmy as he made his way to the cabin. The grass all around them was a milky white with the jelly creatures on top of the grass ready to bite and slash Jimmy and LeRoy. LeRoy fired the gun a scent time at the creatures and several of them flew in the air. But there was so many of the creatures it made little different, they was quietly replaced with more creatures.

Jimmy pulled one of the creatures off his leg and though it a side. They were only a few feet away but the ground was covered with jelly creatures waiting to attack them. Jimmy still thought if he could get to his car and get a few cloths out to make a touch it wound save they lives. Jimmy put his hand on the cold steel of his car, it felt good to him that they had reached the car alive, know he had to get the stuff out of the car with out getting hurt to bad.

LeRoy fired the gun one more time and killed several creatures in their path.

Jimmy reached in the window of his car to get the clothes out of the seat, when one of the jelly creatures slashed his hand.

Jimmy quietly pulled his arm back as blood from the cut dripped on the ground. Pain ran up his arm, he didn't have time for pain he reached in his pants pocket for his car keys.

There are times that survival comes first and not the pain. Jimmy fingers felt the car keys in his pocket, he started to pull the keys out, when suddenly on the roof of his car appeared a jelly creature, then another and another one pop into view.

One of the creature jumped on Jimmy shoulder and another one jumped on Jimmy's head, slashing his flesh with it's claws. Jimmy quietly pulled his hand on again out of his pocket to throw off the creature.

LeRoy seen Jimmy was been attack by the jelly creatures pulled the tiger of his gun with a bang and some of the creatures flew into the air.

Jimmy pulled back from his car and though the last one off of him. Jimmy still wonted to move around so he could get in the truck of his car so he could get the things he need to fight off the creatures.

Berry was watching the creatures move closer and closer to them and Jill was beside him ready to fight them off. Lisa had stepped back to get away from the creatures, but the creatures were all around her and were jumping on her legs and biting her with their claws. Lisa screamed in horrible pain as the creature cut her flesh with their claws.

On the wooden table were once Cessie's body lay suddenly appeared a jelly creature and another and another creature popped in view. One more and another one appeared and jumped on Lisa face and shoulder slashing her flesh with there claws. Lisa stumbled and fell to the grass. More and more creature jumped on Lisa body trying to kill her. Lisa tried to get up but the jelly creatures were covering her up body and legs. She was blooding from several bad cut on her face and head. She screamed loudly as horrible pain ran though her body.

LeRoy heard Lisa screaming and turned to see if he could help her, but he was to faraway to do mach help. Berry also turned, but he and Jill also were fighting off the jelly creatures around them self and couldn't help Lisa.

LeRoy know he had to try and help Berry and the girls, he couldn't fire the gun at these angel, so he tried to move a little closer them and as he did he howl to Jimmy, "Jimmy they in real trouble, we have to help them!"

Jimmy had moved around to the hood of his car and was about to open it, when LeRoy shouted that Berry neared help. Jimmy turned and looked back take the girls by the picnic table and could see they was in real trouble. He needed to get the stuff out of the trunk so he could fight off the creatures. He put his bloody hand back in his pocket trying to get the keys out once again. Jimmy pulled the keys out of his pocket and quietly opened the truck of the car. The hood popped open and he reached inside to get what he needed to fight off the creatures.

Berry and Jill tried to move forward so Leroy could help them with his gun. But it was hard to move; stepping forward into the jelly creatures was like stepping into mud. The jelly creatures tried to hold they foot back from moving.

Lisa was getting very week from being bite by the jelly creatures that was all over her body now. Life getting blood poured out of her body. Lisa though of her mother and father and she didn't wont to fight any more. Her eyes close the fight was all over, she felt no more pain in her body, she lay steal on the ground.

LeRoy was a big tall man with large heave boots. He took long big steps towards Berry and the girls. Because LeRoy was so big the jelly creatures couldn't hold him back from moving forward, but could only slow him down a little bit. The creatures tried to bite him, but they couldn't peach he's big boots with their claws

The creatures tried to jump on Jimmy as he took the things from the truck, but he back off just a enough so they mist him. Jimmy pulled the things out of the car and turned to make his way back to the girls. The jelly creatures were on the roof of the cabin and one after one popped in to sight. There was hundred of them on the roof and the ones near the edge of the roof near Jimmy's car, that was parked beside the house, jumped on the roof of the car so they could attack Jimmy. The first one hit the roof of the car with a thud and then like horrible rain there was five, ten, twenty of the creatures that hitting the roof of the car. Their claws ready to bite and ripe Jimmy flesh apart.

Jimmy seeing the creatures hit the roof of the car and trying to jump on him So he moved back from the car and pulled the creature off him as he moved back. Jimmy had to drop the things he took out of the car so he could fight off the creatures from his body. Jimmy moved back but he didn't wont to leave the things from the car behind. He stepped toward the car so he could retrieve the things from the car, but the creature snapped at his hand trying to stop him from retrieving the things from the car. One of the creature cut his hand with it's claws and blood ran down Jimmy hand, he pulled the things away from the car and now he needed to make his way back to the girls. Jimmy turned and seen LeRoy trying to fight off the creatures with his gun. LeRoy fired again and again with the short gun, but the creatures keep coming at them. So. LeRoy fired again and again with his short gun, but there were thousand of them and they keep coming at LeRoy trying to stop him from helping Berry and Jill.

Jimmy looked back at Berry and Jill, but he couldn't see Lisa. Jimmy mind raced, wear is Lisa he shouted out in his head he couldn't lose her. She was save where he left her, but know he couldn't see her, and didn't know were she had gone?

LeRoy put the last shell in the gun and pulled the trigger the gun when off with a bang but didn't help much. He heard Jimmy behind him and he turned his head to see Jimmy just behind him helping him fight off the creatures. Jimmy thought he heard Berry say Lisa was gone, but he didn't have time to ask what Berry mean by what be said. He had to keep fighting off the creatures. LeRoy turned the gun around and put his finger on the barrel of the gun, so he could swing it like a bat. Berry was along side LeRoy now and he said with a great deal of concern in his voice," We can't go back to the pick nick area, the creatures are coming out of the woods by the thousand, wave after wave of them. There just to many of them to fight off." Berry put his hand on LeRoy shoulder to turn him around and LeRoy turned around so he could go back to the cabin.

"What are you doing?" Jimmy said to Berry, " I need to go get the fire." and Jimmy added, "Were is Lisa?" Jimmy looked into Berry eyes. "I thought she was safe with you , what happen?

"She gone," Berry said, " We've got to get back to the cabin, I'll tell you later." Berry told him..

"We have to fine a save place to go too." Berry said to Jimmy. The picnic area is to dangers now." Berry shouted to Jimmy.

"But we can't go in the cabin, so wear do we go?" LeRoy stated.

"Lisa and I walked on the beach," Jimmy felt a wave of sadness come over him as he thought of the lose of the one he loved so much. Then his mind turned back to the matter of they saved. "Lisa and I had walked to the right of the cabin and there is no boat down there to use, but maybe there is a boat to the left of the cabin that we haven't seen?" Jimmy said as he turned to go back to were the cabin is by the shore line. Then Jimmy thought to himself, Berry said Lisa was gone, It couldn't be, what was he thinking. The creatures didn't kill Lisa? It couldn't be! He looked back at Jill,. she was crying . No, No! Jimmy thought it couldn't be? Jimmy didn't wont to ask were was Lisa. He didn't think he wonted to hear the answer. Jimmy looked around he couldn't see the girl he loved, then with a tear in his eye he looked out over the field. The creatures were out there ready to attack them at any time when ever they wonted too they could with out warren. Jimmy held the bat in his right hand, then he thought , why fight? Lisa wound have wonted him to fight to stay alive. God what did he say? He didn't wont to think any more, but he did. "What did you mean ,Lisa is gone, Berry?" Jimmy asked .

Berry wasn't a very strong man but he had done his best to fight off the creatures and say in control of what was going on. Berry tired and sad because off the lose of Lisa he did his best but it wasn't good enough. Then Berry said we tried to help her, Lisa lost control and knotted the table over, and then she tripped and fell to the ground. The creatures were their and jumped all over her. We tried to help but creatures kill her to quietly we couldn't stop them fast enough. I sorry Jimmy, we love her too. Like a hammer hitting him in the head, when he heard what Berry had said, Lisa was gone killed by the creatures. It was true, Lisa had been killed by the creatures. Tears round down his cheek. Jimmy really did love Lisa Oh, he'd only know her a couple months, but he truly loved her. Lisa was a wonderful, beautiful girl and he'd always love till times end.

As there moved back to the cabin they was still fighting off the creatures as they moved slowly back to the cabin. "Ok!" Berry said, "it's whore a try."

Jill was close behind him as they moved back to the cabin grounds. she was so afraid she was shaking and wonted to hold on to Berry for help. Jill couldn't think clearly anymore. She had seen poor Lisa die in front of her and she might be next.

It was a nightmare; she didn't know what to do anymore. Jill just keep on walking slowly back to the cabin. Were was the help that they had call for, why didn't they come to help them before they all die? God we needed help fast

LeRoy lead the way near the cabin, he looked around to try to see if he could see any of the creatures a head of them. It looked clear to the right and there didn't seem to be many jelly creatures near the cabin, but it was hard to tell because the jelly creatures could be all most invisible to the eye until the creatures popped in sigh. But they could see that there was a few jelly creatures on the roof of the cabin and the left side of the cabin had way more tree then the other side of the cabin, witch made it way more dangers then the right side, because the creatures like to jump from the tree on top of them as they when by.

As they moved close to the cabin a couple of jelly creature jump to the ground and tried to attack them. Jimmy took his bat and hit one of them and LeRoy turned the gun around to shoot them, but didn't because he had the one bullet left in his gun.

Berry was in back and could see the creatures closing in on them from the woods and the creatures wasn't far behind them. As though the creatures were pushing them to the cabin, were they planed on kill them. "Jimmy, LeRoy there's to many creatures to fight off, there coming out of the woods by the thousands, we got to get moving we can't fight that many off.

Jimmy turned to see Berry was right, there was way to many of the creatures to fight off. They'd just have to keep moving down to shoreline, and hope they could find saved so were on the beach. "Jill, come up here with us we'll try to make it to the shore line, maybe there a boat we can use?" Jimmy waved

Jill to run up beside him and Jill did start running forward but beside LeRoy. LeRoy still had the short gun in his hand but he had used the last shell gun and was empty. And know he was using the gun as a cub to beat off the creatures.

Jill ran past Jimmy and moved up beside LeRoy. He was the bigger stronger man and she felt saver with LeRoy beside her.

Jimmy could see Berry was in trouble with the creatures all around him and Jimmy moved back to help Berry fight off the creatures. The jelly creatures were cutting Berry legs and were jumping up to his wrist to cut his body. The creatures were holding on to his legs trying to keep him from moving forward to the cabin. Jimmy moved loser to Berry the jelly creatures tried to hold him back from helping Berry. Jimmy was swing the cub the best he could, but there was so many creatures, he couldn't hit them all in time to move forward to help Berry. Jimmy was only a few feet from Berry but he couldn't move any closer to him because for the creatures. Dam, Berry keep on coming I'll help you but you've got to come closer to me." Jimmy shouted to Berry.

Berry tried but fell to his knee and the jelly creatures jumped on his back trying to cut his flesh as they hit his body. Berry tried to get up but the creatures keep on biting and clawing at his flesh.

Jimmy shouted to Berry, "For God sack get up Berry Don't give up I'm coming!"

But the creatures held Jimmy back from helping Berry. Now Berry was on the ground and the creatures were ripping poor Berry apart. and cutting his flesh with their claws. Berry howled in great pain. He wasn't a strong man and he was losing blood fast. . Blood was pouring out of a large cut on his legs and he was losing straight in his right leg. And the creatures were jumping on his back and head now. Jimmy could see Berry had fallen and was in real trouble with the creatures. Jimmy was trying to go to help Berry but the creatures were doing there best to hold him back from helping Berry. Jimmy shouted to Berry to get up and start moving back to wear he was, but Berry couldn't, the creatures wound let him up.

It was hard going the creatures were trying to hold Jimmy back from helping him.

Jimmy swag his bat fur sly at the creatures, trying to make his way to Berry. All the time shouting to Berry to get up and keep moving. Jimmy was   moving forward but it was very going.

Berry tried to get up but creatures were all over him cutting and slashing his flesh. So many creatures were on his back now. The weight of the creatures was pushing down on him, trying to hold him down. trying to kill him. Berry gasp for help Berry tried to get up but fell to the ground as the weight of the creatures was to much for him know that he had weaken from the cutting of his body. Berry was losing the battle; his eyes round back in his head then was no pain Berry was at peace had came to him, Berry had die.

Jimmy seen him fall, and pushed forward to help Berry. He was close enough to help him now, so he put his hand out so he could grab Berry arm. But by then Berry was covered in jelly creatures had kill him. Jimmy grab Berry bloody arm and pulled hard on his arm to pull him up. Jimmy looked into Berry's eyes, Berry's eyes did not respond. Jimmy waited a scent, but the jelly creatures were jumping on Jimmy back now. He let go of Berry hand, as he was no longer with alive, Berry had been killed by the jelly creatures.

Jimmy had to fight his way back to were LeRoy and Jill was as the creatures were doing their best to kill Jimmy. Jimmy was swinging the bat as fast as he could to clear a path so he could go back near the cabin. Jimmy could see that LeRoy was on the beach and Jill was behind him, so he yell to them to stop so he could catch up with them. "LeRoy, wait for me!"

Jill turned to see Jimmy was fighting he's way back to the cabin. But were was Berry, she couldn't see him. LeRoy also turned his head when he heard Jimmy shouted to Berry but he didn't hear him respond and looked back at Jill to see if she now were Berry was? As Jimmy got close enough to Jill he shouted for them to stop so he could help them, but LeRoy keep on moving down on the beach. Jimmy had fought his way up near Jill and he could see the cold look on her face He looked into Jill's face and they keep on moving forward He didn't have time to tell Jill but he thought Berry was die.

Berry was just a nice young college kid. It wasn't; right for him to die, he was so young, but the weak die and the strong go on. But

I guess you could say life isn't fair. Berry wound have gone on to be a accountant or and business man in his family real state business. if he had survived the creatures attack. His family and friends will miss him now his gone

Now the group of college kids have lost one more, panic came over the group. What, do they do now that they have last Berry? Wear do they go to be in a safe place? If the creatures wound let them go, but no the creatures had them trapped in the cabin grounds and was killing them one by one.

LeRoy when back up the hill to see if he could help Jimmy and seen Jimmy, but he didn't see Berry. "Were is Berry?" he asked

Jimmy seen LeRoy and heard him, he didn't wont to answer, so he said We've got to keep going the creatures are behind me." and then he added "We've lost Berry." he waved for them to keep going.

Jimmy, only a couple of days ago was a college student and know he had become a man fighting for his life and those he'd ask to come to these place of horror. A knight of the round table had a sword and Jimmy only had a baseball bat as a weapon. Jimmy tried to think, his body was tense as a worrier mine be thousand years ago. His sword was a bat, but he needed to think and use his head. Jimmy had made a misstate by leaving Berry, Jill and Lisa the girl he loved. And know his was die thanks to him. He was suppose to be smart, but the creatures were winning the battle.

Jimmy needed to think, but the cheaters didn't give him a change to think, so he better think fast and quit or they all wound be die. Jimmy tried to think, there had to be a way out of these?

Jimmy had said they could fight with fire but the creatures had stopped him from making the torch he needed to fight off the creatures. Know they was running to the beach for help hopping to find a boat, but in Jimmy mind there was no boat, he know there was no boat to the right of the cabin, because Jimmy and Lisa had walked to the right of the beach and there was no boat to be found. He didn't think there was a boat to the left of the cabin but he didn't know that? He need timer to think.

There was a small dock on the left side of the cabin, but he hadn't seen any boat there before. LeRoy and Jill were in front of him now and were making they way to the beach.

For some resin Jimmy didn't feel going down on the beach was the right thing to do. Why he wasn't shore? The beach was small rocky with sandy under the rocks., but Jimmy know the creatures could be hiding ready to jump out of the beach. They did when Lisa and Jimmy tried to walk on the beach before and they had to get off the beach to save their life. So now if they walked the beach they could be surround and forced into the water with no boat to help them. Maybe if they were on the dock they could find something to help them? Jimmy walked to the dock. It was a old wooden dock that when out in the water ten maybe fifteen feet. Jimmy felt it was the best beat right know he thought for them. Even if there was no boat, there wound be something to use to flout in the water and maybe they could make they way to a different shoreline to be save. Jimmy didn't think the beach was the right place to be, shouted to LeRoy, " LeRoy, come back lets check the dock out first."

LeRoy didn't turn around, Jimmy had left Lisa and Jill at the picnic table t so he could go get a torch to fight off the creatures and now Lisa and Berry were die And now the girl he love d was gone too, Lisa.

LeRoy wasn't going to leasing to that little smart ass white boy anymore. He keep on walking and Jill when with him down the beach. LeRoy waved his hand at Jimmy, to get the hell out of hear. He wasn't going to let Jimmy get him killed like the other.

Jimmy asked them to wait but LeRoy keep on walking down the beach. Jimmy walked on the wooden dock, but he keep his eye on Jill and LeRoy as they walked down the beach. Jimmy still didn't think, walking down the beach was the right think to do. What if someone came to help them they wouldn't know be able to find them. It was well know to try to stay were you were until help came.

Suddenly Jimmy thought he heard movement on the roof of the cabin. jelly creatures popped into sigh on the roof above him. Jimmy held the weapon tightly in his hand. A couple of jelly creatures fell from the roof and landed on the wooden deck. Jimmy quietly hit them with the bat knotting them off the deck and into the water below. Jimmy moved away from the part of the wooden deck that was closes to the cabin. And moved to the edge of the deck that was near the water. Jimmy had expected more of the jelly creatures jumping on the deck, but only a few jumped on the deck and Jimmy handle them quietly.

Jimmy turned and looked back at Jill, who was walking down the beach with LeRoy her protector. Jimmy shouted to Jill, " Jill if help comes they wont know were to find us if we move."

Jill looked back as she heard Jimmy shout. She heard what he said but was they save near the cabin? That were the creatures first came out of the wood works and chased them out of the cabin. She shouted, "LeRoy, don't you think we could go back, so if help comes they can find us? LeRoy held the barrel of the empty shoot gun loosely in his hand. He looked in front of him. He couldn't see any creatures on the beach, maybe they would be save if they stayed on the beach? Jimmy had been wrong when he left Berry, Jill and Lisa at the grill sight. Both Lisa and Berry lost their lives because of what Jimmy did. And now Jimmy didn't to be trapped on the wooden deck and let the creatures kill them. He really didn't like Jimmy. Rachel and Lisa was die because of Jimmy. He wasn't going to lesson to Jimmy any more. "No, I'm going to keep going down the beach to safety. I'm not going to lessen to him any more. His not as smart as he think he is, he's just a rich little white boy. He's not telling me what to do anymore.

Jill stopped walking and looked back at Jimmy, who was standing on the dock next to cabin looking back at her. Jill couldn't see a boat on the beach in front of them. Jill was maybe forty or fifty feet away from Jimmy, who was on the dock was waving her to come back were the cabin was on the dock.

Suddenly she thought she could hear the sound of police car coming with it's siren blasting as it drove down the cabin road. Jill had a chill go up her spine as she hear the sound of the on coming police cruiser coming up the duty road to the cabin. Jill looked back at Jimmy and started running back to him on the dock .Jill's arms waving wildly as she ran to him Jimmy watched Jill running to him and he went to meet her at the end of the dock. Jimmy held the weapon tightly in his hand. Jill was running to him, then they hear the sound of the siren stopped. It was quiet, two dam quiet, something was wrong. Then Jimmy remember, they must have came across the body of poor Rachel laying along side of the duty road and stopped to check it out. Jimmy pulled Jill warm body close to him and looked up the road to see if he could see the police car coming, but he couldn't see anything coming. It wouldn't be long know and they would be hear to help them.

LeRoy turned to see Jill going back to the cabin wear Jimmy was standing on the dock. dam fool, she's going back to Jimmy to be killed by the jelly creatures. He turned back and looked down the beach he couldn't see that far down the beach, but he couldn't see a boat on the beach . Well LeRoy couldn't see any creatures on the beach either. Maybe he had made a mistake going down the beach?

Then LeRoy heard the sound of the creatures popping up into view all around him. LeRoy tried to get a grape on his gun tightly, but he dropped the gun on the ground when one of the creatures cut his leg with their claws LeRoy then reached down with his hand to grab the short gun by the butt of the gun As LeRoy bent down to grab the gun the jelly creatures jumped on his back and attack his legs. He hauled in pain as they cut his leg. LeRoy twisted and turned trying to through the creatures off his back, but he slipped and fell to the ground. He screamed in pain as the creatures pilled on his back, bighting and slashing his flash. He got to his knees and tried to stand up, but the creatures tour at his legs and he fell back to the ground. And started swinging at the creature with his long arms trying to knot them off his body as they attacked him. The creatures jumped on his back and legs as he tried to get up once again.

Jimmy looked down the beach and seen LeRoy being attack by the jelly creatures. Jimmy had his arm around Jill and he let go of her, as Jimmy's body tense, and like it or not he had to be ready to go into battle once again. Jimmy with his hand lightly push Jill in back of him and doing the best he could to protect her and try to help LeRoy at the same time. He lifted his weapon and moved forward to help LeRoy, but the dam jelly creatures popped into sight on the roof of the cabin and the creatures started to pope in front of Jimmy as well. And didn't wont to let him get by to help LeRoy.

The jelly creatures started jumping off the roof of the cabin trying to jump on Jimmy's head. Jimmy swung his bat knotting them away from him, but ever more of them jumping off the roof trying to stop him. Jimmy swung his bat as fast as he could, but there were just two many of them to fight off. He had to stop and fight them off first. Jill was right behind Jimmy and yelled for LeRoy to get up and fight. Jimmy had to take a step back wound to regroup. So he shouted to LeRoy to keep on fighting and he'd be there as soon as he could.

Then a couple of the jelly creatures jumped on Jimmy's head and he twisted and turned throwing them off.. Jill screamed for Jimmy to be careful and not get hurt. The creatures were still jumping off the roof of the cabin and it made it hard for Jimmy to advance. So far Jimmy wasn't hurt that bad, but he hadn't made it but a couple of feet forward and the creatures had stopped him from going any further.

LeRoy had fallen a couple of time and was bleeding badly from the face and legs now. The jelly creatures wear advising on Jimmy and Jill slowly pushing him back so he was almost moved back beside Jill. Jimmy and Jill both turned to looking down the beach at LeRoy. He was on the ground again and the creatures were all over him once again. Jimmy shouted, "LeRoy get up fight back don't let them beat you. Get up and fight back, dam it!" LeRoy was on the ground and he couldn't grab the short gun as the creatures were attacking his body so hearing Jill and Jimmy shout at him to get up he lifted his big body up and started twisting and turning his body as the creature lashed at his big black body.

They were so many of the creatures attacking him it was almost impossible to get up, but he did and he started swinging his big arm to through the creatures off of him. LeRoy took a step forward as the creature slashed at his legs and he stumble and fell to the ground once again. He twisted and turned on the sand and then he got to his feet once again. But now he was bleeding form his back and legs from the cuts the jelly creatures had inflexed on him. Blood pored down his legs and onto the sanded beach.

LeRoy, lift the gun behind and tried to get off the beach to safety. His legs was shaking know from the pain of being cut so badly, but he wasn't going to give up now. LeRoy took a step forward in the soft sand and stumble and coot his balance and took another step. He was big and strong not like the other before him their little creatures wasn't going to kill him? LeRoy stumbled and fell once again. He quietly started to get up as more blood poured out of the cuts on his body. And once again e was on his feet. LeRoy was badly bent over if pain but he tried to keep moving forward. As he was bent over so much do to the pain and lost of blood, his hands touched the sand and he was young his hands to help him stay on his feet, but being so low the jelly creatures started jumping on his head and body now. LeRoy slipped and fell once more was on the sanded beach and the creatures were trying to ripping his body apart. He heard Jimmy shouting at him he tied to get up, but he was so weak it was getting harder to get up now. LeRoy didn't wont to give up, but he was getting weaker every mount now. LeRoy got to his feet once again and took a step, his legs were shaking because he was so weak. It took all his strength to keep going just to take a step or two forward, now he couldn't tell wear he was going, these time because the blood was blinding him. LeRoy tried to throw them off, but it was getting harder to do so, as he was so weak now.

The creatures were trying to tear at his face and head now. Blood pouring down his face and still blinding his eyes. LeRoy was bleeding very badly now, he was on his feet and every step took a little more out of him total strength. He had moved only a couple feet and he was badly hurt now. The lose of blood was making him very weak and he stumble forward in the sand trying to keep on his feet was a big deal now.

LeRoy thought of Rachel and how much he loved her and the good life he had lead, and what a wonderful family he had. LeRoy thought of his mother and father calling him home and then Leroy thought of the beautiful face of

Rachel the girl he loved, he thought he could see her ghostly figure motion for him to come with her. LeRoy put his hand out to touch Rachel's hand and then he was so week he fell back on the sand as life's blood poured out of his body, on the sand around him. LeRoy eyes rolled back in his head and his eyes closed and the darkness in gulfed him. He was at peace with the world now his body was sell he had die.

CHAPTER 21

"Hello Alice," Burt talked into the mike, " I think I'm almost there. The road has smoothed out of a wild and I think I can see the cabin was just up in front of me, Alice." Burt turned the police car siren on. It came on with a loud rouging sound.

There were fewer pot holds in the road as he approached the cabin, but there were still alot more pot holds in the road he had to steer around. Once he cleared the pot holds Burt stepped on the gas to speed up the cruiser. If he could get the speed up to thirty it wound help speed up the call. The needle of the speed odometer read thirty, he didn't dare to go any faster

Burt could see a turn in the road in front of him and what looked like a opening to the cabin. He stepped on the aciculate to speed up the car. Just before the turn in the road there was a large maple tree to the left of the road.

Burt eyes widen as he thought seen something laying under the tree. It looked like a body of a person. Burt pulled the cruiser up along side what appeared to be a body. Burt pulled the cruiser down under the tree along side the body on the ground. He looked out of the window of the car at the body. It appeared to be the body of a young girl, and she was covered in blood.

Burt picked up the mike, "Alice!" Burt waited for her to answer.

"Yes, Burt." Alice replied.

"Alice, I've stopped just before the turn in the road and I think the Orland's cabin is just up ahead." He lower his voice. " I've found a body of a what appears to be a young black girl along side the road. She's in a large pool of blood, I think she's die." Burt posed and looked down at the body of the young black girl. the poor girl's body had been torn apart by something. Most likely a animal of some kind?

"Alice, I'm going to getting out of my car and investigate the matter." He opened the car door of his police cruiser and grabbed the clip board in his right hand. Alice wound wont a report on the killing. Burt looked around he couldn't see anything around that had killed the girl. So he walked over to wear the body on the ground was to check it out. "Alice, I'm out of the car and it's quiet. I don't see anything that might have killed the girl. I'm going to check it out and call you back in a couple of minutes, over and out." He let go of the button on the mike.

"Ok, Burt be careful.'" Alice replied.

Burt was out of the police car now, he had looked around and very thing seem quiet, so he left his short gun in the cruiser. Burt looked down at the torn body of the young black girl. He didn't wont to step in the blood of the girl but he needed to see if he could find sum interaction on the girl. He stepped into the blood and bent down to check out the girl's body.

The girl was wearing a blouse with blue jean. He checked the right front porch of the jeans and his fingers came across a roll of money. Burt didn't add it up but it may have been around sixty dollars in her porch and nothing else. Burt thought to himself. Young girl wear tight fitting jeans and don't have room of much indentation on them. Hopefully she had a drivers license on her. He keep looking of the license. Burt put his hand on the die girl's back and started to turn her over so he could look for a driver license. And stopped he thought he heard some thing in the tree above him. As he looked up something struck him in the face and another and another fell on his head slashing Burt's flesh. He hollowed in pain as the jelly creatures slashed at his face. He dropped his note book and his hands went to his face and head. His fingers sunk into the shimmy oozy jelly creature. "What the hell!" he shouted out loud with surprise as his fingers sunk into shimmy creature. It was like putting his hand in a bowl of jelly, he couldn't get a grip on the creature. So, Burt scoop the jelly creature up and the sticky slimy creature was pulled off his face, and he throw it off his face and on to the ground.

But as he pulled off the creature, more creatures jumped on his shoulder and back, biting and clawing at his flesh. Blood pour down his face from the cuts. Burt did the best he could to pull the creatures off his face, but know he was blinded by the blood pouring down his face. Burt backed up screaming in pain as the creature tore at his face. And now the creatures were biting and clawing at his legs. Burt tried to move back away from the tree, he couldn't see any more as the creatures had cut his eyes out. As Burt moved back his foot hit the body of the die girl on the ground and he fell to the ground with a bang. The creatures pounded on him as he hit the ground cutting and ripping and his body. Burt twisted and turned trying to though the creatures off him, but there was so many on him now he couldn't get them off of his body fast enough. The jelly creature tore at his neck ripping a large hole in his neck. Blood pour out of the cut and down his body. More and more creatures jumped on poor Burt now. He tried to get up but he was so weak know it was hard to fight back even move was hard now. Suddenly he stopped moving, Burt had lost the fight he fell back and didn't move. He was in pain no longer. Life's blood poured out of his body.

Jimmy and Jill were standing on the front of the dock of the cabin hopping to hear or see the police car coming down the road. Then they hear the chattering of the creatures. And it was coming from down the road wear the police car could be. Jimmy heard the noise of the creatures and looked at Jill with a puzzled look on his face. Jill looked back at Jimmy with a panic look on her face. Had the creatures kill the rescue offices on his way to helping them? Jimmy put his hand on Jill's hip and started slowly moving back down the dock by the cabin. Jill held back a bite, hopping again hope that some one wound come. But all his heard was the noise of the jelly spider (creature) and it was getting mind she thought to herself. Help us God!

CHAPER 22

"Burt, Come in!" Alice said as she talked into the mike. Burt hadn't reported in, so she started call him, hopping he would answer her call. " Burt, report in please, you're over due." Still no answer, Alice didn't like the idea that she hadn't heard from the deputy. Alice call again and again, still no answer. She called several or more no answer. Burt wasn't answer or couldn't answer? It was time to call the Sheriff.

Burt, wasn't the best deputy, she know that but the Sheriff told him, that he might be going into a very dangers place and to be careful. It was time to call the Sheriff. There was a good many times Burt had reported in late in the passed, but these time she had the feeling something might be wrong! Burt was going in a place that he was told might be dangers to see if he could help so college kids that might be in trouble. And now he could be in trouble himself? "Sheriff, come in!" Alice said in to the mike.

The Sheriff had his portable mike on his shirt and picked it up when he heard Alice voice." Yes, Alice, what going on?" the Sheriff replied back.

"Sheriff, I think something wrong, I can't get a hold of Burt. He was suppose to call in minutes ago. Burt told me a few minutes ago he'd came across the body of what appeared to be a young die black girl along side the road, and he was getting out of his car to check it out and report back to me in a couple minutes. He hasn't call me. Alice was nerves now and she repeated what she said once more.

"Sheriff and he hasn't called in yet Sheriff and he's way over do. I've tried calling him several times and he hasn't answer my calls back, Sheriff. I'm very worry, something very wrong, Clayton."

"Ok, Alice," the Sheriff replied, " Were just about done here. I'll go down the road and have help with me too. I'll be on my way in a couple of minutes, Alice. I'll try to call him and you keep on trying to call, Alice. And if you hear from him call me right away, Alice." The Sheriff said good- bye and hang up the mike.

The accident at the intersection in the road was pretty much cleaned up. The ambulance had taken away the injured persons to the nearest hospital. And the tow truck had taking one car to the garage to be repaired and the truck was coming back for the other one later.

The Sheriff walked over to the fire chief and told him he was going to need his help going down the duty road to the cabin. And that he'd sent his deputy down the road to see if so college kids needed so help and he hasn't heard from his deputy about the call and there could be something very wrong down at the cabin by Black Lake. The Sheriff, know Chief Morgan a little from the past calls. And the Sheriff told him there could be trouble with what might be a wild animal, and that one person may already be die. " Morgan, do you have any guns if need we need them?" The Sheriff asked the fire Chief.

The fire Chief thought a bite then said, "We don't carry guns you now that Clayton, but one of my men as a rife in his truck we can use if need be." The chief told him. "And we do have one in the glove box in one of the fire trucks, that all, Clayton."

"Good, we may need them Moran, " the Sheriff went on to tell him, " It could get very dangers, you know we'll need them. You keep you're men safe, Morgan"

"Are you sorry you're trucks can make it down that dam dirt road Chief?" the Sheriff asked him. That's a off full narrow road down there, Chief?" Sheriff Clayton asked him.

"Hell, Clayton we can plow our way down that dam road no problem. Our big wheels well just roll over them little pot- holes with no problem, Clayton. We've done it many times before." the Chief told him. "I'll tell my men to get ready to roll out and they'll all have to be on the inside," then the Chief added, " Is one truck ok, or do you need more, Sheriff?" the fire Chief said. "One well be fine, Morgan." the Sheriff told him. The fire Chief walked off to get his men ready to go down the dirt road. Then the Chief turned back and shouted to the Sheriff, "We could go first and plow our way through the trees branches that are to low and may it a bite easer of you, if you like Sheriff?" Morgan told the Sheriff.

"No, Morgan, thanks, but they may be big trouble and I'll go first." the Sheriff told him. The Sheriff turned back and got in his police cruiser and the fire Chief got his men ready. The Chief got his best men on the one fire truck that was going down the road to the cabin and the big engine of the truck rowed as it started up to go down the dirt road. And the siren started blasting once again.

The Sheriff looked at his watch there was plate of time to make it down the dirt road before dark. The Sheriff picked up his mike on his shirt and pushed the butting.

"Burt, come in, these is the Sheriff Clayton. we need you to report in! Were on our way to help you." Sheriff Clayton said, hopping that Burt was still alive. No answer, he got in his police car and turned the key. He was on his way to help the living? Jeff was one of the Sheriff's deputy jumped in the front passenger's seat with his short gun in hand.

The sounds of the siren screeching and the blowing of the hang was loud, but from the cabin the sounds were muff lily lost in the deep forest that surrounded the dirt road and the pounding of the noise the truck made harder to hear the sirens as it made it way down the dirt road.

Jill and Jimmy were looking down the dirt road hopping to hear the noise of police car coming down the road, but the trees and the wind blocked the nose from making it to their ears. They heard nothing just the quiet and the on coming of the creatures moving closer. And even more important the jelly creatures that looked like monsters deformed killer spider didn't hear the sound either. But then as Jimmy took a step back wounds and the creatures stopped chattering for a moment he thought he heard the sound of a siren coming down the road then it stopped and the chattering started up once again. Jimmy and Jill moved back as the creatures advanced on them.

CHAPTER 23

And even more important the clear looking monsters jelly like creatures that looked like a deformed four legged spiders with tube like legs and a round clear jelly like body and also a clear much smaller round head with no eyes and a clear sharp claw for a mouth that could kill.

If there were a Devil, he would look upon the deadly creatures as his allied in crime. The Devil might smile, as another beastly human died by the claws of the jelly creatures.

The jelly creatures started chattering and slowly moving to the wooden dock wear Jill and Jimmy was standing. and the creatures with one thing on their little twisted mind, to kill the two legged beast, Jimmy and Jill. They would kill the beast so they would keep there home in the cabin by Black Lake.

Jimmy seen the creatures advising toward them, and they started to move down the wooden dock very slowly. Jimmy looked around of something to help him in the fight.

Jill had felt save when she was with LeRoy. He was tall and strong, and when she was along side of him, nothing could hurt her. And now that LeRoy was gone, killed by the jelly creatures, that attack him on the beach. Jill didn't fell save anymore. Jill felt cold and afraid she thought she was going to killed next by jelly creatures, just like all the rest that had die before her. She turned and looked at Jimmy, oh he was nice looking but right now she needed someone to pretext her for the killer creatures and she wasn't shore Jimmy was the right person to do that? God, was she going to die. Jill didn't wont to she had her whole life ahead of her. Not now, she couldn't die? But the creatures keep on moving closer getting ready to attack them

They had walked along the beach and nothing had happen to them. Then Jimmy had to shout for her to come back to him, and like a fool she did. Jill left LeRoy on the beach along to go running back to little Jimmy. LeRoy, her friend for life was left along on the beach to fight the jelly creatures off by himself. If he hadn't stopped when she ran away from him to go back to Jimmy, LeRoy might be alive today. if it wasn't for Jimmy? Jill looked back at little Jimmy. He was dirty with torn clothes and holding a baseball bat for a weapon in his right hand. He wasn't like LeRoy, strong and big. Jimmy had a boyish face and he was big and strong like LeRoy. He was little college boy and he couldn't protect her like LeRoy did.

Jill's hands were shaking, her heart pounding, she was almost paralyze with fear. She liked Jimmy, but she didn't fell save with him like she did with LeRoy.

No thanks to Jimmy, they were trapped on the dock with the jelly creatures advising on the getting ready to attack them and either kill them or push them into the water wear they would drown.

Jill pushed away from Jimmy, she didn't wont to die with him. Not with small little Jimmy. Jill looked at Jimmy, he was a small little warrior waiting to fight the creatures. And he'd get killed by the jelly creatures and take Jill with him to die too.

Jimmy looked back at into Jill's eyes and could see she was frozen by fear. He took her arm and they moved slowly back on the dock. Jimmy had no chose left now, fight or run! He held his weapon tightly in his right hand ready to fight, as the creatures were on the wooden dock now getting ready to attack him. Jimmy looked around as he moved back down on the dock. He seem a old life preserver hanging on the dock and picked it up and kicked it with his foot down on the wooden dock near the end of the dock were they was going. Jimmy was beginning to know how the jelly creatures worked they evil ways. Jimmy could look out over the grassy field and wouldn't be able to see the creatures in the grass, but they were there hiding, only to pope into sight and attack them when they wont to. Jimmy looked out over the field and now the creatures wear hiding. The jelly creatures seamed to all most melt into to the grass or what ever they was on at the time and then when they wonted to reappear they could come back to the solid form they once was and attack you with out warning.. They had done it before in the cabin appeared from no wear to attack them. Jimmy had heard them chattering again and now they were on they way to attack Jill and Jimmy. Jimmy had seen the jelly creatures suddenly appear on the wooden dock in front of them, like a evil creatures might do before it attacking them.

What appeared to be a save place on the dock, had became a place of hell. Jimmy looked at Jill, and he thought she was losing control, because she pushed away from him and also she had a look of panic on her face. He could see she was shaking badly. And Jimmy said, to her in a loud voice almost shouting at her," Jill, I need you. If we are going to make it out of hear alive. Please, help me!

"Jimmy could see the jelly creatures as they advanced on them.

Sheriff Clayton had pounded his police car as he road down the dirt road full of large pot-holes. Hell figure the car didn't mine anything, if Burt and the college kids were in danger, so he destroyed a fringing police car it was wreath it. Sheriff Clayton was making good time going down that dam dirt road full of large pot –holes. His police car banged, and shook as it hit the pot-holes. The Sheriff turned the siren off after short time down the road to the cabin to Black Lake. As far as the Sheriff now The Sheriff knew that his poor police car was being pounded to peaces by the dirt road with all it pot-holes. And when these was over he'd have to have the front end of his car fixed and most likely much more done to his car. The Sheriff, keep his eyes on the road as he made his way down the dirt road As the Sheriff's car made it's way down the road, the over hanging branches of the trees almost touched the roof of the police car and the fire truck pushed it way though the tree as it made it way down the road. Suddenly the Sheriff though he see way up in front of his car, what appeared to be Burt's police car along side the road. Chief Morgan was looking forward and thought he see a car up ahead of them He pointed to what he thought was the car under a maple tree to his driver so he to could look at what he thought was a car under a tree. The big fire tuck was plowing it's way throw the thick tree branches. the chief picked up the mike and said , "Sheriff I think we coming up on what might be you're deputy's police car." Then the Sheriff responded back," O k! Morgan I thought I seen to car too, I'll see if I can take a second look and see if I can seethe car ahead of you." then he told his driver to pull as far as he could to the right so he could look pass the fire tuck, which he did pull the car to the right. Dam the Sheriff could see Burt police car parked under a tree. Then he thought to himself, he told Burt to be careful, so what happened that Burt couldn't report back. The Sheriff picked up the mike and with his other hand flicked the switch on the radio.

"Burt come in , were hear to help you hold on we're coming." there was no answer, just hissing o f the radio. The Sheriff put his hand out the window and waved to the fire truck in back of him that he had found Burt 's police car. "Morgan pull up past Burt's police car and stop and I'll check the seen out and see what I can do to help." The Sheriff told the Fire Chief.

Jimmy was watching the jelly creatures move down the dock after him. He tried to think, the jelly creatures were not hard to fight, they could only attack and cut him from the front of they body with their sharp claws, and for the most-part didn't move very fast and when they did could turn their body around very quietly to bite him. They were easy to hit and kill, but there was so many of them he couldn't kill them fast enough to do any good. Jimmy knew the creatures could swim. He took another step backwards down the dock. Jimmy could see there were jelly creatures on the roof of the cabin getting ready to jump on him., so he moved back even more. His heart was pounding the adrenalin flowed throw his body, he was no longer a college kid , he was a worrier ready to fight for his and her life now.

A jelly monster jumped off the roof of the cabin and one landed on his shoulder and he pushed it off with his left hand. and they still keep coming by the thousands down the deck in front of Jimmy. He quietly swung the bat in his hand and knotted the creature in the water. Then there were on after one jumping from the roof. Jimmy swung the club fusels knotting the creatures off the deck, but they keep coming at him. There was just to many to fight off. Jimmy moved back to the end of the deck. Jill looked at Jimmy, thinking what do we do now were at the end of the dock. She started shaking, her face turned white with fear. And she said to Jimmy, "I'm not a ever good swimmer." Jimmy looked back it Jill and said nothing Jimmy could see Jill was terrified he had to do something soon. Jill shrieked in pain as the creatures were slashing at her leg trying to cut them creatures were jumping at their waist and other was jumping off the roof, trying to jump on their heads. Jimmy kicked the life preserver into the water it hit the water with a splash . Jimmy turned and looked at Jill she hadn't told him she couldn't swim very much, but the jelly creatures were on her legs and head, jimmy pushed her back she almost fell into the cold water of Black Lake, Jill got her balance and keep from falling in the water. Jimmy strong hand touched her stomach. Jill thought to herself. What are you doing?, as she looked down and seen his hand on her stomach ,but he was way to fast for Jill could react and shouted, " No, Jimmy!" but he pushed her back once more with his hand. Jill was at the very edge of the dock and her heals were off the wooden dock in mid air. She tried to keep from falling in the water but Jill was losing her balance. Then Jimmy pushed her harder once again and Jill when flying off the dock in the air. Jill hit the cold water with a splash and in Jill in seconds started going under in the cold water, her hands waved in panic as she went under the icy cold water of the lake. As she hit the water the jelly creatures were all around her flouting on top of the water. As Jill hit the water the jelly creatures that were all ready swimming in the cold lake moved to see what had hit the water were they was swimming, as they did so they surrounded Jill pushing her down under the water ever deeper. Jimmy had no choose he dove into the cold lake as the creatures tried to swam him. There were hundreds of jelly creatures that surrounded them and the weight of the jelly creatures along seem to pushed down on them and keep them from them to the sir fish It had been twenty scents that Jill and Jimmy were under water deeper in the icy cold water. Jill tried to get control of herself, so she started swimming to the surface, but jelly creatures keep her from doing so. They cover the top of the water were Jill was trying to swim to the surfs of the water of air but there was so many jelly creatures on top of the water they stopped her from trying to get to the top so she could get the much need air. The weight of the jelly creatures that was covered the top of the water was to much for Jill. There was so many they made the water look almost a white sheet of jelly creatures swimming so close together Jill couldn't brake though to the surface of the water to get much needed air.. She tried disparity to brake through sheet of jelly creatures, but she was not strong enough to do so and she wound need breath of air very soon. Jill arm and legs moved franticly trying again and again to brake though to surfs. Wear was Jimmy, she needed his help soon? Thirty second with by: she held her breath!

When Jimmy hit the water, the creatures were on his head and back and were knock off. Jimmy went down deep in the water hitting the bottom hard.

Jill thought she heard the sound of a siren of a police car coming. But now she as under water fighting of her life. In her struggle her mouth open and the old water of the lake felled her mouth. Wear is Jimmy? She started to panic as water poured in her mouth and started to fell her lungs.

Jill is a tall beautiful girl with long silky white legs. Most men loved a tall girl. Jill simple wonted to lead a nice life. And it some point get married and have a family and a nice husband. She didn't care to be rich just be a wife and mother and be happy, that's all. Being tall had it's down points, a lot of guys shorter then her didn't ask her out or to dance. Jill had nice long legs and a small round breast.

She looked nice in a bathing suit and turned most men heads. Jill worked as a nursing and was going to college to become a R.N. She just wonted to be happy and have fun. Jill like Jimmy maybe it was because he didn't seem to care about being her boy friend that bother her the most. Jill wonted to be like and loved, she just didn't know about Jimmy. Maybe it was because of her father who left her and her mother at a young age. Sixty seconds: went by: No air! Jill tried to hold on not to take in any more water. She tried to cough it out, but know she had very little air in her lung at all. Wear was little Jimmy she didn't wont to die. One minute: when by no air:

Her body stiffed, she was going in shock. Jill arms opened up and spread wide and so did her legs. Her mouth open up one last time. The cold water of the lake poured in her lungs and started to fell. Two minutes went by; NO AIR! Ten second is a long time! A author a writer can think of a story in his mind in ten seconds. A inventor can come up with a big idea in ten seconds. You can marry and have a family in ten seconds. A man can tell you he LOVERS YOU, in ten seconds.

Jill eyes stayed straight ahead she was going in shock Jill's body started to stiffing as she went into shock. Two and a haft minutes when by; : No air!

The SIREN BLASTED , above the water as rescue team approached the cabin by Black Lake . Sheriff Clayton had the mike in his hand as he was looking forward in his police cruiser. the Sheriff spoke into the mike, "Chief Morgan, what do you see up front, anything?"

CHAPTER 24

Sheriff I think I see your deputy's cruiser and it look like there is a body on the ground under the tree up in front of us " Chief Morgan took a second look, yes it was a police car parked under a tree just a few hundred feet in front of his fire truck, " Sheriff I think it is the deputy's car and it don't look good. I see two bodies in front of the cruiser I'll pull by it and let you take a look Sheriff." the Fire Chief said.

Sheriff Clayton could see Burt's police cruiser in front of him now. He turned the siren on. The noise blasted the surrounding tree with a blast of the hollowing of horn. The fire Chief in the truck behind him and hearing the police car siren go off turned his siren on in the fire truck also. Sheriff Cleyton did the best he could to speed he's police cruiser up on the dirt road. It seemed much longer then it actually was to reach Burt's police car along side the road as it was but as soon a he got up to Burt's car the Sheriff could see poor Burt's bloody body laying on the ground not far from what appeared to a die black girl in a pool of blood die also. Sheriff Cleyton pulled he's cruiser up along side Burt's car and opened the door and jumped out the to check it out. The Sheriff could see that poor Burt and the girl were die. The Sheriff looked at his other deputy and told him to stay there and him was going to check scene out and make his report on what happen, if he could. There was a large puddle of blood here Burt lay. The Sheriff had no choose he put his boot in the blood and bent down to check on poor Burt's body. Dam he know it! Burt was die! The Sheriff thought

168

to himself, Sorry Burt I could have know better. then he turned to check out the girl. laying on the ground not far from Burt's body. The Sheriff looked around what animal could do a thing like these. Poor Burt's body was torn apart by what ever it was?

"Sheriff is very thing ok?" the deputy asked him.

"No, deputy I think their both die. keep a look out something killed them it might come back, cover me." The Sheriff told his deputy. The Sheriff moved over to wear the girl body was. The body was torn apart like Burt's body. It was hard to tell but it looked like the body of a young black in her twenty, five feet ten maybe. The Sheriff touched her hand, there was no plugs, she was die too. Sheriff Clayton looked around what the hell killed them? The cabin couldn't be that far up front , he couldn't help Burt and the girl it was to late, they was die but what about the kids in the cabin was they die too? The Sheriff got up and walked back to he's car. He picked up the mike Morgan my deputy and a young black girl have been killed hear. I wont you to leave a couple men with guns hear and we'll go on to the cabin, ok?" the Sheriff said.

"Sore, sorry about you're deputy Clayton" the Chief replied.

"Maybe we'll have better lock with the kids in the cabin. Morgan, be careful?"

The Sheriff started to get back into his police car and waved his deputy to do the same. The deputy got in the police cruiser and turned the key, the engine started up and the Sher8iff pointed ahead to the cabin by Black Lake. The Sheriff looked down the road and into the woods, what the hell going on hear, he thought to himself. Well he'd fined out soon. the Sheriff put his head on his gun. He'd check the cabin out to see if he could find anyone alive. It was time to call Alice Cleyton picked up the mike, " Alice, I found Burt," the posed a second then went on to say, " He's die, Alice, I found a young black girl's body not far from him. And she die also." it wasn't easy for Sheriff Cleyton to say, Burt wasn't the best deputy, but no one could die like that! He when on to say "You're going to have to call the cornier and tell him about the body, Alice. And better caller the State Police and tell them we need back up. We have two people killed buy some animals don't know what? but we need back up some Alice. God know what going to happen now! I've got to go, I'll call you back as soon as I can." and then he add, "I hope, I don't find any more people that have been killed like these ,I just don't know right now Alice." The Sheriff was almost crying when he said that. I'll call you later, and he added, I love you, Alice." The deputy had to stop the cruiser he couldn't get buy Burt's police car and the fire tuck was in front of Burt car and had to back up so The Sheriff could get by.

Burt's car was in the way and he couldn't get by the Sheriff waved for the fire tuck to back up. to get out of the way and then the Sheriff told his deputy he was going to have to push Burt's cruiser out of the way.

The deputy put the car in gear but Burt's car was blocking the road and he couldn't get his cruiser by. So the Sheriff told the deputy to get out of the way and he was going to use his car to push Burt's car out of the way, so he could move on by and go see if they could find someone alive at the cabin. But the police cruiser had a hard time on the dirt road.

The fire Chief and his men went back in fire truck and were getting ready to go down the dirt road. Chief Morgan could see the Sheriff was having a hard time pushing Burt's car to the side to the side so they could get by. So the Chief thought he could use his fire truck and push both car's. The fire truck was big enough to push both vesicles. The fire Chief honked his horn as the

Chief moved his truck bumper up to the Sheriff police car.

On the dirt road the Sheriff and his deputy couldn't get enough traction to push Burt's car to the side but the big fire truck did easily.

The big fire truck hit the back of the Sheriff's car pushing it into Burt's car off the road so they could get by and go check out the cabin. Once Burt's car was pushed off the road the Sheriff turned the wheel to straighten the wheels of his car, so he could drive to the cabin. Once the Sheriff had pushed Burt's car off the road he speed down the as fast as he could to cabin.

The Sheriff made a turn to right and then in from of him was the cabin to Back Lake. The Sheriff could see a clearing as the tree seemed to open up and the road smoothing a little and there was the old dirty cabin in front of him. And there was a pick nick table and a grill the college kids broth to the cabin.

Dam, the Sheriff was almost there and he could see another body lying on the wooden table. He stopped the car and got out with the rife in his left hand. What the hell going on, he thought to himself?

The Sheriff got out of the cruiser and moved slowly to the picnic table and there was a body of a young girl with long brown hair laying again the wooden table. The Sheriff motioned of the fire Chief to stay back, as he had no gun on him. The Sheriff eyes widen with fear as he looked around, and then he seen another body of a girl laying just a few feet away. He lifted the gun up, but he couldn't see anything, it was quiet.

But something had killed all these people, but what or who? They both looked around, the fire Chief was a big man just under three hundreds pounds and just in back of the smaller Sheriff with the rife in his hand. It was quiet, what killed Burt and the college kids was gone or now, but not far away.

Then the Sheriff started walking to the cabin with the Chief just behind him when they spotted another body of a young man laying in the deep grass. The Sheriff bent down to check the body out. The young man was killed just like the other, not far from the two dead girls. The Sheriff tried to think as he and the fire Chief once again started walking to the cabin. Cleyton had been told by Alice, there was seven college kids that when to the cabin. And as they when down the road they found the first body of a   black girl along side of the dirt road. And not   far from that they found the car of one of students with it's tires slashed a few feet away from the girl. And when they got to the picnic table they found the second die girls by the wooden table. And not far from that they found another body of a white young man in the grass. So, now that made four body that was found that was die and there was still three unaccounted for. college kids. They all was ripped apart by some animal. The Sheriff and the Chief stepped up on the porch of the cabin. The door was partly open, and the Sheriff pushed the door open the rest of the way. He looked in side the cabin. The Sheriff could see sleeping bags on the floor and surplice, but no body on the floor. Cleyton and the Chief walked in the cabin and looked around. There was another room in the back of the cabin and on the floor was a large pool of blood, but no body. It looked like to the Sheriff that some one had been cared out of the cabin as there was a trail of blood going to the door. Sheriff pointed to the blood so the Chief could see the trail of blood. "No body in hear Morgan." the Sheriff told him and turned to when out of the cabin door.

One of the fire man shouted, "I found anther one it's a girl, Chief."

The Sheriff looked at the fire Chief and said it must be the girl that was in the cabin see the trail of blood leading to body of the girl. The Sheriff pointed to the blood and the body , but these one had been cover with a blanket unlike the other, "She must have die first Chief." the Sheriff told Chief Morgan.

The firemen had spread out and were looking around to see if they could find anyone else. And Cleyton deputy went down on the beach to look around. The Sheriff and fire Chief walked out on the dock along side the cabin to the lift. As they walked down the dock they could see little drops of blood, some thing had happen on the dock. there? Cleyton turned and looked out over the water, then he heard his deputy shouting to him. "Sheriff!" the deputy screamed to him. "There is another body down hear. it's a black man." The Sheriff and the Chief looked down to the beach wear the deputy was and a good two hundred feet or so down the beach and they could see the deputy had found another body on the beach, these time a black man.

They turned back and started walking back down the dock to go back to the beach to check out the next body. When they reach the deputy and the body of a black man the Sheriff bent down to check out body. It had been killed just like the other. The body was that of a tall young black boy about twenty five years old, it was poor LeRoy. On the other side of the cabin there was a car parked it's tires ere slash also. They looked and found the car belonged to a Jimmy Bently another college student.

Sheriff thought he heard something a sound coming from the woods, a chattering sound of some animal and then it stopped. The Sheriff turned his head to hear the sound then it stopped. He could tell what kind of animal it was by the sound?

The firemen were starting to put the body of the died in body bags. and hours later a man in a black suit came up to the Sheriff, he was a doctor and said to the Sheriff. "I check the body's of the people kill they all die the same way. Killed by some cutting of some animal torn by the claws ripping the flesh by some kind of beast with claw like a knife of some sort. I'll know more were I check them out later, Sheriff." The doctor told him.

Sheriff Cleyton and fire men had been at the location of the cabin by the lake and found Burt and five college kids died around the camp, they had put the body in body bags and loaded them in the ambulance to be taking to the nearest hospital . Cleyton had told the men to rope off the sign and they'd be back tomorrow to check the area out and see if they could find what killed them. There was still two kids unaccounted for and thought to have drowned in the lake or something?

The Sheriff put his hand on Morgan shoulder and said to him. " Hell of a day ,a dam night mar, Chief, I've been a Sheriff for twenty years never seen anything like these Chief, we might as well call it a day, it's getting to dark to do anything and we'll have to come back first thing in the morning." The Sheriff ked around, the fire men were getting in the fire truck and his deputy had fished roping off the area. The Sheriff turned back to Morgan and said, " I'll have the divers take a look around tomorrow and they may have to do some diving for the body of the two kids that are lift, a girl named Jill and a young man named Jimmy. And hopefully they can find the bodies.

"Yah, you're right Cleyton it's getting to dark, any idea what might have kill the kids and poor Burt, Sheriff?" The Chief said.

"Dammed if I know," the Sheriff replied. "I've never seen anything like these and hope I never do again. " They turned and started going back to their vehicles.

The Sheriff slide back in the front set of the police car and pick up the mike in the car. " Alice!" the Sheriff said. " Alice, come in. This is the Sheriff talking."

He waited a couple minutes, then he repeated the call to Alice.

Alice picked up the phone. "Yes, sheriff I'm hear, what can I do for you?"

"Do you have the names of the college kids at hand?" he when on to say and didn't give her a change to answer. "We have two college kid unaccounted for. I think it is a young man named Jimmy Bentely and a once petty girl, I think is named Jill some thing, I didn't know.

"No, but wait a minute and I'll get it Sheriff." Alice replied.

"That fine Alice, I'll call you back in a couple minutes. We're calling it quits for the night. I know it's late Alice but we've never had anything happen like these before, all these people being killed like these. I'm on my way back now Alice see you in a few minutes, thanks, out" he hang the mike up

The Sheriff turned the key and the engine started up. He put the car in drive and stepped on the gas.

Sheriff Cleyton had been the first to go to the cabin and now he was the last to leave the scene of the killing Burt and the young college kids. Dam, what a mesh these was all those young kids killed. What next? Cleyton turned the wheel of the car and started down the dirt road. As the drove down the dirt road you could see the dirty police car and the back of the Sheriff and his deputy heads. The Sheriff had take off his hat, but the deputy had his hat on.

What the Hell! Some thing had appeared in the set behind the Sheriff. And there was another on the back of the Sheriff seat. A jelly Creatures!

The police car keep on driving down the dirt road.

CHAPTER 25

The next day the evening papers banner story report read , Five college STUDENTS KILLED by wild animals in the Black Lake areas and two are missing presumed die.

"These is Roger Long channel Fourteen New with late braking new!" Roger held the mike phone close to his mouth as he when on to say, "Sheriff department reported finding the body of five college student at the old Orland cabin by Black Lake. I'm hear at the Sheriff station and Sheriff Cleyton is hear with me." Roger moved over were Sheriff Cleyton was standing and put the mike between him and the Sheriff and said, "How did the students die Sheriff?" Roger moved the mike to the face so he could answer him. The Sheriff didn't wont to talk to the report but it was part of his job too. So he said to the reporter in a cram voice, "I'd rather not say we are still investigating the matter."

"There are roomer about a wild animals like wolfs that kill the students." and he when on to say like Is that so, Sheriff?"

"I can't say it's very early in the investigating." the Sheriff said bolting .

"So they didn't drown?' the reporter said

"No! "the Sheriff said to the reporter. then he when on to say "I'm sorry but I have work to do, thank you for coming" And he touch his hand and pushed there port to the door.

It was a sunny day Howard didn't care, how could the sun shine when his only son he love so much was missing and hell could be die! How dare the sun shine! Howard and his wife June didn't wont the hear or read the new. Hell he didn't wont to hear the new , they could say the word he didn't wont to hear. His son was die!!! God no! It had been a long day at the store, Howard went though the mooching of his job at the store. But he felt as though something was missing. His son Jimmy was lost at Black Lake and God five of his friends had been murder by some animal. Howard didn't wont to think about it, but he couldn't help it, he did! He now his wife June was very up set and it wound be hard on her too. Maybe he'd call her and see how she was doing or ever better call her sister and ask her if she wound come and visit her sister at a time like these God he was sixty years old and never had anything like these happen before why now?

Howard hadn't heard for his friend, Ned the police detective from New York how had moved to Maine a couple month ago. Maybe he try to call him and ask if he heard anything about his son. It's crazy but did he wont to know? Howard shook his head these had to be the first time in his life he wasn't shore what to do. He thought to him self, God help me. Hell he's close the store a hour sooner and go home and be with his loving wife June and wait for a call he didn't know if he wonted to hear the answer. It was the longest day of his life just waiting for the phone to ring. not knowing what they was going to say. Howard tried to sleep that night but it was hard not to think about his son and what happened to him, was he safe?

Howard was up at five o'clock, made coffee and just set in the chair waiting for the phone to ring, his wife June was a sleep up stairs, she need her rest it had been hard on her too. Seven o'clock Howard turned the T.V on some detective show, he didn't wont to watch the new affair of what he might hear.

June came down stair at a little past seven o'clock in her bathrobe she still was a beautiful woman. Howard turned and said, " Hi honey, how you sleep?" June walked over beside him and replied back, "Fine dear, so what do you hear from the new these morning." she looked at the T.V. it was on some detective show "You don't have it on the New, dear how are you going to know about own son if it's not on the station?" June looked into Howard's face, see could see he was up set. and she said, "We have to now dear, I know your up set so am I but we just can't turn our head and wont it to go away!" June pick

up the remote and pushed the button. and change the channel to the
New. The T.V. changer to channel fourteen the New station and the
New deck came on with a pretty young girl behind the deck. She had
short brown hair with a pretty round face and a great smile. She was
new lady Joan Walker she had a plant female voice. "Lets go way up
in northern to Fort Kent Maine with Roger Long," The T.V. picture
turned to Roger holding the mike in his hands, he was in the small
town of Fort Kent. general store behind him. You could hear Joan 's
voices but you seen Roger's face on the T.V. "Roger what have you
found out about the young college kids that was killed on the Orland
road?"

Roger put the mike to his mouth and said, "Joan, we learned that
five body were found killed by so animal, there not saying what kind
yet and two people are missing as of now. Their still looking for them
,Joan"

The T.V. switched back to Joan in front of the new deck. "And
what do the police say about the missing college kids, Roger?" Joan
asked

"Well the police haven't said much but I talked to Sheriff Clayton
a few minutes ago and hear what he said." The T.V. picture switched
to his report her was with Sheriff Clayton once again. "Sheriff can you
tell us what is going on to find the two missing college kids?" Roger
asked the Sheriff.

"Well I can't say much, but the State Crime devising will be hear
later and they will take over for the most part. We're looking for the
missing kids on the land and in the lake. We have a couple driver on
the lake looking for the college student and we're going to keep on
looking tell we find them."

"Sheriff, what have you found new that might help in finding the
college student that are still missing?" Roger asked the Sheriff. "Well
I didn't know if we've found anything new yet, but we're bring in more
people to help in the shirt for the young college student." the Sheriff
said

"And what about the killer animal that is still out there some wear
waiting to attack once again, is it save at the cabin by the lake?" Roger
asked.

The Sheriff didn't know if he like the question, but he answer it,

"We have armed men all around the champ. And so far we haven't see any wild animals that might attack us." The Sheriff answered.

Then Roger thought and said to the Sheriff, "Have you or your men gone into the forest to look animals that attack the kids?" Roger asked.

"Not at these time, we're looking for the student first and later we'll see if we can find the animals." The Sheriff when on to say, We've caller the Game warden to come in to help in the finding of the animal that might have killed the kids. "then the Sheriff when on to say, " Most likely that will be later after we find the students."

"These is Roger Lane reporting from Fort Kent on the death of the college students and the two that are still missing at these point, Joan!"

Then the T.V. picture turned back to the woman behind the deck in the station and she said , "Thank you Roger."

June turned away from looking at the T.V. New, "Well they haven't found our son yet, Howard." she could see her husband didn't like looking at the T.V. because he was affair of what he might hear. "I call Lisa mother, and told her how sorry we were of the lose of her daughter. She seemed to be a very nice person, Howard." June turned and looked at Howard, and said "They have lost there daughter and sons, Howard, we haven't yet!" she when on to say, "We have to be strong, Howard, he might be alive you know? "then she said "Pray to God for his help!"

Howard looked at June he had been praying for his son that all he could think about. June turned and started walking to the dinning room and said to Howard, "I'm going to try and call all the parents in the party and talk to them, I wont to try to call Rachel parents next they don't live far. The dinning room were June walked into was a nice room with a dark hard wood floor a oat dinning table and matching two window china cabinet. There was a telephone seat to the right of the door. June pitch up the phone and pushed the number to make a call.

Howard watched June on the phone, if at the start they told him his son was die, he could, dell with it, but not knowing would he ever know if his son was die or not. It was like a night mare. He didn't wont to think, but he couldn't stop! Dam he know his wife was hurting too. She had been in the kitchen all the time just cooking anything just to keep her mind off what was going on. .Howard got up walked into the living room. his wife had gone to start cooking dinner ready in a few minutes. Howard thought he hear the phone ring in the study just off the dinning room, he walked in the room the light was turned off just the sun light lite the room. The old phone set on the little table and started ringing. Howard, not thinking it could be bad new of his son pick up the phone and .as he did looked back to see if his wife hear the phone. Howard looked down at the colored phone on top of the table, as it rang one more time his hand when his fingers when around the phone and lifted the receiver picking it up and put it to his right ear and said, "Hello! "He heard hissing of the phone, then he hear the voice say at the other end of the telephone

"Dad, I'm alive!"

THE END